Never Close Enough

By Anie Michaels

Edited By
Krysta Drechsler

Never Close Enough

© Copyright Anie Michaels 2013

Author's Notes

This story is set in a beach town called Lincoln City. Lincoln City is a real place in Oregon, and it holds a dear place in my heart. I have been there countless times, and have many fond memories tied to this town. I did, however, take some artistic license when creating this story.

If you are familiar with Lincoln City, you will probably notice some things described in the book that are not true to life. All of the settings in the book were written from memories, but I might have pulled bits and pieces of other cities together to complete the book in the way it played out in my head. So, please do not let the small things bother you, and go with it.

Chapter One

Ella

There were certain days one wasn't supposed to spend alone; holidays, anniversaries, graduations, and most importantly, birthdays. Birthdays had always held special rank with Ella Sinclair, so she found it ironic that here she was driving in what could only be described as hurricane conditions, towards the beach, stifling back sobs, alone, and on her thirtieth birthday. Just hours earlier she had the bad luck typical in her life, to walk in on her boyfriend as he and some chesty brunette were in the middle of some crazy Kama Sutra pose that could only lead Ella to believe that the slut was not only a whorish home-wrecker, but also some crazy yoga instructor for people with no bones. Perfect.

He and Super-Slut were so involved in their activities he probably wouldn't have even noticed he'd been caught except Ella had backed into a bookshelf as she tried to stumble out of the bedroom, causing all kinds of ruckus as books and knickknacks fell to the floor. His head turned and their eyes met. Ella saw a flash of what she thought was remorse in them, but she didn't recognize anything else about him, as if she were looking at a stranger. She couldn't add it all up in her mind: Kyle? Buried in some other woman? Who was he?

She grabbed the suitcase she had placed by the front door that morning and left before he had a chance to catch her. As she flew down the stairs she could hear him calling her name, but didn't know how to make herself stop, or allow him to see her so embarrassed.

So now it was two hours later and she was still on her way to the beach house they were supposed to be spending the next week at celebrating her birthday. Only she was very much alone and still replaying everything that had

happened back at their apartment. What had happened?
She knew things weren't perfect with Kyle, but it had never
occurred to her that he was cheating. This week was
supposed to be their chance to reconnect, to get back the
spark that had been slowly dwindling between them. She
had been sure that all they needed was some time alone.
All the space between them would fade away and they'd get
back to the couple they'd been in the beginning. Back
when even an inch was too much space between them.
Back to nights of snuggling on the couch, watching movies
and talking until one of them, usually her, passed out. Back
when things were simple.

It was really raining now and sheets of water were
pounding her windshield, making it almost impossible to
see and definitely not safe to drive in. She took the next
exit and came up to a bar with "Tilly's" flashing in neon
lights. This was just as good a place as any to take shelter
from this terrible rain and she could definitely use a drink.
She ran quickly from her car to the wooden doors with
handles made of small logs, a rustic touch that signified her
proximity to the beach.

Inside there were only a few people scattered throughout
the room. Two men were playing pool, a man and woman
sat at a table near the juke box, and a few more men were
sprinkled at the bar. Ella took a few seconds to shake the
water off her coat, hung it on the coat rack near the door,
and headed to the bar. The bartender was a woman who
looked to be in her mid-sixties with short hair that was once
brown, but now was more gray than any other color. When
Ella sat down, the woman headed her way.

"Hey there, what can I get for you?"

Ella wasn't a big drinker and always felt a little silly
ordering drinks for fear of sounding like an imposter of
some sort.

"I will just have a vodka sour, please."

"Sure thing. Can I see some I.D.?"

"Of course." Most people liked getting carded, but Ella felt the novelty wore off by twenty-three and it seemed silly now. She handed her I.D. over, hoping she didn't seem annoyed.

"Well, my dear, you're entitled to a birthday drink on the house!" The woman said with a smile on her face. Oh, right. Her birthday.

"Oh, well, that's nice. I had honestly forgotten about my birthday. Today hasn't gone the way I thought it would," Ella said while looking down at a coaster she had started spinning on the bar.

"Well, I will go get you that drink and, if you'd like, you can tell me about it. My name's Tilly Masters and I'm a really good listener."

"Tilly, as in the flashing signs outside Tilly?" Ella asked.

"The one and only. This is my bar and I make the rules, so you get a birthday drink."

Tilly walked away to make her drink and Ella reached into her purse to find her phone. There were seventeen missed calls and five text messages, all from Kyle. Ella debated for a moment whether she wanted to read any of them or not, but gave in to her curiosity.

Ella, please come back. Where are you going?

Please talk to me! Why won't you answer your phone?

Ella, I'm worried about you. Tiffany doesn't mean anything to me. Answer me!

Please call me so we can talk.

Ella, at least let me know that you're ok.

Ella sighed and quickly typed a message out.

** I am safe. I went to the beach. Please stop calling and texting. I need some time. I will call when I am ready to talk. **

"Here's your birthday drink, on the house," Tilly said as she set the drink down on the coaster Ella had been spinning. "So, tell me what's got you so down on your birthday, Honey."

Ella looked at Tilly and decided that being a pseudo-shrink to patrons was part of the job description of a bartender, so she spilled. "I came home early from work and found my boyfriend having porno sex with a very limber, woman-jellyfish hybrid." Ella took a sip of her drink, looked down at her glass, and sighed. "We were supposed to be coming to the beach for my birthday to get away, to reconnect. But when I saw them together I sort of shut down, grabbed my bags and ran." Ella looked up at Tilly, who stared blankly at her waiting for more information, so she continued.

"It never occurred to me that Kyle could be cheating, that there was a *Tiffany* out there I should be worried about. I didn't even yell. I said nothing. I almost felt like I had walked in on strangers accidentally. I should be angrier, right? I should be throwing things. I should be ruining his clothes and spray painting his car with four letter words. But I'm just not."

"Well, Honey, what are you feeling?" Tilly asked gently.

Ella took in a deep breath, held it for a second, and let it out loudly.

"I don't know. I guess I'm just sad. I don't know if Kyle was *The One*," Ella said with emphasis, "but I certainly wasn't looking for anyone else." Ella paused and took in a shaky but deep breath. "It hurts to think that he could be with someone other than me and someone so opposite of me." Ella thought about the chesty brunette. And even though she hadn't taken a thorough look at the woman, she knew *Tiffany* was everything she wasn't. Busty, brunette, tall, and flexible to boot. Ella was shorter, with blonde hair that came down past her shoulders, and had curves where she should, but they were nothing to get excited about.

"Well, it sounds to me like he didn't know what he had and he doesn't deserve you anyway. Good riddance to bad rubbish," Tilly said.

The swinging double doors behind the bar suddenly opened, which had both Ella and Tilly turning to look at the man who walked through them.

"There was a leak in the main line to the dishwasher, causing a pressure problem, which is why nothing was getting clean. I patched it, but you might need to get an actual plumber in here to check it out soon, if you don't want it to cause problems again," he said.

"Thanks, Son. You're a life saver," Tilly said as she affectionately rubbed his arm. Tilly turned to Ella and said, "This is my son, Porter Masters. He comes around sometimes to fix things that need fixing, like a good son should."

"Hi. I'm Ella Sinclair," she said as she reached her hand out to him. He took it and she was surprised at his commanding handshake. Not hard or rough, but firm and purposeful. She looked him in the eyes as he shook her hand and couldn't help but notice how stupidly handsome he was. He was tall with dark hair that wasn't short, but wasn't long, and didn't really have a style. It simply fell where it fell and looked messy on purpose, like he spent much of his time running his fingers through it. Her eyes roamed over his body that wasn't hidden by the bar. His simple t-shirt was stretched deliciously over the muscles in his arms, and she caught her glare lingering on them longer than it probably should have.

"Nice to meet you," he said in a way that left her feeling like he was used to his mother introducing him to women at her bar, and that this handshake was one of many he'd been roped into. He turned back to his mother and said, "I'm going to go take a look at the lock on that door in the bathroom before I leave."

"Ok, thanks" Tilly replied. He walked toward the small hallway that had a sign above it that said "Restrooms". Tilly looked back at Ella and said, "Sorry he was so gruff. He's a nice guy, it just takes a while for him to warm up. His daddy died when he was a boy and he took on the "Man of the House" role. I think he grew up a little too fast. But he's the most loyal loving son I could ask for."

"It's ok. I'm probably not the best candidate for conversation tonight anyways." Ella grabbed her purse and put a single on the bar. "I better get out of here if I'm ever going to find my rental. Thanks for listening and thanks for the birthday drink," she said to Tilly.

"No problem, Honey. Come on back before you leave town. We have a real good lunch menu. And I hope you have a good rest of your birthday," she said with a smile.

"Thanks, I will try." Ella got up and headed to the door, pulled on her coat, and headed out into the rain. She jogged the short distance to her car, got in, but when she put the keys in the ignition the car wouldn't start. That was an understatement. The car wouldn't do anything. It didn't even *try* to start. She looked around and noticed that her headlight knob was still switched on.

"Damn it!"

Ella slumped down until her head thumped against the steering wheel and she tried not to think about why everything had to fall apart at the same time. Tried not to think about how Kyle should be here to help her figure out what is wrong with her car. Tried not to think about how alone she felt at this very moment. She let out the breath she'd been holding and opened her car door to head back into the bar. This time she didn't bother to take her coat off, just headed to the bar, and sat down on the stool she had just vacated. Tilly handed another woman a drink that looked a little too tropical to enjoy while a monsoon raged outside and came back to Ella.

"Ella, what's wrong?"

"My car won't start. I think I killed the battery. Do you have a phonebook so I can call a tow truck?"

"Oh, I don't think you'll get a tow truck out here for a battery in this weather. There's only two or three in the area, and they will be busy responding to accidents from the rain."

"Well that's just great," Ella said.

"Hey Mom, that lock is fixed," Porter said as he came out of the hallway, heading towards the bar.

"Great, Honey. Thanks. Hey do you have jumper cables in your truck? Ella's battery died."

"No. I loaned them to Bob the last time he was in here."

"That's ok, I will just call a cab," Ella said as she shrugged.

"A cab?" Porter laughed. "There aren't any cabs out here. You'd have better luck hitch-hiking."

"Ok, well, that's not an option," Ella replied, a little annoyed that he obviously thought she was out of her element – which she was but he didn't need to be so smug about it.

"No problem," Tilly said. "Porter was just finishing up here, so he can take you wherever you are going, right Porter?"

Porter stared blankly at his mother for a second, obviously irritated by her offering up his services. "Yea, sure, no problem. Where you headed?"

"I'm staying at a rental in Lincoln City on Elm Street," Ella said. "But really, it's ok. I'll manage."

"Well, don't be so stubborn; you can't walk. It's at least ten miles down the road," Tilly said. "I would take you myself but I don't close for another few hours. Porter will take you; he doesn't mind." She smiled sweetly at her son with a look that implied he didn't have a choice.

"Let's get going then," he said. Ella followed him out the door. She stopped at her black Toyota to grab her bags out of the trunk, just one suitcase and one duffel bag. She noticed he hadn't stopped to wait for her, so he was almost to his truck on the other side of the lot. She picked up her pace and made it to the passenger side just as he was shutting his door. She took a deep breath before she got in and tried to plaster a polite smile onto her face to give the illusion that she was thankful for the ride. She had a feeling that the next few miles in a car with this man would be less than pleasant.

Porter

This was so typical of his mother. She was always volunteering him for projects or favors for friends, especially if the friends were pretty women. It didn't matter to him that Ella was pretty, or even beautiful. He noticed her small frame and how her blue eyes locked on his when they shook hands. He noticed the way she smelled like vanilla, but it didn't matter. He wasn't looking for a relationship; he was never looking for relationships. Sure, he'd had his fair share of women, especially when he was younger, but he'd never felt the need to date anyone seriously. He never felt compelled to be in a relationship and only considered dating the few women he had because he knew his mother desperately wanted him to be married and wanted grandbabies. None of the women ever stuck though, and the longest he'd been with one woman recently had been merely a couple months.

"So, what's the address of your rental?" He asked.

"Oh, um, I'm not sure. I will look it up right now."

Porter rolled his eyes in the dark, knowing she couldn't see him. He saw her fumbling with her phone and tried to hide his annoyance.

"Ok, here we go. It's 2358 Elm St in Lincoln City."

"Alright, that shouldn't be too hard to find," he said.

"Thanks for driving me. I'm sure this isn't how you envisioned spending your Friday night."

"It's no problem. But you should really carry jumper cables with you, so you don't end up stranded."

"You're right. I shouldn't rely on the kindness of strangers," she said with a little edge to her voice.

"I guess you're lucky I am a kind stranger and not some lunatic who happened to be at the right place at the right time to take advantage of you," he snapped.

"Oh, well thank my lucky stars! I do say, you're a regular hero," she said, her voice oozing with sarcasm. "Look, I've had a pretty rotten day and I don't need you lecturing me. So either take me to my rental, or I can get out and walk the rest of the way."

Porter thought about arguing further, but decided to save his breath. It was only a few more minutes to her place, and then he could leave her in peace, and it wasn't her fault that his mother was always trying to set him up with women. They traveled in silence the rest of the way, and when they found her place, he pulled into the driveway threw the truck into park.

"Do you need help in with your bags?"

"Um, no. Now, I just have to figure out how to get in."

"What do you mean? You don't have the keys?"

"No, I don't have the keys. I found this place on the internet and the owners told me in an email that they keep the key hidden on the property. I just have to find that email real quick."

"Let me get this straight," Porter said, irritated. "You are traveling alone, without jumper cables, taking rides from strangers, unaware of the address of your rental, and without any keys to get it? Are you out of your mind?!"

"Excuse me?" she gaped at him, pissed off that he would talk to her that way. "I have keys, they are just hidden out there somewhere," she gestured out the windshield of his truck. "According to this email," she said, pointing at her phone, "they are under the potted flowers on the back porch."

Porter said nothing, but opened his door and jumped down from his truck. He stomped through the rain, up the steps of the front porch, and around to the back. A few seconds later he returned and headed towards the front door. He saw her grab her bags and she met him at the front steps. He opened the door, fumbled around for a light switch, found it and turned it on, but nothing happened. He flipped it up and down a few more times, somehow hoping that it would start working after a few tries.

Porter let out a frustrated growl, "I don't suppose you know how to turn on the electricity, do you?"

"Not exactly," Ella said hesitantly.

"How can you be so irresponsible to get yourself into this situation to begin with?" Porter nearly shouted.

"Listen," Ella said, turning towards Porter matching his annoyance in her tone, "I didn't plan any of this! Today is my birthday. This was supposed to be my getaway. My boyfriend was supposed to be with me, handling all of these details. It's not my fault that I found him having sex with someone else not four hours ago. He decided to abandon our relationship to have crazy-bendy sex with that slut, and it looked like better sex than we'd ever had together. So tell me how fair that is?" Ella took a deep breath in, seeming to for her next verbal assault. "I am sorry if helping me has been an inconvenience for you or I haven't lived up to some standard of responsible behavior. I was just trying to get away from what seemed to be my life falling apart!" She was breathing heavily, and he could tell she was trying to hold tears back. Seeing her that way shifted something inside of him.

Porter didn't know what to say. She was obviously upset, and he wasn't sure how much of that anger he was responsible for, but he wanted to make it right. He might not be the world's friendliest person, but he wasn't an ass.

"Look, Ella, I am sorry," he said, running his hand through his damp hair. "I had no idea any of that was going on. I don't know what's wrong with your boyfriend, but he sounds like an idiot if he'd do anything to mess things up with you. And I'm sorry for yelling about the cables and keys. I guess it just bothers me thinking about what could have happened if I hadn't been around."

But that was the strange thing. It did bother him, more than he was comfortable with. He wasn't used to worrying about anyone and he didn't usually go out of his way to help anyone besides his mother. But the idea of some schmoe off the street driving Ella home and helping her into her house made his blood run fast through his veins. For now, he was just glad he had been around when she needed him. "Let's go inside. You can sit down and I will get the power on for you."

Chapter Two

Ella

Ella was ready for the day to be over. She sat quietly on the couch in the living room, alone in the dark, trying really hard not to crumble into tiny shards of blubbering female. She would have plenty of time for a formal breakdown; she just needed to hold on to her sanity for a few more minutes. The lights came on suddenly and she heard Porter's footsteps coming up the stairs.

"I found the fuse box and got everything turned on. You should be good to go here," he said as he stood at the threshold from the basement to the kitchen.

"Thanks again, for everything. I am sorry I got a little crazy out there earlier. It's been a rough day," Ella said, trying to hold back tears threatening to break free.

"Forget about it. Sorry you're having an awful birthday. Listen," he started slowly walking into the kitchen, heading in her direction. "Tomorrow, if you'd like, I could get my cables back from Bob. I'll take you back to your car and give it a jump."

"No, Porter, really. You've done enough. I appreciate it but I can figure it out."

"The way I see it, I sort of owe you for snapping at you outside. I shouldn't have done that and I apologize."

Ella didn't really want to take him up on his offer. After everything that had happened she was a little embarrassed that she had thrown a grown-woman tantrum and wanted this whole experience to be behind her. She gave him a weak smile and said, "Thanks for that Porter, apology not necessary, but I accept. I will figure everything out tomorrow. I have bothered you enough."

Porter looked her directly in the eyes for a short moment, looked out the window towards the ocean, and then headed toward the door. "If you change your mind you can always call my mom at the bar. She will get me a message. Her number is listed, so you should be able to find it if you need it," he said as he came to the door. He reached for the doorknob, opened the door, and then turned back to her. "I hope you enjoy your stay here, Ella. And I hope you realize while you're here that any man who cheats isn't worth the tears you will likely shed over him. You're a beautiful woman and it's obvious that he's made the mistake by taking you for granted. So try not to spend too much time being heart broken." He pulled the door all the way open and walked out into the rain. Ella walked him out of the house and down the porch steps, manners always winning out. She watched him back his truck up and then pull it out onto the long driveway. Once his truck was out of sight, she turned to go back into the house.

Ella looked at the beautiful house and felt a wave of sadness. This was supposed to be the romantic house where she and Kyle found each other again. She had specifically chosen this house because it had a gorgeous wrap-around porch with a swing that faced the ocean. When she had found the house online she had imagined spending nights on that swing with Kyle, drinking wine, holding hands, watching the sunset. Now she was pretty convinced she would be swinging alone, but still drinking the wine.

Ella closed the door and felt a little confused about the one-eighty Porter had done. On the drive over he had seemed like she had been a huge annoyance to him, and now he was giving her relationship advice and compliments? Weird. It was sweet of him, but it caught her off-guard. She locked the door and headed back into the living room where she had left her bags. She looked at the clock over the mantel, nine o'clock. It was late enough that she didn't feel like a total loser for going to bed and she really couldn't find a good reason to be awake any longer. She took her bags up the stairs and walked all the way down to hallway to the master bedroom at the end.

She walked in and all her sadness came rushing back. The four poster bed with white chiffon curtains cascading all the way to the floor was exactly as she had seen in the pictures. It was such a romantic bed and it had been her every intention to spend many hours in it with Kyle. She had daydreams since booking this house about the two of them loving each other there, talking about their future, remembering why they were with each other. She sat on the bed and gave in to the quiet sobs that she'd been holding in for the last hour.

She leaned all the way back on the bed, covering her face with both hands. She rolled on her side and pulled her knees to her chest, as violent cries racked her body. She cried at first because she was confused. What had she done wrong? Why did he need to sleep with someone else? As she cried, she remembered walking in on them and her confusion turned into anger. Why hadn't he tried to talk with her before he cheated? How long had he been sleeping with her? Was she the only one? Ella immediately felt ill. She hadn't even considered the possibility that he'd been with more women than just the Flexi-Whore.

She thought very seriously about calling him and having this conversation with him. But knew she would just be a crying mess and she didn't want him to know how upset she was. She wanted to be calm and collected when they spoke, and not give him any indication of how truly wrecked she was. Besides, what could he really say to her at this point? All she wanted was answers, because the resolution was clear: they were over. She loved Kyle but she would never stay with a man who cheated on her. She had enough self-respect to know that he had given her up when he'd decided to be with someone else, but that realization hurt as well. He'd chosen someone else over her, consciously or not.

She cried for the loss of the relationship. She cried for the betrayal. She cried for the hopelessness she felt that anything would work out the way she'd planned. She got up from the bed, opened her suitcase, and pulled out a nightgown. She went into the master bathroom and as her sobs started to subside and she readied herself for bed.

As she came out of the bathroom, she went out onto the attached balcony. She noticed that the rain had let up, and although she couldn't see any stars, she could hear the ocean. She closed her eyes and listened hard for the rhythm of the waves coming onto the shore of the beach. She knew from the web page that the house was very close to the water and she was grateful that at this very moment. The steadiness of the surge of the ocean was calming her nerves. It gave her a little satisfaction to know that there were things in the world she could always rely on, like the ocean. The constant give and take of the tide, and although the waves move away from you, they always come back. She felt she could be steady like the sea; even though there were storms and swells, she could find her rhythm again.

Porter

Porter had no idea why he'd said those things to Ella. He'd meant them, he just wasn't used to words popping out of his mouth that he wasn't prepared to say. She probably thought he was some weird, manic man who swung like a pendulum from totally irritable to charming and sweet. He hadn't meant to come across that way. He could feel that she was on the verge of a major breakdown and he wanted to try to ease some of her pain. Hell, he'd wanted to stay and hold her through her sobs. But he knew that was an irrational compulsion and that she would think it more than a little weird for some stranger to want to hold her while she cried over her boyfriend. But he'd be damned if he didn't feel a pull towards her.

The way she had looked when he had come up the stairs from the basement, vacant and still, but so beautiful, had almost caused him to stumble over his words. He knew it was time for him to go, but wanted to find any excuse to see her again. That alone made him wary of his judgment. She was beautiful, but his need be near her, to see her again, was not a feeling he was familiar with. So he threw out the lame offer to help her get her car running again and she'd declined, like any sane woman should. He was having a hard time getting past the idea of not seeing her again. She might not be looking for someone to help her, but he was going to see her again, if only to be close to her.

Chapter Three

Ella

Ella woke the next morning and looked through the chiffon fabric out the glass French doors to the balcony. The fabric made the world outside her bed look foggy and muted, which mirrored how she was feeling. She debated staying within the sheltered walls of the four poster bed all day, but the thought of walking the beach this early in the morning was too enticing.

She dug some black yoga pants out of her suitcase, put on her University of Oregon sweatshirt, and threw her hair up into a messy bun. Then she grabbed her running shoes and walked down the stairs. The sliding glass door in the living room opened up onto the back of the house that lead directly to the beach. She sat on the porch steps and put her shoes on.

There was nothing Ella loved more than the Oregon coast. People who lived in Oregon didn't come to the coast to swim and they didn't come to the coast to tan. They came for the view. It was magnificent. Straight ahead she could see the beautiful ocean, with blue-gray waves rolling up onto the shore. Looking to the North there was a tall wall of earth and rock, and Ella knew at the top of that wall there was a peaceful spot of grass and flowers called High Meadow. She had only been to the top once, but it was the closest to Heaven anyone could get on Earth as far as she was concerned. Looking to the East and South, she was totally surrounded by the trees that made Oregon famous. Everywhere you looked, it was green. It was trees. It was moss. It was ferns.

Right now everything was veiled in gray, waiting for the sun to decide if it was going to appear. As an Oregonian, Ella considered herself lucky if the sun came to the beach with her, but she wasn't going to count on it. There was quite a bit of debris on the sand, from last night's storm, she figured. It would make some lucky person's day to find a bounty of kindling and firewood for the bonfires that were traditional on the beaches in Oregon, because it was the only way anyone could stay warm.

Ella walked towards the water, listening to the waves and the calls of the seagulls. She stopped before she hit the really wet sand and just gazed out over the sea. The view was humbling and inspiring. She had never felt so small and insignificant, or so important at the same time. She needed this message, this reminder, that everything is constantly moving and changing and evolving. She could see the fluidity of the water, the perpetual motion. She could also feel the sturdiness of the sand, which was deceiving since it was hardly solid. Tiny particles bound together to forge one seemingly strong surface. That's how she felt at this moment, like many particles that had been held together for so long, but now threatened to separate. She could feel herself start to fall apart. It was a breakdown she wasn't willing to have again, not after the crying she had done last night. She'd had enough. She took in deep breaths of salty ocean air and let the sound of the waves wash over her and calm her nerves.

She walked along the water, stopping every now and then to admire the view or pick up an interesting shell. As early as it was, there were few other people on the beach, and the ones that were out were jogging or walking their dogs. After she had walked quite a ways, she decided to turn back. She had been out for at least an hour, and had done some good thinking and sorting of her feelings. Self-respect was important to Ella, and she knew there was no way to go back to that relationship and maintain a shred of dignity. She knew she would have to call Kyle and deal with him. And the sooner the better, she decided.

As she came back up to the house, she was halted by the sight of a man on her porch. She knew immediately it was

Porter, even though he had his back to her. She stood in place for a few seconds taking the opportunity to admire him from a distance. She had seen plenty of him the night before but now she wanted to really look at him. The first thing that stood out to her was his wide shoulders and strong back. He was a man with a tall frame, and his shoulders were wide, broad and imposing in a terribly sexy way. The strength that was concentrated in this one area was impressive, and the muscles continued down his arms making them a very fine feature she couldn't help but admire. He was leaning back against the porch railing, wearing jeans with a black, short-sleeved shirt. His legs were crossed at the ankle and he was talking to someone on the phone.

Ella decided to stop staring at him and see what it was he wanted. She continued up the path to the porch, and when Porter finally spotted her he held up one finger in the air to indicate 'just a minute'.

"Yeah, listen, Mitch. I patched the line last night, but it needs someone who knows what they're doing to fix it," he said to whomever he was talking to. "That would be great. I will let her to know expect you later on today. Okay. Thanks, man." Porter hung up the phone and turned towards Ella, his face transforming into a friendly smile. "Hey, you're up early."

"Good thing, too, cause here you are. What are you doing here, Porter?"

"I know you said last night that you would figure everything out, but I really just couldn't leave you stranded without any help to get back to your car. Please just let me help you. I know you don't need the help. You'd be doing me a favor, because if my mom finds out I just abandoned you, she'd kill me."

Ella smiled up at him and said, "She would, wouldn't she?"

Porter laughed, "Yes, so please let me drive you back to

the bar."

Ella turned toward the house and said as she walked away "Fine, but I have to take a quick shower first. Make yourself at home." Ella had no way of knowing but she was pretty sure he was watching her walk away, so she made sure she gave a little extra sway in her hips. As she climbed the stairs, she heard him moving around the living room.

A few minutes later Ella came down the stairs, grabbed her purse off of the counter and said, "Ready?"

"Yeah, let's go." Porter headed toward his truck and Ella followed after locking the door. He went to the passenger side and opened the door for her.

"Such a gentleman today, Porter. Or are you Porter's much nicer and chivalrous twin brother?"

Porter laughed, shut her door, and got in on his side. "I know I was a little harsh last night. I didn't mean to be. I apologize, again. My mom has a habit of making me, how shall I say, overly available to any woman who is single, attractive, and seems nice. She's an eternal optimist and thinks one day I will settle down with someone and have a family."

"So," Ella looked at him from her side of the truck, "you think I'm attractive and nice?" She asked just to watch him squirm.

Porter fumbled a little, ran his hand through his hair and said "Well, I mean, I'm not blind and anyone who can see you would agree that you are gorgeous." He held her eyes for a moment more, but then turned back to start the truck.

Ella watched Porter maneuver out of the driveway and felt like she couldn't hide her surprise at his words. She wanted to make him smile and laugh, but wasn't expecting him to respond so sincerely. She had really only had one serious relationship with Kyle and a few short-term boyfriends in college. None of them had given her a compliment that had made her breathing falter and heart race. She tried to maintain her cool composure, but was sure he could hear her finally let out the breath she was holding. "Well, I guess we'll both have to deal with each other's good looks then," she said giving him a shy smile. "So, where is this Bob and will he give you your cables back?"

"After I left your place last night I went to Bob's house and got them. You know, just on the off chance I could convince you to let me help." Porter said.

"I see," Ella said, thinking it was adorable that he had planned this the night before, "so now just off to your mom's bar?"

"That's the plan."

"So, tell me what you do for work. Oh my gosh," Ella said quickly, "You're not missing work for this, are you?"

"No, it's fine. I work for myself." Ella let out a sigh of relief, glad she wasn't compromising his work. "I'm a contractor. So I will do almost anything that involves tools, power equipment, and lumber. You name it, I can build it."

"Not to mention, you fix dishwashers."

"Oh no. I am no plumber. Along with my mother's keen eye for pretty girls, she also feels like I am far more capable at handy-man duties than I really am. You want a deck? I can do that. You need an addition built on to your house? I'm your man. But I do not mess with the plumbing or electrical. She just thinks way too highly of me."

"Aw, she just loves you, I'm sure. Plus, you probably charge her a lot less, right?" Ella said laughing.

"I guess that's a good point. I might have to raise my rates among family," he said smiling back at her. "So, tell me, what do you do?"

"I own my own boutique in Portland. I opened it a few years back and it's been doing pretty well. I am pretty hands on, so I put in quite a few hours at the shop. But it is the best feeling to be your own boss, right? That's something we have in common." She looked over him and their eyes met as he turned to look at her.

"Yeah, I agree. I really like that I get to choose how I am going to spend my time and that I can make my own plans. But there's also a lot of pressure. I've got three guys working under me. I know that if I can't pull it together and do right by them, their families will struggle. That's a big driving force behind my work."

Ella agreed quietly and nodded her head at him. What he had said really resonated with her. She often felt the same pressure. Although she only really employed two other women who were both working through college, so the pressure wasn't as high. However, she not only understood what he was saying, but admired the fact that he was aware of his responsibility to his employees. He sounded so grown up and responsible, and surprisingly to her, that was a huge turn on. In spite of his acute bout of grumpiness displayed the night before, he was being completely friendly and open to her today. She was doing her best to reconcile the fact that he was someone she would normally be very attracted to, had she been in a place emotionally to have an attraction.

"So, tell me Porter, how old is Lincoln City's most eligible bachelor?"

"Bob is at least 65," Porter said deadpan.

"Oh, really? I guess that's not too old for me, as long as he has money."

"Oh, he's loaded," Porter said, finally breaking a smile towards Ella.

Chapter Four

Ella

Porter had taken her to her car where he was currently hooking some cables up to their batteries. He seemed more than capable, so Ella let him handle the task. She felt her purse vibrating and then realized that the phone had been on silent since yesterday. She took her phone out and saw 'Kyle' on the screen. She hesitated, but then thought she'd have to face him sooner or later. "Hello?"

"Ella! You answered. I'm so glad. Listen, we need to talk," Kyle said

"Kyle, I don't really think there's anything to talk about."

"Of course there is, Ella. I am so sorry about what you saw. I don't know what I was thinking. That never should have happened."

"What shouldn't have happened, Kyle? You cheating on me or me walking in on you in the act?" Ella's voice was rising. She knew Porter could hear her and that he was politely pretending not to listen to her conversation.

"All of it Ella, I shouldn't have cheated on you and I am so sorry you had to see what you did. I know I totally messed everything up and that you deserve better. I don't know how to explain everything that's been going on."

"Start from the beginning Kyle," Ella said softly, not entirely sure she wanted to hear it, but the need to hear answers to her questions won out.

"Ok, well, you remember about three months ago, when I went on that business trip to Miami?" Kyle asked.

"Yes," Ella remembered him going to Miami for a week and nothing seemed suspicious.

"Well, when I was in Miami, I met Tiffany at one of my conferences. I swear to you I didn't go there with the intention of sleeping with anyone. When I first met her, we were together for work purposes, and things just kind of happened. We went out to dinner with some other people at the conference, we had some drinks, and we just talked all night. We spent the week together and before I left we slept together. I am so sorry Ella."

"Why didn't you tell me? And this has been going on for three months?!" Ella yelled.

"No. Yes. No. Jesus!" She heard a loud smack like he had slammed his fist into a table, and then she heard him inhale deeply. She waited for him to calm down and he eventually continued. "We only slept together once in Miami. After I came home I wanted to fix things with you, Ella. Things have been off between us for a while now; I know you felt it, too. I wanted to make sure that I was giving us the shot we deserved, the shot you deserved. This wasn't your fault Ella. It was mine. Anyway, for the last three months Tiffany has been emailing me at work, asking me to come back to Miami to be with her. At first it was friendly, but she started getting really insistent. I kept trying to tell her that I wasn't sure about her and me and that I needed to see what was happening with us. I told her that we were going to the beach, and that I was hoping it would help our relationship, that it would fix us. And I really was, El. I wanted to not feel guilty anymore and to be happy with you." Kyle was quiet for a few seconds and Ella could hear him trying to gain control. She could tell he was near tears. Ella had a few rogue tears slipping down her cheeks. This was not what she was expecting.

"Tiffany showed up here yesterday afternoon unexpected," Kyle continued. "I wasn't expecting her to be here and I wasn't expecting to feel the way I did when I saw her. I just kept thinking about how far apart I feel from you and how close she was. She *wanted* me Ella. I haven't felt that from you in years."

"Don't you dare try and turn this around on me, Kyle! I was trying just as hard as you were. I was feeling alone too. I never found some convenient yoga slut to make me feel better!"

"I know. Damn, Ella, that's not what I meant. I should have talked to you about it. I shouldn't have slept with her. I will never be as sorry about anything else in my life. But it happened and I can't take it back. Believe me, I would."

"Where is she now, Kyle? Is she still there with you?"

"No, I made her leave after you walked in on us."

"Was she the only one?"

"Yes, I swear."

Ella believed him and she was relieved to know that he had only been with one person. She took a deep breath and exhaled slowly.

"I think we are over, Kyle," Ella said softly.

"We can work through this El. Don't give up on us."

"I think you should move out of the apartment."

"Are you going to stay at the beach?"

"I think that's best."

"I'll be out by the end of the week."

"Bye, Kyle."

"Bye, El."

Ella ended the call put her phone back in her purse. She used her hands to knead the back of her neck and felt no amount of pressure would relieve the tension she felt in her body.

"Everything ok, Ella?"

Ella turned around and looked at Porter. She had forgotten he was so nearby and knew he'd heard the whole conversation.

"Well, if by 'ok' you mean 'totally fucked up', then yes. Everything's dandy," she said with more sadness in her voice than anything.

"Anything I can do to help?" Porter asked.

"Buy me a drink?"

"Ella, it's nine o'clock in the morning."

"Ok, fine, buy me a drink in twelve hours."

Porter laughed, "Ok, I can do that. You want to get in your car and see if it'll start?"

"Sure," she replied. She got in and sat with one leg in the car and one leg out. She put the key in the ignition and it turned over without a problem. She smiled excitedly and said, "And you said you weren't an electrician."

"Well, I guess I missed my calling." Porter walked over to her car, unhooked the cables, shut her hood and then went to her open door and leaned on the frame of the car, boxing her in slightly. "Seriously, are you going to be ok?"

Ella shrugged, "I think so. It's over, and honestly, it's been over for a while. He went about it in a pretty shitty way, but we were destined to end. I've been trying to put it off, trying to fix whatever was wrong, but maybe it's better this way. Relationships should take work, but it shouldn't *be* work. Maybe once it's broken it's too late. We've been broken for a while. I just want to go back to the house, take a hot bath, and relax."

Porter looked down at Ella, and then took a step backwards, reaching for his keys in his pocket. "Do you need to follow me back to your house or do you remember the way?"

"I remember the way. Thanks Porter, for everything. I don't know how I would have gotten here to fix my car without you. I am going to hold you to that drink tonight."

"You're on. I will meet you back here in twelve hours, sharp," he said with a smile.

Ella smiled back at him and then closed her door. She backed out of the parking space and waved to Porter as she pulled away. Was she really going to meet him tonight at the bar? She didn't necessarily think anything scandalous would happen, but she was newly single and he was single too. Would she be giving him the wrong impression by meeting him? What if he was expecting something from her? Well, honestly, if he had wanted something from her he had certainly had a few opportunities. So if he hadn't tried something already, she was probably in the clear, right? Did she want to be in the clear?

She had *just* broken up with her long term boyfriend, but she didn't feel as upset as she thought she should. She was a little sad, and a little angry for the way it had all ended, but she wasn't destroyed. Was there something wrong with her? She decided that not being an emotional wreck was ok, and that meeting a nice man who had helped her tremendously for a drink wouldn't be the end of the world.

Porter

Porter watched her car pull out on to the road, and smiled as he removed the cables from his battery and put them in the bed of his truck. He turned towards the bar and headed inside and felt the sides of his mouth turn up. She had a way of making him smile. He felt bad that she was going through something rough, but he also felt good about being able to help her feel better. As he walked into the bar, he saw his mother bring an order to a table of older, retired men. He recognized them as regulars, and knew that they came here almost every morning to eat breakfast and flirt with his mom. It was harmless and his mom was good at making anyone she came into contact with feel special. It didn't surprise him that she could bring customers back day after day.

Tilly saw him come in and after giving the men their food and a thousand watt smile, she met him back at the bar. "You want some coffee, son?"

"Yeah, thanks"

"What are you doing here this morning? I usually don't see you until the afternoon," Tilly asked as she poured him a cup of coffee.

"I picked up Ella and brought her to get her car. She just left."

"Well, isn't that nice of you," Tilly said, trying to hide her smile from him.

"Calm down, Mom. It was nothing. I didn't feel right about leaving her there without a way to get back."

"That was very nice of you, Honey. I'm sure she appreciates your help."

"She did. She has told me 'Thank You' a few too many times," he said as he took a drink of his coffee. It was delicious. His mom made the best coffee. He'd have to come here in the mornings more often. It tasted even better because he knew his mom wouldn't take any money from him. Free coffee only partly made up for all the times his mother tried to fix him up with unsuspecting women.

"Maybe she'll think of a way to repay you," Tilly said with a wink.

"Mom, honestly, you're ridiculous. Ella just broke up with her boyfriend. Five minutes ago. In the parking lot. She doesn't need you trying to put your nose in her business and neither do I."

"I am simply suggesting that maybe she doesn't need to be alone right now, perhaps you should keep an eye on her."

"Ok, Mom. Well, as it happens, we are meeting here tonight for drinks."

Tilly got an excited look on her face, "That's my boy!"

"That's my cue to leave. You're too much."

"Have a good day, Son! See you tonight," she said as he got up from his stool.

"Love you, Mom. Call me if you need anything." He walked behind the bar and gave her a kiss on the cheek before he headed to the door.

Porter shook his head as he walked to his truck. His mother was relentless. Sometimes he thought he should just find a woman he tolerated to marry just so his mother would back off, but he knew that was a bad idea. He'd never really met a woman he wanted to spend more than an evening with, let alone a lifetime. Would he want more than an evening with Ella? The thought had crossed his mind. He was attracted to her, that was simple. Her blonde hair was enticing, and looked soft enough to touch whether it had been up in a bun this morning, or swirling in the wind last night. Her small frame was highlighted by her curves and he had tried not to get caught admiring her body. She was slender with just enough roundness to hold onto. He doubted he'd get an opportunity to hold on to anything of hers and that was ok. He wasn't into rebounds and he wasn't a desperate man. He could spend time with a beautiful woman as a friend without expectations. It didn't mean he couldn't think about getting ahold of her.

Chapter Five
Ella

Ella spent the rest of her day relaxing and she enjoyed it immensely. She had taken a much needed bath in her giant jacuzzi tub, gone out for lunch, and then stopped to do some grocery shopping so she could eat meals without having to leave the house. Then she grabbed the latest book she had been reading and headed to the beach. It was a warm and sunny afternoon and reading on the beach had been calming and relaxing.

The evening came and brought cool breezes with it that forced her back inside. She figured she had better start getting ready to meet Porter at the bar. She had been thinking all day about how she should approach this situation. Was she preparing to simply meet a friend at the bar, or should she be treating this like a date? What should she wear? She was pretty sure it wasn't really socially acceptable to be going on dates on the very same day you break up with your boyfriend, but she wasn't sure she cared about what was acceptable. She didn't feel newly single. She felt newly freed. She thought she would spend the day thinking about Kyle and being sad about their abrupt ending, but she found herself thinking more about Porter. She remembered the way he looked when he'd come to her house this morning in his black shirt that clung to his strong arms and how his hair seemed to always be perfectly messy.

She decided that regardless of how long she'd been on the market she was going to make sure she looked nice when she met Porter at the bar. There was nothing wrong with wanting to look your best, right? She had packed date outfits for her weeklong stay and she wasn't about to let them go to waste. This might be the only opportunity she got to wear them and what did she have to lose?

When Ella was done getting ready, she did one last check in the mirrored closet door. She had chosen to wear her favorite skinny jeans, a cream-colored lace camisole, and a sheer burgundy cardigan. She also had her suede boots that came up just below her knee which matched the creamy color of her cami, and added three inches to her height with a stiletto heel. Her hair was hanging in big, loose curls, and she had put on just a little bit of mascara and tinted lip gloss. She looked at her reflection and was pretty satisfied with her appearance.

As she drove towards Tilly's, she tried to ignore the nervous feeling she was getting in her stomach and kept thinking about how this definitely wasn't a date. Just as she knew it wasn't a date, she was sure that Porter didn't think it was a date either. He knew she'd just ended everything with Kyle. Hell, he had been standing right next to her. She just needed to reassure herself that this was nothing but a friendly meeting of two people for drinks. However, when she pulled into the parking lot, her head and the butterflies in her stomach started having a serious disagreement.

She saw Porter sitting on the lowered tailgate of his truck and he looked ridiculously hot. She debated turning the car around and going back to the beach house. She thought she was ready to do this, but she wasn't expecting to be so surprisingly attracted to him. She saw recognition in his eyes when he saw her car, so now the brilliant idea to bail was no longer an option. She parked her car a few spots over from Porter, took a few deep breaths, and then managed to get out of her car. She walked towards him and he was looking in her direction waiting for her.

He was wearing a pair of dark blue jeans that seemed to be just the right amount of tight in all the right places. She thought his shirt earlier had shown off the muscles in his arms, but these jeans were highlighting muscle definition in a completely different area, accentuating his sturdy legs.

She had never really noticed a man's thighs before, but she was definitely a fan of his, and now a fan of whatever brand of jeans he was wearing. His legs were almost like tree trunks. If he looked this good in his jeans from the front, she was sure the view from the back would be deadly. She would have to remind herself to not check out his ass. Because honestly, people who are just friends meeting for drinks don't check out each other's asses. She was almost positive that no good could come of that.

He was wearing another black shirt. This one buttoned up the front and he rolled up the long sleeves up to just below his elbows. There was obviously no shirt on the planet that could make his arms look bad. She was totally and completely out of her element and throwing herself into a situation with a man who was too good looking; it could only mean trouble.

"Hey Ella, glad you could make it." She saw him look at her, and definitely saw his eyes move up and down her body, finally settling on her face. "You ready to get that drink?"

"I am definitely ready for a drink. Let's go." They turned and started for the door. "Did you work today?" She asked.

"Well, sort of. I worked on my own project. So it's not a paid job and I only work on it on my free time. But it's work."

"What is it?" She eyed him curiously.

"A boat," he said as he opened the door for her. She felt his hand cup the small of her back as she walked through the door and it made her stomach drop. That was a very date-like thing for him to do.

"You're building a boat? Like, a *boat* boat?"

"Yeah, I am."

"Hmm. That's impressive. Is it a small boat? Big boat?"

"It's not terribly small. It's a twenty-five foot sailboat. Built it from scratch."

She cocked an eyebrow at him. "I stand corrected. That's *very* impressive."

He smiled at her, "It keeps me busy. What did you do today?"

"A whole lot of nothing. Took a very relaxing bath, and then read on the beach for a while. Nothing fancy."

Ella followed him up to a small table in the center of the bar. He motioned for her to sit at one of the chairs, and he leaned down next to her with his mouth right next to her ear. "I am going to head to the bar. What can I get for you?"

"I will take a Long Island, please," she managed to squeak out, shivers running throughout her body, terribly affected by his breath on her ear.

"Sure thing."

He headed for the bar and it took every ounce of self-control to not watch him walk away. She didn't need any more reasons to be attracted to Porter. She had more than enough to deal with at the moment. She was concentrating very hard on looking straight ahead when a man sat down in Porter's chair. She glanced up at him and gave him a confused look. He was about her age with blonde, thin hair creeping out from underneath a greasy trucker hat.

"Hey there, sweetie. Haven't seen you around here before," he said with a grimy smile plastered on his face. "I would remember seeing a hot little thing like you running around town. My name's Josh. What's yours?"

Politeness won out as she introduced herself, "My name's Ella."

"Well, Ella, that's a pretty hot name. It matches your hot little body. Why are you here all by yourself? Let's get out of here and I'll show you a real good time."

Ella opened her mouth to tell him off, but was cut off by Porter's voice.

"Walk away now, Josh," he said quietly but with force. "Get up and walk away."

"What's your problem, Porter? This one belong to you?" Josh asked with a smirk.

"She doesn't *belong* to anyone, but she sure as shit didn't come here to get hit on by some drunk, middle-aged, in-need-of-a-shower townie. If you know what's good for you, just walk away."

Josh stood up and took a few steps closer to Porter, so their faces were only inches apart. Porter didn't budge. "You think you are so much better than all of us, Porter? Don't be fooled, man. You're a townie, too. So you better just watch who your flinging insults at." Josh turned and walked out of the bar.

"Are you ok, Ella?" He asked as he set the drinks down on the table. "I am sorry about Josh. He's been a jackass for as long as I can remember. Don't let him get to you. He won't be back."

"I'm fine," she offered him a small smile. "I was just about to tell him to go to hell, but you kind of took care of that for me."

"I'm sorry if I stepped over some sort of line here. But honestly, I can't blame the guy for trying to hit on you. As soon as you got out of your car tonight, I knew I was going to have a hard time keeping you to myself. You look amazing."

Ella wasn't sure she'd heard him right, but she was pretty sure they had crossed over into a date-like territory. She could definitely play this game with him. "Your chivalrous nature shows its face again. Twice in one day, I must have done something good to deserve the attention of such a gentleman."

"Oh, you've got my attention, all right," he said with a half grin.

"Good," she said with a shy smile. "So how long has your mom owned this bar?"

Porter took a pull from his beer before he answered. "When I was twelve my dad died. A few months later my mom got a check from his life insurance and she used part of it to buy this place. It was in terrible shape, so my mom and I worked for a few months to get it open. So I guess she's had the place for about twenty years now."

"I am sorry about your dad. That must have been hard on you, being so young."

"It got easier as time went by. I think the hardest part was just how sudden it was. We never had a chance to say goodbye at all. He was driving down the highway here in town. A logging truck took a turn too sharp. Flipped over right onto my dad's truck. He never saw it coming."

"That's terrible," Ella said softly.

"Yeah, but it happened and we made it through. I don't think my mom will ever move on, though. I mean, she hasn't ever been on a date in twenty years. I think she's still madly in love with him. She flirts with the customers all the time, but not seriously. Sometimes I wish she would date again, that way maybe she's stop focusing on my love life," he gave a small grin.

"She obviously just wants you to be happy," Ella said. "And she obviously thinks the world of you."

"Yeah, well, I can tell by the way she's looking at you that she thinks you're pretty special, too," Porter said pointing with his beer towards the bar. Ella looked over and saw Tilly with a giant smile on her face looking right at the two of them. Ella laughed and gave a small wave in Tilly's direction. She winked at Ella and then went back to her customers.

"So, tell me how you've managed to remain single all these years," Ella asked, looking down at her drink, a little embarrassed to be asking such a personal question.

"That's simple. I never met a woman who held my attention or who I wanted to pursue seriously. I've dated here and there, but usually it's just one or two dates at most before I lose interest."

Ella laughed a little, "Ok, so if I never hear from you

again, I shouldn't take it personally?"

"Do you want to hear from me again?" He asked looking her right in the eyes, suddenly serious. His question caught her off guard. She wasn't used to men being so forward or up front with her.

"I wouldn't be opposed to it," She said looking right back at him.

"Ella, I don't want to push you, given your circumstance, but there is no way I am letting you leave tonight without knowing that I'll get to see you while you're in town. I know you just broke up with your ex, and part of my head is telling me you're off limits because of it, but most of me is just really happy that you pulled into this parking lot last night. I can't ignore that."

Ella took in a sharp breath and managed to respond with a breathy, "I'd like that." This was all a little crazy, but she couldn't help it. Porter was openly and obviously interested in her, and for once she wasn't going to question what she was feeling; she was going to trust herself and her instincts. He was responsible, treated his mom well, and was sexy as hell. A lethal trifecta. She could spend a few days getting to know him while she was here. No harm, no foul.

Chapter Six

Porter

There had been no words to describe the instant possessive feelings that had come over him when he turned and saw Josh drooling all over Ella. He wasn't a violent man, and would avoid confrontation usually, but at that moment he wasn't opposed to physically removing Josh from the bar. Luckily for him, Josh made the right decision and left Ella alone. The moment Ella had stepped out of her car, Porter had known he was a goner. She looked amazing with her hair curled around her face, and she was wearing those damn boots that made her legs and ass look spectacular. Porter knew he was in for a rough night of playing it cool and being the gentleman, but all bets where off when he caught another man looking at her. He would be the only one to talk to her while they were together.

They had a few drinks and it became clear to Porter she was having the same visceral attraction to him. He caught her eyes roaming over his arms a few times, and she always gave him a sweet smile whenever he locked eyes with her. The red color of her sweater was making her blue eyes almost glimmer. "So," Porter took a drink of his beer, "I've told you about my family; let's hear about yours."

"Well, there's not a whole lot to tell. My mom and dad are still married and they still live in the same house they have lived in all my life. My mom works for a school district on the board of directors, and my dad use to be the CEO of a marketing company in Portland. He retired a few years back and now just spends most of his time hiking and fishing. I have a little sister, Megan, and she and her fiancé live near Portland, too."

"Do you and your sister get along?"

"I guess you could say that. There is 8 years between us, so we were never really at the same stage in life. I have no idea why my parents had us so far apart. I think she might have been a surprise," she laughed a little. "Megan is really sweet and good at of a lot of things. But I think she really just wants to be married and have a family. She met her fiancé, Patrick, in college and they've been inseparable ever since. They will both graduate from college this June and then they plan on getting married next Spring." Ella took another sip of her drink. "She always knew what she wanted and she just went after it. She's fearless that way." The description of her sister made him smile.

"You're pretty fearless, too. You got into a car with a complete stranger last night and let him drive you home. Then you let him into your house that had no lights. He could have really taken advantage of you," he said with a smirk.

"Hey, that was alcohol-fueled desperation, mixed with a little stupidity, I suppose."

"Well, consider yourself lucky. If I hadn't been here to help you, another man would have helped you out, and I'm definitely the best looking man in town," he said, trying to feign cockiness.

"Oh, really? Lucky me then. I guess I got the better end of the deal."

"I don't know about that. I got a pretty good deal, too. I mean, you're here with me, right? I may be the best looking man in town, but there's never been a more beautiful woman in this bar." Porter watched as a very slow smile moved across Ella's face and a small blush filled her cheeks. Her smile made his heart beat faster and the lightness he felt from it was addictive. He felt that given the opportunity he would do anything to see her smile. He took another pull from his beer.

"You know," Ella took a sip of her drink, "if you keep saying sweet things like that and I'm going to start thinking this is a date." She put her drink down but kept her eyes on Porter.

"You think this should be a date?"

"No. I just ended a very long relationship and you're a handsome stranger. I don't think this should be a date. But I think it feels like a date and I think I want it to be a date."

Porter definitely wanted a date with Ella. "Listen, I want it to be a date, too. But when I date women, I pick them up and we go someplace nice, not a bar."

"You don't like your mom's bar?" She seemed surprised.

"That's not what I meant, but there is something to be said for not having your mom spy on you while you're out with an attractive woman. It's usually a mood killer."

"Usually?"

"Let's just say there's little in this world that I think could distract me from you. So, even though my mom is probably behind the bar telling all her customers about us, I couldn't care less and would stay here if it's what you wanted." Ella's eyes wandered to the bar. He saw her smile and he knew that he was right about his mom.

"She does look a little preoccupied by us," she said as she looked back at him. "Ok. I'm game. When and where is this date going to happen? I'm here all week," she winked at him.

"Are you doing anything tomorrow night?"

"Looks like I'm going on a date with you."

"Great." His smile widened as satisfaction rolled through him.

"Let me see your phone," she said as she held out her hand to him. Porter gave her a strange look, but once he handed it over he realized she was programming her phone number into it. "There, now you can call me if anything comes up or you need to cancel or something."

"That was slick," he smirked at her, laughing. "I have never gotten a woman's phone number without even asking before."

"I'm sorry. Was that too forward? I haven't given my phone number to a man in years. I guess I didn't even think about it." She looked worried.

"No, I am glad you gave me your number, but I won't be canceling on you," he said with promise. He kept his eyes on hers hoping she understood how much he wanted their date to happen.

"Ok, well, use it if you need to."

"I will," Porter paused. "Do you mind if I ask you about the guy?" Ella was mid-sip and coughed a little bit at his question.

"You mean Kyle?"

"Yes. The ex."

"Um, ok. What do you want to know?"

"Well, how long were you together?"

"Four years."

"Wow, that's a long time."

"Yes, it is. It is the longest I've ever been with someone. Seems like kind of a waste of time now. What's your longest relationship?"

"Right after I graduated from high school I dated a girl for a little over a year. I wasn't a very good boyfriend. Eventually she realized that and dumped me."

"What made you such a terrible boyfriend?"

"I guess I just didn't give her all the attention she wanted or deserved. I've found it very difficult in the past to move past the 'get to know you' stage of a relationship. She wanted more, and I couldn't give it to her at the time." Ella tilted her head to the side and smirked at him.

"Her loss," she smiled.

"Nah, the next guy she dated she was with for a few years and eventually they got married. I like to think of myself as a stepping stone to her happily ever after." Ella wrinkled up her nose at his words.

"It sounds so sad and pathetic when you say it like that. I get the feeling you enjoy your bachelorhood. I don't buy into your pity party."

"Well, you're right and you're wrong. I enjoy being a

bachelor, but only because none of the women I've ever met have I wanted to spend more than a few evenings with, and I'm ok being alone. I guess it's going to take a special person to grab my attention and hold on." Porter took another drink of his beer. "And you live with this Kyle guy? What are you going to do about that?"

"I asked him to move out of our apartment while I'm here at the beach. I guess that might have been a little harsh, and come to think of it, I don't know if I want to live in that apartment anyway after what I saw. Maybe I will just let him know to take the bed."

"That bad, huh?"

"Um, yes. I have never seen actual gymnastics performed during sex before. Someone should have been in there holding up score cards."

"It couldn't have been that bad." Porter laughed out loud.

"Oh, yes, it was. I will never be able to watch the Summer Olympics again."

"Ok, well, I will make sure our date tomorrow doesn't involve any gymnastics meets."

"I would really appreciate it. So, what are we going to do?"

"It will have to be a surprise, I suppose," he said with a smug grin.

"Well, I think I had better head home now. Thanks for meeting me here tonight. I needed something to take my mind off things and you are a very handsome distraction." Ella looked at Porter for just a few seconds and then rose to grab her purse off the back of the chair digging for her wallet.

"I've got the drinks, Ella, my treat. Let me walk you to your car." Porter followed Ella out to the parking lot. "So, how about I pick you up at your place around five tomorrow evening?" He asked as they approached her car. He held his hands out for her keys and even though she gave him a curious look she handed them over. He took the keys, unlocked the door, and opened it for her. She smiled shyly at him and took her keys back as he handed them to her. He had pulled the door open in front of him so that it was between them, and she stood on the other side.

"I will be ready at five," she said. He watched as the breeze blew her hair around her face making the curls bounce in the wind. He wanted to reach out and touch her hair, tuck it behind her ear, but he didn't want to make her uncomfortable. He really wanted to kiss her, but felt it might be too soon. He knew that he would have to let her set the pace. They stood at the car staring at each other, then finally Ella made the first move. She leaned forward placing her hand on Porter's arm for balance, and gave him a small kiss on his cheek. She lingered there for a few seconds and he could smell her hair. The vanilla scent seemed to follow her everywhere. He turned his face into her cheek and he could hear a small sigh escape from her that made fire run through his veins.

"I can't wait for tomorrow," he whispered in her ear. She slowly pulled away from him and a blush had warmed her cheeks. He brushed a thumb over her cheek and said, "Drive safe."

"You, too. See you tomorrow." She slid into her car and he shut the door once she was inside. She backed out of her spot and gave small wave to him as she drove away.

Porter watched her drive away and headed back inside to settle the bill. Tonight had gone better than he had expected, minus Josh making his appearance. He knew Ella was beautiful and that he was going to be attracted to her. He hadn't expected to like her company so much, or to feel like he already had some sort of claim on her. He thought they had just brushed the surface of the deep connection he was sure they shared and had very few ideas on how he was going to keep his hands to himself tomorrow night.

Chapter Seven

Ella

The non-date with Porter had been surprisingly comfortable. She had been worried that he would expect too much from her, or even worse, not expect anything and really only be meeting her because he felt sorry for her. He seemed happy to be there with her, interested in what she was saying, and it had been a total turn on when he'd stood up to the creep who tried to hit on her.

She'd driven back to the house with her face still tingling from his touch. She had definitely reacted to his hand on her face and his mouth so close to her ear. She had immediately felt giant butterflies crammed in her stomach and she couldn't really remember the drive home. She'd made it in the house, and after she'd put on some pajama shorts and a tee-shirt, she crawled into bed. She was checking her email on her phone when she got a text message. She didn't recognize the number but knew it was from Porter.

Hoping you made it back to the house safely.

She felt a slow smile inch across her face.

Yes, I most certainly did. Thank you.

No problem, I had a great time tonight.

Ella was trying to gauge how brave she was feeling, and decided that the beauty of texting was you didn't have to look the person in the face while you said embarrassing things to them. She gathered her courage.

**I did, too. I'm kind of regretting going for the cheek

*though. Wishing I had just gone for it and gotten a real kiss out of you.***

Ella waited for a response and it seemed to take forever. She realized she was holding her breath when there was a burning in her lungs and she remembered to exhale. Finally her phone pinged.

I could always drive over to your house to rectify the situation ;)

She couldn't believe he had just used a winky face. Was he flirting with her? It made her giggle a little bit at how juvenile she felt. Is this what teenagers did these days?

That's kind of you, but I am already in bed.

Well, I think I would able to work in those conditions, for your benefit, of course. I wouldn't want you losing sleep berating yourself for not giving me a proper kiss goodnight.

She couldn't help the enormous smile that was plastered across her face. She had a hard time reconciling the fact that this funny and sweet man who was flirting with her over text messages was the same man who was yelling at her for being irresponsible the night before. She wasn't sure what had made him turn into this charming man, but she was glad she got to see this side of him.

Fortunately for both of us, the alcohol I've consumed will help me sleep. So that will save you a drive all the way over here. I do appreciate your attentiveness though.

**Alright, I will let you sleep. But in regards to the kiss, don't make the same mistake tomorrow. Goodnight,

*Ella.***

She still had a stupid grin on her face and thought that there was no way she was going to be able to stop herself from getting the kiss she was after tomorrow night. She pulled her covers up to her chin and snuggled into the soft sheets, feeling more lightweight than she had in months. She fell asleep smiling, thinking about Porter's gentle touch on her face.

The next morning she woke to beautiful bright light shining through the sheer fabric of the bed. It appeared as if the weather gods had smiled upon her and given her a sunny day at the beach, which was a rarity this time of year on the Oregon coast. She stretched her arms and legs and after remembering the sweet way Porter had said goodnight to her at the bar and their text conversation, the butterflies returned with full force. She was going to have to try to keep her mind occupied for the day unless she wanted to slowly torture herself with replaying the whole scenario in her head over and over again. She decided to take a jog on the beach to clear her mind.

It wasn't terribly early, but the beach was still relatively empty. Ella had the whole beach to herself for the most part, and took joy in the openness it afforded her while she ran along the shore. She had her iPod on and was using the upbeat dance music to keep her pace up. There were a few large, white, puffy clouds in the sky, but the sun was out in full force and it felt wonderful against her face. After a while, when she felt like she'd run long enough to counteract the drinks she'd had the night before, she found her way back to the house and sat on the porch steps admiring the crashing waves. She had been thinking about absolutely nothing when she suddenly felt her phone vibrating in the pocket of her jacket. She saw her sister's name on the screen and answered with a smile.

"Hey, Megan, what's up? How is Patrick?"

"Patrick is good. We are getting ready to go and look at a venue for the wedding. We are torn between getting an outdoor or indoor venue. You can never be too sure about the weather here, but we just want to see what's out there. Ya know?"

"Totally. Maybe you can find a place that has both, so that you're safe either way," Ella offered.

"You are brilliant, sister of mine. Anyway, I was just calling to see how your romantic birthday trip was going." Ella's stomach dropped. She had been disconnected from her family and the real world for the last three days, and it hadn't occurred to her that she hadn't told anyone that she and Kyle had broken up.

"Well, that's an interesting story. Do you have a few minutes?"

"Yeah, I don't have anything planned until later this afternoon. Is something wrong? You sound weird."

"Yes, everything is fine, but Kyle and I broke up on Friday."

"Wait, what?" Megan sounded just as confused as Ella had expected.

"Well, it turns out that Kyle was seeing someone else and I walked in on them together on Friday. So we decided to end the relationship."

"End the relationship?" Megan parroted.

"Yes."

"Ok," Megan said slowly, drawing out the word while her brain processed all the new information. "So, Kyle was cheating on you? And you walked in on them, like, together?"

"Yes. I saw them together, bolted, and came to the beach alone."

"Oh my gosh, Ella. Are you ok? Do you need me to drive to the beach to be with you?"

"No, no, no. I'm fine. Don't drive all the way out here.

Besides, it's for the best."

"Ella, Friday was your birthday. This all happened on your birthday? I'm so sorry." Ella could hear the genuine concern in her sister's voice and she had to remind herself that in reality she should be more upset about what had happened. Anyone else in her situation would still be crumpled on the floor, eating ice cream by the gallon, crying over the man she had lost. It wasn't typical that she felt relieved and content; it was strange. "And what the hell is Kyle's problem? Who is this slut he's having an affair with?" Ella smiled at her sister's loyalty.

"Megan, it's a long story. He met a woman at a work thing and they slept together. She showed up at our apartment on Friday and I had the unfortunate luck to walk in on them mid-romp. I left. He called. We broke up."

"Wow. So now what?"

"I don't really know, Meg. I'm here at the beach and I'll be here until Sunday, while Kyle moves out of the apartment. After that, I guess it's back to life as we know it." The thought of going back to Portland made her a little nervous. It made her think about Porter and what might happen between them. She felt silly for even thinking about him, seeing as how they hadn't even had a real date. Still, the idea of being two hours away from him made her feel uneasy.

"And you're sure you don't want some company? I could drive out there tomorrow and stay the night. We could have a girls' night," Megan said in a sing-song voice, trying to convince her. Ella started to refuse, but then thought about how long it had been since she and her baby sister had really had any time together alone.

"You don't have class?"

"I have one early class tomorrow morning and I could drive out after. Then I don't have class again until Wednesday."

"If you're sure you want to and it won't be any trouble,

I'd actually really love to see you."

"Great! I will be there late morning; just text me the address. I'm excited to see you, Ella. I am so sorry that Kyle turned out to be such a jackass." Ella laughed.

"Thanks Meg, I'll see you tomorrow, then. Oh, don't tell Mom and Dad. I haven't called them yet."

"I won't, promise."

Ella ended the call, and was genuinely excited to spend some time with her sister. She took a moment to text the address of the house to Megan and then sent a second text to her:

Do me a favor. Text Kyle and tell him to take the bed with him.*

She got up from the porch steps and decided she would spend the next few hours relaxing, reading her book, and taking her time preparing for her date that evening. She had gone to the closet upstairs and picked out her date outfit with a little trepidation simply because she didn't know what they were doing. She decided that she would go for a little dressier than the night before seeing as how this was a 'real' date. Around one o'clock she had run out of things to do and got an idea. She got her phone and started looking up numbers for salons in Lincoln City. She called a few until she found one that could fit her in right away. She figured that a little pampering was deserved and she also hoped it would help alleviate all the nerves that were building up. She grabbed her purse and headed out the door.

A few hours later Ella was back from the salon and she felt amazing. The women who worked at the salon were so thankful that Ella had saved them from a slow Sunday; they made sure she looked her best when she left. She had told them the story about her breakup and how Porter had come to her rescue, albeit reluctantly, and that now he was taking her out on a date. The women were almost as excited as she was about it and it showed in their work. Ella's hair had been expertly braided from the top part, around the front, and down the side creating a waterfall of hair that came together at a delicate and low side pony. The ends had been curled and the finished product looked completely feminine. Her makeup was minimal with a little shimmery eye shadow, mascara and a pale pink lip gloss. Her freshly manicured nails matched the pink in her lips. She looked at the clock and saw she had a half hour until Porter came to pick her up. She headed upstairs and smiled with excitement to think about the final touch of her preparation. The Dress.

She had seen this dress when it came in on a shipment for her store, and she fell in love with it right away. It was a medium blue, strapless, sweetheart dress with a black lace overlay that covered her shoulders with capped sleeves. The sweetheart neckline accentuated the swells of her breasts and did fabulous things for her cleavage. The blue shell of the dress came to a few inches above the knee, and the lace extended a few inches below, giving the illusion of skin with the without being scandalous. The last detail was a skinny little black belt that sat right at her waist.

She looked in the mirror and decided that if this dress didn't work for Porter, nothing would. She pulled on her black matte pumps and did one final check in the mirror. Now she just needed her date to arrive.

Chapter Eight

Porter

Porter had spent the day doing anything he could think of to keep himself busy, but nothing he did could keep his mind off of Ella. He thought about everything from the way she smelled, to the way he instinctively wanted to protect her, but mostly he thought about how crazy it was that he felt any of this three days after meeting her. As he pulled up to her house, he definitely started to feel a little nervous. He couldn't remember the last time a date had been this important to him, or a woman, for that matter. He knew Ella was different; he could feel it. He was a few minutes early, but got out of his car and headed to her door. He stopped as he saw his reflection in the window by her front door and did a check to make sure he looked all right. He hadn't spent a whole lot of time getting ready but he was confident he looked acceptable. He had chosen his dark jeans, a white shirt, and a black suit jacket. It was simple, but he really didn't have the tolerance for anything fancy. Besides, he was sure if he was going anywhere with Ella, no one would be looking at him anyway. He made it to her door and rang the bell. He listened for any indication that she was coming and eventually heard the tell-tale sound of heels on stairs. A few seconds later she opened the door and Porter felt as if the floor had dropped out from under him.

It was over for him and he knew it. Ella stood before him, and affected him unlike any other woman he'd ever seen. She managed to be absolutely sexy, thoroughly beautiful, and was completely unaware of it. She looked at him and he knew she waiting for his reaction, hoping he approved of her. He slowly let his eyes roam from her face, all the way to her feet and up again. Porter managed to clear his throat and say, "You're going to kill me with that dress, Ella." She blushed and then to add insult to injury, she did a turn.

"It's just a dress, Porter. Is it ok for what we're doing tonight?" She said as she finished her spin. Porter wasn't sure how to answer, because every thought he was having started and ended with her body, and what her dress did to it.

"You look amazing. I'm not even sure amazing covers it." Porter saw the familiar pink rush to Ella's cheeks and decided it was best to just leave instead of standing on the porch and staring at her all night. "You ready to go?"

"Yep. Where are we going?"

"I thought we could go out for dinner and drinks. Ever been to Inn at the Spanish Head?" He saw Ella smile.

"I haven't been there myself, but I remember when I was younger my parents would go away for the weekends to the coast and they would stay there. I always thought it sounded grown-up and fancy."

"Well, it has a really nice restaurant. Hopefully it will live up to your expectations." He waited for Ella to lock the door and then they walked to his truck. He opened the door for her and then after she was safely inside, he closed the door and went to his side. As his truck made its way onto the main road Porter stole a glance over at Ella and felt himself smiling. She was looking out of her window at the ocean and she looked completely relaxed. Her hair was pulled around to the opposite side and from his view all he could focus on was the bare skin of her neck. The gentle slope from behind her ear, to where her neck met her shoulder, to the delicate lace that covered her bare skin; it was all he could do to keep from running a finger along it. He could only imagine how soft her skin felt there and he thought it probably felt a lot like silk. The more he thought about her, the more images popped into his mind. First his finger was along her neck, then his mouth, slowly moving along the curve she left open for him. His thoughts were interrupted by Ella's voice.

"What did you do today? Work on your boat at all?"

"No. I need a part, so I am waiting for it to come in. I didn't do a whole lot today, just kind of caught up on some stuff that I had been putting off." What he didn't tell Ella was that he had spent the entire day making sure that his house was clean enough to entertain, on the off chance that they decided to go back to his house after dinner. He hadn't had a woman in his house for months, not even his mom, and he was pretty sure he needed to do some serious cleaning before he attempted to bring anyone over. "What about you?"

"Well, I went to get pampered for our date, which was amazing. I also spoke with my sister, and she's going to come up tomorrow to stay for a night. It's going to be fun. We're going to be total girls, and watch movies, and eat junk food," Ella said while smiling; she looked excited to spend time with her sister.

"A little sisterly bonding? Sounds fun." They chatted about a few more things before they pulled up to the restaurant. As they walked through the parking lot Porter found his hand on the small of Ella's back. He hadn't purposefully touched her but it seemed as if he had little control over it. His body just wanted to be close to hers. Luckily, it didn't seem like she was opposed to his touch because she offered him a small smile. They walked up to the hostess Porter said, "Hi. We have a reservation for Masters."

The hostess, who looked to be still in high school, looked at her clipboard and said, "I see your reservation right here and we were able to get you the table you requested." Ella looked up at Porter.

"You requested a table?"

"You'll see," was all he said in response.

They followed the hostess and Porter watched Ella for any signs that he'd made a good choice of table. He had asked them to reserve a table on the far wall of the restaurant that was made of one giant picture window. The view from the table looked out over the ocean, above a bluff. Waves were crashing up on to the rocks below, and in just a few minutes they would be able to watch the sunset from their seats. The restaurant had done well and even managed to light a candle on their table as he'd requested.

"Porter," Ella said with a voice that sounded breathy and full of wonder, "this is amazing. I've never seen anything so beautiful." She turned to him and the smile on her face could have stopped his heart. He would go to any lengths tonight to make sure he saw that smile. He pulled out her chair and motioned for her to sit. After they were seated, he ordered a bottle of white wine. They were looking over their menus when he heard Ella give a small gasp.

"Oh, wow." She was looking out over the water. The sun was beginning to set over the water. The sky had brushstrokes of red, yellow and orange, with splashes of pink mixed in. There were a few gauzy clouds along the horizon. Ella rested her chin in her palm, looking as though she was content to watch the sunset all night. He watched her, and took the opportunity to appreciate the way the orangey-red hues of the sunset were making her hair turn a golden color, which made her crystal blue eyes even more alluring and reflective. She was so beautiful and she seemed to have no idea.

All through dinner Porter felt at ease with Ella. They spent the time talking and never found themselves in awkward silences or lacking topics of conversation. He asked her about college and found out that she had majored in business at the University of Oregon, which gave her the foundation she needed to open her own shop in a trendy area of Portland that was known for its small shops and boutiques. She asked him about his college experience and he gave her the truthful answer.

"When I graduated from high school, I never really felt like college was the right choice for me. My mom and I had a little money from my dad's life insurance, but I didn't feel like spending it all on college when I wasn't even sure I needed to go. I got an apprenticeship with a local carpenter, and everything just sort of fell into place. I had spent a good portion of my high school years fixing anything that broke in the bar, or fixing problems at our house. I was good at it, and it seemed silly to go to college. Kids usually go to college to figure out what they want to do in life, find out what they're good at. I already knew."

"That seems like a smart choice. It seems like you've got a good head on your shoulders. Your mom probably has something to do with that," Ella said.

"My mom did anything and everything she could for me. Things could have gotten really bad when my dad died, but she was strong and I never felt like I was at a disadvantage for only having one parent. I couldn't imagine anyone doing a better job than my mom," Porter said proudly.

"Yeah, your mom seems amazing, but I can't imagine what it was like to lose your dad, that must have been hard."

"It was at first, and there are still times when I wish my dad was around, but we managed." Porter felt like the conversation had taken a depressing turn and he wanted to maintain an upbeat mood. "So tell me where you see yourself in five years."

"Well," Ella thought out loud, "I guess I would like to have a second store, somewhere local so that I could be involved, but feel like the business was growing and thriving. I hope I am married by then, with a baby coming soon." Ella smiled and dropped her head into her hands. "Oh my gosh, I cannot believe in five years I will be thirty-five! I am just starting to get used to being thirty." She raised her head and looked at Porter, laughing.

"Thirty's not bad. You've still got time."

"Yeah, I know. It all just kind of hit me when you asked." She took a drink of her wine. "So, where do you see yourself in five years? Wife? Kids?"

"Honestly, I don't know. Dating has never been a priority for me before. I just assumed I would be an eternal bachelor. I'm not opposed to a family, in fact," he smiled up at Ella, "the idea becomes more appealing to me every day. I guess I will just have to wait and see what happens."

"Your mom would be very disappointed if you never gave her any grandchildren. You can't disappoint her," Ella joked.

"You're right. I should probably just marry the next woman that catches my eye."

"I'm just saying, time is passing by you, and so are women. If you aren't paying attention, your future wife and mother of your children could slip away and you would never be the wiser."

Porter looked into Ella's eyes and said, "Trust me, once I find her, I'm not going to let her go."

Ella

Ella could have stayed at the restaurant with Porter forever. She couldn't deny the warmth that had spread through her body when she saw the table he had reserved for them. The candlelight and the sunset; it was picture perfect. If one of her friends had described it to her, she would have rolled her eyes and thought the guy was obviously trying too hard. But with Porter it seemed sweet and totally sexy knowing that he had thought this date through and planned ahead of time. She was enjoying talking with him and learning about his life, and more than that, she was enjoying looking at him. He looked amazing in his black suit jacket and dark jeans. She was now convinced that there was no shirt or jacket in the world that could hide his masculine form, and she was willing now to give in and just ogle him.

Between taking bites of the delicious dinner, sipping drinks and engaging in conversation, the two of them were fully engulfed in what Ella could only describe as Dinner Table Sex. She was finding ways to brush her hand against his, and she felt him gently caress her calf under the table with his foot. The buzzing that was coursing through her body as they sought out each other's touch was bringing her to new levels of arousal and a slow, achy knot was forming in her core.

She stared at his gorgeous body, not bothering to hide the fact that she liked what she saw, and she knew that he was enjoying his view as well. When did dating become this much fun? When she and Kyle started dating everything was calculated and expected. She knew what the next step was before she took it, and knew what her role was from the get-go. But here, with Porter, she had no idea what she was in for, and it was thrilling. She knew that he was sweet and thoughtful, protective with a hint of aggression when challenged, sexy, and strong. She also knew that he felt as out of his element as she did, but he was enjoying it just as much as her, if not more.

When their waitress came to clear their dinner plates she asked if they were interested in dessert. Ella looked to Porter with raised eyebrows and he said, "I have some pretty decent cheesecake back at my place, if you want to go back there."

Ella's insides seemed to implode with excitement. "I could go for some cheesecake," she answered in a calm voiced that betrayed every heartbeat that raced through her veins.

As they were walking back to Porter's truck, Ella felt him take her hand and link their fingers together. It was such a small gesture, but it had caused her heart to falter slightly and a smile spread across her face. Who got this much excitement from holding hands? Had she been missing something with every other man she'd been with? She was starting to realize that every experience with Porter was going to be more exciting and exponentially more arousing than any other she'd had with other men. And that was terrifying. As they approached the truck Porter unlocked her side and opened her door for her. He dropped her hand so she could climb in the truck and she ached for the warmth he took with him. She turned to face him and before she could think too much about it, she rose up and lightly touched her lips to his. She kissed him softly and she felt him respond to her mouth with his. It lasted only a few seconds before she pulled away. She opened her eyes to look up at him, "Thank you for dinner, Porter. It was so beautiful."

He answered her by leaning down to take another kiss. His lips met with hers and his hand came to cradle the side of her face. This kiss was sweet and effectively made her forget everything except the feeling of his lips on hers. She felt him ask to deepen the kiss and it was all she could do to remember to breathe. He now had both hands on her, pulling her into the kiss, caging her in, and she loved it. Their tongues were flirting with each other and when she instinctively nibbled on his lower lip she heard a masculine groan escape from him. He pushed her back up against his truck as he took the kiss even deeper.

She reached her hands around his waist and up his back. She could feel all the hard muscle she'd known was there. He continued to kiss her senseless and she realized that even though she had started this, she was no longer in control. They were all hands and staggered breaths.

He broke away from her mouth and spread kisses from just behind her ear, down the side of her neck and she melted. If he hadn't been holding on to her, she would have crumpled to the ground. "Porter," she breathed quietly, "this is crazy."

"You're bare neck has been torturing me all night," he said between kisses.

The idea that he had been thinking about kissing her there all through dinner sent a new wave of courage through her. She found his mouth again and this time she wanted to explore. She kissed him with force, running her fingers through his hair. It felt smooth and soft between her fingers, but gave her satisfaction when she pulled on it to bring him closer. She felt his hands move past her shoulders, down her spine and settle on the small of her back. She gave a little moan to indicate her need for more and he moved his hands over her ass. She could feel him pull her towards him, even though there was nowhere left for her to go. They were as close as two people could be fully clothed in a parking lot, but she needed to be closer.

She pulled away, breathing heavily and leaned her forehead against his, "Porter?"

"Ella?" he breathed.

"Can we still go back to your place?"

Porter exhaled loudly. "Definitely. Let's go."

Chapter Nine

Ella

On the drive to his house, Porter kept her hand securely in his. It felt as if once he'd gotten ahold of it, he wasn't going to let it go and that was definitely ok with her. She wasn't sure when she'd decided to lose herself in Porter, but somewhere between the dress, and the door, and the dinner, she'd decided to let herself have one night. She felt entitled to a rebound. That's what most twenty or thirty-somethings did after a break-up; they made rash decisions and spent one night with someone to ease the heartache. But this felt different. It didn't feel like heartache and it didn't feel like one night was going to be enough of Porter. Not after the way his hands had captured her face, or how his arms seemed to mold around her body, and the way all her nerves seemed frazzled after one small kiss. Not to mention how the one small kiss morphed into many deep interlaced kisses. Ella caught herself blushing at the memory of the kisses they shared only a few moments ago. She exhaled loudly, trying to shake the butterflies from her stomach. She stole a glance at Porter and saw that he was wearing a small grin as well. She felt him gently rub his thumb along her hand and the butterflies simply multiplied.

Porter pulled onto a gravel drive that took them off the main road, and the road seemed to wind along, dodging trees and curving around coastal brush. After a short drive a small house appeared and seemed to be the only house down the road.

"Is this you?" Ella asked, pointing ahead at the house as they neared.

"Yup, this is my house."

Ella didn't know exactly what she was expecting, but she was definitely taken by surprise when she saw his house. It looked to be at least three stories high, the top half had shingled siding in a medium colored wood, while the bottom half was a warm forest green. The trim around the house was white, as well as the shutters. There were two elegant wooden columns that held up the roof of the front porch. The third floor boasted a very large picture window, and Ella thought that being so high up, there was probably a pretty awesome view of the ocean, which was just about a half mile from his road. The house looked to be the perfect mixture of masculinity and femininity. The colors were warm, but the angles were sharp. The lines were clean, but it looked incredibly inviting. "Porter, this house is amazing," she said with unmasked sincerity and awe.

"Thanks, I worked really hard on it. There are still a few projects I want to complete, but it took quite a bit of work."

"Did you fix it up a lot?"

"You could say that. I built it from the ground up." Ella shot him a surprised look.

"You built that house?" She asked shocked.

"Yeah. I used the money I got from my father's life insurance when I turned eighteen and I bought the land. Then I just spent the next couple years building it as I went. I lived with my mom during the build, so most of my income went directly into the house, as well as all my free time."

"I'm not going to lie Porter. That is incredibly sexy."

Porter laughed, "What is? My house?"

"No. The fact that you built it."

Porter shrugged his shoulders. "It wasn't that difficult. This is what I do for a living."

"Porter, not everyone can build a house," she said as she smiled at him.

"Well, I don't want to bring you here under false pretenses," he had a huge smile on his face. "I didn't do any of the plumbing or electrical."

Ella laughed, "Ok, I guess in that case you've been bumped down to 'mildly attractive'".

"Well, maybe I can improve my rating with the cheesecake I have inside."

"That is highly likely," she said with a smile.

They got out of the truck and Ella was still gripped by the beautiful house he had built. There was definitely something ridiculously sexy about a man who had built his house with his own hands. She was sure it was programmed into a woman's DNA to be attracted to a man who can provide shelter, but this was more than any fort or lean-to. This was a piece of art, crafted by a man who obviously had the patience and commitment to see the project through. There was something to be said for a man who was simply capable. If he could build a freaking house, what couldn't he do? Probably very little.

She followed him up to the front steps and watched him unlock his door. She used the opportunity to admire him from the back. Of course, there were the broad muscular shoulders that she had recently had the pleasure of rubbing her hands along while he kissed her senseless, but now she could also see the great ass in his jeans. She had never really been one to longingly stare at a man or his backside, but Porter's ass was worth staring at. He walked into the house and flipped on the lights.

Ella followed him into the house and was lead into a great room that included a living room, dining room and kitchen. She came into the living room with big, comfy, plush couches facing a large flat screen TV. Past the living room was a state of the art kitchen with white cabinets, crown molding, and a large island in the middle with a light colored granite top. To the left of the kitchen area was a smaller dining room with just a little table to seat four. The bottom floor had light colored hard wood floors throughout, no curtains, and no pictures hanging on the wall. It looked like a bachelor pad, but it was beautiful.

"Wow," Ella said as she walked around the big room. "This is amazing Porter. How long did it take you to build it?"

"Well, I guess from the beginning to when it would have been sellable, it was about three years, but that was with just me doing most of the work. I had help putting up the frame and pouring the foundation and all that, but it was mostly just me. I would work all week, and then come out here at night and work until I couldn't see straight. I would come out on weekends, too. Once it was essentially done, I would tweak things, or redo things all together, until I felt like it was just right. Once I felt like there wasn't really anything else for me to do, I started the boat."

"That's right, the boat," Ella remembered. "Again, Porter, I am totally impressed."

"Wine?" He asked from the kitchen.

"Sure, that sounds great."

"Red or white?"

"White, please." She wandered around the big living room, looking at his handy work, thinking how beautiful everything was, but that a woman's touch could really soften the place up. She took a seat on one of his big-cushioned couches. She smoothed her dress down her legs as he brought her the wine, placed a plate on the table with a slice of cheesecake on it, and sat down on the other side of the couch. She took a sip and eyed him. She gently rubbed the cushion next to her, signaling him to move closer to her. He took a sip of wine, looking at her, gave her a smirk, and crooked his finger at her, asking her to make the move. Ella laughed, rolled her eyes, and scooted over so that she was right next to him, smoothing out her dress again.

She took a sip of her wine and felt him tuck a loose strand of hair behind her ear. Just that simple touch made everything simmer inside and she instinctively closed her eyes, relishing in his touch. Trying to maintain a little composure, she opened her eyes and looked at him. "So, do you cook in that magnificent kitchen?"

Porter laughed, "No, not really. I have limited cooking skills. I can grill and I can handle a box of mac'n'cheese every now and then. Anything more complicated than that, and I just either go out, or I head to the bar."

"So, you didn't make this cheesecake?" Ella said with mock surprise motioning towards the cake on the table.

"Nope, my mother made that. Want a bite?"

"Definitely. I was lured here under the pretenses that there would be cheesecake," she said laughing.

"Then cheesecake you will get," Porter lifted the plate, scooped up a piece, and held the fork up to her mouth. She took the bite and immediately closed her eyes as she groaned.

"Oh my god, Porter. That's amazing," she said as she chewed. She heard him laugh and when she looked back up at him he was wearing a half grin, but his eyes looked darker. She licked a piece of stray cake off her lip and she heard him inhale sharply. The way he was looking at her was turning the simmering into a rapid boil. "Here, let me," Ella said. She put her glass down, took the fork and plate from him, and fed him a bite. He took it, but kept his eyes on hers as he chewed. "Don't you like it?" she asked, frowning at his less than enthused reaction to what she deemed to be the best cheesecake she'd ever tasted.

"It's very good, but I've had it before. And besides, you're the most delicious thing on this couch." She watched as he put his wine down and then leaned over towards her. She knew what was coming. He hesitated just before his lips met hers to give her the opportunity to stop him, but she simply closed the gap between them. He was scooting closer to her and she could taste the cheesecake on his mouth. He took the plate from her hand and placed it on the table all without breaking their contact. Once both of their hands were free from obstacles, they immediately moved to exploring each other. His hands, once again, were wrapped around her face, cradling her cheeks and urging her mouth closer to his, while hers were roaming up his chest and over his shoulders.

As she felt his shoulders, her hands ran into his jacket and she started sliding her hands down his arms urging the jacket off of him. He wriggled out of it and dropped it on the floor. He leaned forward and wrapped his arms around her waist and pulled her into him, chest to chest, and her knees came to rest on the couch between his thighs.

"I told you this dress was bad news, Ella," he said as he moved to kiss the side of her neck. "And I can't get enough of this spot here," licking and sucking on the little curve where her neck met her shoulder. He ran his hands up and down the sides of her body from her waist to her arms, his thumbs skimming over her breasts. His mouth moved from her lips, to her neck, and back to her lips. She couldn't form any words, but she couldn't help the whisper-quiet moans that escaped her. Tiny whimpers that caught her off guard because she wasn't in control, not even a little bit. She was on some sort of sexual auto-pilot, and even though she could feel every tremble and every connection their bodies made, she was not the one making the decisions as to where her hands were roaming, or which part of his body she was kissing. She was everywhere and nowhere. And she loved it.

He surprised her by grabbing her waist again, moving over her to lay her down along the couch, draping his body over hers. The weight of his body was considerable, but felt safe and secure. She reached her arms behind his back, up through his arms, pulling him closer to her. His hand skimmed down her side again, but this time on the way back up, his slid his hand along her thigh pulling her dress up with it. The coolness of her exposed skin was heated instantly by his large hand. She couldn't help but wonder if she should stop this before she regretted anything, but he seemed content where he was. The longer he spent kissing and nuzzling the more relaxed she became with her new, more revealing dress. She reminded herself that this was ok. She had every right to enjoy this man who was obviously feasting upon her. If anything, she deserved it.

With new found courage, she found the hem of his shirt and started to glide her hands up his stomach and was astounded at what she felt under the fabric of his shirt. She pushed his mouth away, pulled up his shirt so she could see his stomach and asked, "Are you for real?" His stomach was rock hard with absolutely no distinguishable roundness. She knew he was in shape by the muscles she's already drooled over, but this was ridiculous.

He looked a little confused by the abrupt interruption of her question.

"What do you mean?"

"Um, I guess I'm just wondering why you look like some sort of god carved out of stone?" She asked seriously.

"Like what you see, do you?" He smiled at her and flipped his nose on the tip of hers. She blushed at his question, suddenly shy.

"I can't think of any complaints," she smiled at him.

"Hmmm, well, good," he replied sinking down for another soft kiss. He rested his elbows on either side of her head and used his hands to brush her wayward hair off her forehead. He locked eyes with her and quietly asked, "Are you ok with all of this?"

"What do you mean?" She whispered.

"This. Us. Are you ok with all of this happening? I don't want to rush you into anything you're not ready for," he said.

"I've given myself permission for this one night," she replied as she ran a hand through his silky hair. She saw a strange look in his eyes. She almost thought it was a hint of anger, but it was gone as soon as it appeared. He crashed his lips down on to hers again, his tongue taking wide sweeps through her mouth, dancing with hers. She felt him inhale so deep, it seemed as if he was trying to get as much of her in his system as he could, to flood all of his senses. He suddenly pulled away from her, so quickly it startled her. He stood over her while she still lay sprawled out and half covered on the couch. He reached a hand out to her.

"We better make the most out of it then," he said. She reached out to take his hand, and once she was upright, he led her towards the stairs.

Chapter Ten
Ella

Ella allowed Porter to lead her up the stairs, all the way to the third floor. When they made it to the top of the stairs, she found herself in a room that easily took up the whole floor. She was faced with the wall of windows she had noticed from the driveway. It was already dark, so all she could really see from the window was the flashing of the lighthouse down the beach. She watched him turn on a bedside lamp and then he turned back to her.

His bedroom, much like the first floor, was lacking in the decoration department. His walls were painted a dark navy blue. There were beige colored, wooden chair rails along the walls, which were beautiful and alluded to the fact that a master craftsman lived here. There was a door that looked like it led to the master bathroom, and then she caught a glimpse of what looked like a huge walk-in closet that any woman would weep over. She didn't have to ask to know that the inside of the closet would be made of cedar with plenty of built in shelves for storage. She almost gasped out loud when she laid eyes on his bed.

"Did you build your bed?" she asked motioning towards it. He nodded in response and then came towards her. "It's really beautiful." It was a huge, king size, cherry wood, sleigh bed with plush cream colored bedding. The head and footboards were flat, not curved like a traditional sleigh bed, and it made the bed look incredibly masculine. She saw him coming towards her with determined eyes and a shiver ran through her. "Is there anything in this house that you didn't build?" she asked, trying to cover for the fact that she was nervous about being with him. He came around behind her and put his hands on top of her shoulders gently. She felt his mouth come down lightly on her neck with a half kiss, half nibble.

"If it's made of wood," he said quietly, "I built it." His words vibrated on her neck and she let out a small moan.

"Oh God, that's sexy," she said as she rolled her neck further to the side to allow him more access. "That closet over there is sexy, too. I might have to let you build me one," she said lazily as his mouth went to work on her sensitive neck.

"I can think of a few sexy things, too," he rubbed his hands down her arms and perched his chin on her shoulder.

"Oh yeah?"

"Like your legs in this dress. Your ass in this dress. Generally, you in this dress. You're killing me."

She turned her face towards him and whispered, "Then why don't you take it off me?" She felt his fingers grip the zipper in the back and slowly pull it down. He eased his hands into her dress at the shoulders and slid it down her arms, letting it drop all the way to the ground and gather around her feet. She turned around in his arms and was met by his mouth. There was no hesitation here. Every question of reassurance she was asking him, he was answering as their tongues swirled around each other. His kiss was fierce and it was making it difficult for her to breathe. She grasped at the bottom of his shirt and pulled it up. He leaned forward and she got it over his head, ruffling his hair that constantly looked ruffled anyway. She looked up, ran her hands slowly through it, and found herself looking into his eyes. "I can't believe that two nights ago you were yelling at me about jumper cables." He smiled at her and nudged her nose with the tip of his.

"Sorry about that, again."

"I couldn't believe how mad you were."

He sighed and then rested his forehead against hers. "I couldn't believe that you were all alone and unprepared. And I wasn't really mad at you. I was uncomfortable. It caught me off guard how instantly I was protective over you." He paused and took a deep breath. "I don't usually do this, Ella. I'm not usually this invested in someone, and the fact that I didn't even have a choice really irritated me. I was instantly drawn to you and there was nothing I could do about it." He dropped a small kiss on her lips. "I don't want to do anything about it. I just want to be here with you and spend the night making you happy." She tried to breathe, really tried, but every breath was shallow and edging on frantic. She wasn't sure what was going to happen tomorrow, or what life was going to be like once she went back to Portland, but she knew that at this moment, she wanted Porter. He was offering a night of excitement, pleasure and happiness, and she desperately needed everything he wanted to give her.

She tipped up on her toes and pressed her mouth to his with a new urgency, hoping to alleviate some of the need she was feeling. She needed to be close to him, needed to be wrapped up in him. He matched her in aggression when he returned the kiss, and startled her as he grabbed both of her legs behind her thighs and picked her up. She instinctively wrapped her legs around his waist and let him carry her to the bed where he gently set her down on the edge. Without breaking their connection, he grabbed her around the waist and scooted her back, using their kiss to guide her down onto the bed. The feeling of his large body pressing down on her was heady and she found herself arching up to increase the pressure. It was as if her body was trying to eliminate the space between them.

He broke away from their kiss, only to trail more kisses down her chin and neck, continuing down between her breasts. He lifted his head for a moment to gaze at her body, then continued to place kisses up and down her stomach. "You have an amazing body," he said between adoring kisses. She arched up further to meet his mouth, still not close enough, and he reached below her swiftly unhooking her bra. She helped by pulling it down her arms. Once she was free, she wrapped her hands around his neck to pull his mouth back to hers. His large hand found her breast and he began to knead it in a circular motion that was mirrored in every part of her body. She was swirling everywhere. Her hips were moving in circles, her mouth, too. Her body was connected to every move he made.

His mouth landed on her nipple and she couldn't help the cry that came out of her mouth. Her head fell back and her knees drew up around his hips. As he worked one breast with his mouth, he started on the other with his hand, rolling and pinching her nipple. She was shamelessly grinding everywhere. Her hands were in his hair, her hips moving, trying to find friction where they could. A fire had started in her core and she was desperate for relief from the flame. She needed more.

"Porter," she practically growled.

"Hmmm," he replied, unwilling to leave his station, taking his job very seriously at the moment.

"Porter. Pants. Off." She didn't have time for full sentences now. He lifted his head and smiled at her, but she frantically grabbed his pants and got to work on the belt. Within seconds she had him unbuttoned and was pushing his pants and boxers down his legs. He helped by using his feet to free himself of the last of his clothes. She found him to be fully hard and a new wave of arousal hit her as she began to stroke him between her thighs. If she had thought he was ridiculously masculine before, holding him in her hands only solidified her earlier notions. He was all male. She couldn't help but feel like she might have earned a little sexual karma and was now getting her payout for all the crap she'd been dealing with.

He moved down her body and she felt him slip from her hands. She frowned, groaning at his absence. He must have heard her because he brought his face back up to hers, kissed her behind her ear, and whispered, "We've got all night, Ella." He made a slow trail down her body with his mouth, stopping to suck each of her breasts into taut points. He continued down, kissing the softness of her stomach. When he reached her panties, he made an appreciative moan. "These are sexy as hell, Ella."

"Glad you approve," she said happily, glad she'd taken the appropriate precautions to pick out the sexiest of her panties. They were black lace, to match her dress.

"Oh, I definitely approve, but they have to come off now."

"What a pity," she laughed. He grabbed both sides of her lacy thong, and as he pulled them down, his face followed until he was clear down by her feet. He paused, slowly picked up one of her feet, and lightly kissed the side of her foot, looking directly into her eyes.

"You are beautiful, Ella," he said quietly, and she believed him. She gave him a shy smile. She wasn't self-conscious of her flaws at the moment, because she could see in his eyes that he liked what he saw. He continued to kiss up her calf, all the way up her thigh. When he moved to the inside of her leg, she tensed, knowing where he was headed. She hadn't been with many men, but she was never really comfortable letting anyone go down on her. She had always been so self-conscious and it was entirely too intimate for her liking. She had never really enjoyed it and didn't want to ruin what was, so far, an exceptional sexual experience. She opened her mouth to stop him, but he met her eyes before she could say anything and he simply stated, "Relax." She thought about stopping him still, but then something in the back of her mind told her to just let go. Her head fell back against the bed and any argument she had was immediately erased at the first glide of his tongue.

Fire. White hot fire. Burning out from her core, throughout her limbs, up her chest. She was immediately thrown into a pool of liquid heat that she had never experienced. With every flick of his tongue she felt a new flutter or a new fire being lit within her. "Oh God, Porter. Don't stop." He paused for only a second to respond.

"Don't worry, Ella. I've got you." Then he was back to using his mouth to push her towards oblivion.

He was relentless; He endlessly licked, sucked, and nibbled at her. Her breathing was haggard, and she was making nonsensical noises that fell somewhere between moans of pleasure and worried whimpers. She was grasping around her, looking for something to hold on to, to ground her, to keep her from floating way. She found his hands, and held on for her life, or so it felt. He linked his fingers with hers. He used her hands to pull her body down towards his mouth, adding even more friction and pressure to his already writhing mouth and her already gyrating body. The effect was an immediate burst of pleasure that traveled her body, and the initial tidal wave was followed by a slow roll of warmth that seemed to melt her as it traveled and rippled over her. He stayed on her while she rode the wave, coming down with a loud sigh. She felt his warm mouth leave her, but she couldn't form words to vocalize her displeasure in his absence.

He was back to kissing his way up her body and she was lazily running her hand through his hair again. Half way up, he leaned over to his bedside table and grabbed a condom from the drawer. He held it up to her, "Want to help me with this?" He was grinning at her, and she smiled back, taking it from him. She opened the package and reached down for him, rolling the condom down his length. She looked back up at him and pulled his face back to hers and kissed him with a new sense of relief. The urgent need she had felt earlier had been eradicated with her orgasm, and now she was a liquid cloud, floating on the bed, lazy and willing to do anything to get Porter to this place with her. She wanted him satisfied and she wanted to be the one to get him there. She deepened the kiss and felt his arms squeeze around her at the small of her back, tilting her hips up perfectly. She wrapped her ankles around his back and felt him ready for her. She squeezed her legs, gently guiding him into her, slowly and fully.

"God, Ella," he breathed.

"I know," she said, kissing him again.

He was in control now and this was for him. She let him lead her wherever he wanted and he was obviously not in any rush. His rhythm was slow and sinuous, gradually building in intensity. His hips rolled and he kissed her. The steady thrusts were bold but soft, and she found herself climbing again. She pulled on his shoulders, again trying to grasp anything she could. "Let it go," she heard him whisper in her ear, and it was her undoing. She fell again, but this time it was smooth and silky. She felt him speed up his thrusts and knew he was close to coming apart as well. She did everything should could to get him where she was, meeting his hips with hers, and kissing him harder. When he finally came, he stilled and buried his face in her neck. They laid together, slowly coming down from their highs, breathing each other in.

"Am I crushing you?" He finally asked.

"Not at all," she replied, lazily trailing her hand up and down his back. He lifted his head, nuzzling the side of her face, and then his eyes met hers.

"That was amazing," he said, waiting for a response.

"Yes," she said as she cupped the side of his face. She was too exhausted to explain the depth to which he had touched her or the heights he'd pushed her to. He dipped down and kissed her lightly as her eyes closed. He rolled off of her and she was immediately cold. She heard his moving around, and guessed he was removing the condom, but she couldn't open her eyes to see him because her eyelids were suddenly thousand pound weights. She felt him grab her around her middle and pull her back to his front, cuddling her in tight to him.

"Sleep," was all she heard him say, and he didn't have to

tell her twice.

Chapter Eleven
Ella

When Ella's eyes fluttered open the first thing she noticed was the strong arm still wrapped tightly around her waist. She smiled as images flooded her mind, reminding her of what had transpired between them just hours earlier. Who'd have thought that in the little beach town, after being stranded at a bar, she would meet the man who would give her the best sex she'd ever experienced? Not only had Porter made her feel totally comfortable and sexy, he'd paid her special attention and gifted her two orgasms which had never happened to her before. In the past she'd been lucky to get one. Where was the Porter who claimed he wasn't interested in women? The Porter she'd slept with obviously had extensive sexual experience.

She looked around for a clock and saw the time was three a.m. She was unsure of what the protocol was at this point. She'd never had a one night stand before. She was pretty sure she wasn't supposed to hang around and she was definitely supposed to be gone by morning. She gently started scooting towards the edge of the massive bed, lifting his arm slowly trying not to jostle him. She managed to make it out from under his arm and was almost off the bed completely when she felt his arm grab her around her middle and yank her back to him.

"Ahh!" she yelped in surprise.

"Nope," he said sleepily.

"Nope?"

"Nope. As in, no, you're not leaving."

"Porter, really, I'm fine. I will just call a cab. Go back to sleep." He growled and then shifted up on an arm so he was leering at her.

"There are no cabs here, city girl. I drove you here. I will drive you home. You're not sneaking off in the middle of the night like this was some sort of drunken college hook-up," he looked a little insulted. She reached up and brushed his crazy hair back from his forehead.

"I'm sorry, I'm not trying to be difficult. I've just never been in this situation before. I thought it would be easier if I was gone when you woke up."

"What do you mean easier?"

She took a few seconds to put her thoughts together. "You know I've just ended a long term, serious relationship. I guess I'm just confused about what happened between us, where we stand, and it seemed logical that if I left before we had to talk about it, I could avoid the conversation all together." Her face scrunched up with embarrassment.

"You said you wanted one night, Ella, and I was totally willing to give that to you, if it was what you wanted. Is it still what you want?" He rolled on top of her and looked her in the eyes. "If you're really ready to go home and leave it at that, I will get up and drive you home right now. But that's not what I want." Ella took in the deep brown eyes gazing at her and she felt truly confused.

"What is it that you want?" She whispered.

"I want to see where this goes. I don't want to pressure you, or scare you, but I don't think I could let you walk away knowing I'd never see you again," his eyes were still on hers, expectantly.

"Ok." The word was out of her mouth before she had even a second to think of a response. A slow smile spread across his face and she knew she couldn't walk away either. This all seemed a little crazy. Surely no fling that starts two days after a previous relationship ends will last very long, but at this point she will take whatever she can get from him. He was addictive. He interrupted her thoughts by taking her mouth again, and he gave her a long, thorough, searing kiss. Her heart rate spiked and the butterflies were back flying around in her stomach when he suddenly rolled off of her and got up off the bed, treating her to the visual of his naked ass walking to his closet. When he came back out, she was disappointed to see he had put on boxers. He tossed a tee shirt and boxers at her.

"Get dressed," he said, "then meet me downstairs."

"Porter, it's three in the morning. Why are we getting out of bed?" The bed was exactly where she wanted to be with him.

"I promised you cheesecake, and I got a little distracted before I fully delivered. Let's go eat some cheesecake." What woman in her right mind would turn down cheesecake in the middle of the night with a ridiculously handsome man?

"Ok, I'll be right down," she smiled.

Porter

She came down the stairs wearing his shirt and boxers, and he had never seen a sexier woman. All his clothes were big on her, seeing as how he was a giant compared to her. She had to roll up the boxers at the waist making the shorts very short, accentuating her incredibly toned legs. The shirt hung loosely off one of her shoulders, showing off her sexy neck again.

Last night had been incredible, and he would always remember the way she looked at him as she laid on his bed naked, waiting for him to love her. He'd planned to make the night as much about her as possible, but he hadn't anticipated that there was no way to be with her and not give her everything. She was intoxicating, and if he spent every day for the rest of his life trying to make her feel as beautiful as he thought she was, he would die content. It was easy making love to her, and he knew it would be addictive, too.

While she had been getting dressed in his clothes, he had dished out two plates of cheesecake. He handed one to her as she approached him. She smiled at him and leaned back against the counter, taking a small bite. He mirrored her and leaned back against the counter of the island.

"This is the best cheesecake I've ever had," she said between bites.

"My mom is a pretty good baker. I like the cheesecake, but her blackberry cobbler is out of control."

"Maybe my sister and I will go to the bar for dinner tomorrow night and try some."

Porter laughed. "You'd literally be walking into a mom war zone. She knows about our date, and she will not let you enjoy your meal without harassing you about it. You're better off going someplace else."

Ella shrugged her shoulders and took another bite. "I don't mind your mom. When we talked on the first night she was really sweet to me. Besides, maybe I can pry some information out of her about you."

"Hey, I'm an open book," he smiled.

"Right, but I want to know the stuff you'd never tell a girl you're dating," she blushed after he realized she's implied they were dating, and Porter loved the way the blush affected her skin. He was pleased that she hadn't tried to correct herself or backtrack, she was testing the word out. He pried his eyes off her and made himself look away, not wanting her to notice he was staring. He was going to have to bring her around gently. Let her get used to the idea of being with him, and not get too pushy. He felt like that would be the hardest part – letting her come to him. "You know, embarrassing stories from when you were younger, silly nicknames, stuff like that."

"Portly."

"Huh?" Ella said with a big bite of cheesecake in her mouth.

"Portly. That was my embarrassing nickname. I was a little chubby in grade school, and my mom used to call me Portly. Not in a mean way, kind of in an endearing way. Anyway, one day I forgot my lunch and my mom drove it to the bus stop and had my lunch out the car window yelling, "Portly! You forgot your lunch!" Needless to say, all the kids at the bus stop heard her, and that was my nickname until about eighth grade." Ella began to giggle, covering her mouth with her hand. It looked like she was trying to get it under control, but she just kept giggling. It morphed into a full blown laugh, complete with gasping breaths and tears forming in her eyes. Eventually she had to put her plate down, and was bent over holding her stomach. Porter was smiling, watching her lose herself in laughter. She was enjoying his childhood trauma way too much. Her laughter tapered off, and she picked up her plate again, although a few more chuckles made it past her. She took a bite, and wiped the tears that had escaped.

"So, I guess eventually they couldn't really call you Portly anymore, huh?" she asked, smiling.

"Nope," he said with a sly smile.

"I had an embarrassing nickname," she was focused on her cheesecake again.

"And?" He drew the word out, expecting an answer.

"I'm not telling you."

"What? I just gave you an insight into my agonizing formative years, and you're holding out on me?" She kept quiet for a moment more, thinking about her response.

"I am strategically withholding information that I might find useful and to my benefit sometime in the future," she declared firmly.

"Tell me," he demanded with a smile.

"Not a chance, Portly."

He pounced on her, tossing his plate on the counter and jolting up. She had pretty good reflexes, and was running from him instantly. He could tell she didn't really know which way to go, so he had the advantage of knowing the floor plan. When she headed out of the kitchen she went right, so he went left, effectively leaving her alone in the living room, but giving her nowhere to run. He was standing near the front door and the stairs. If she wanted to go anywhere she would have to go through him. He could wait her out. She was bouncing from foot to foot, looking like a baseball player about to steal third base. He relaxed from his hunched position, stood up straight, and crossed his arms over his chest.

"You're trapped, Ella. You can stand there dancing around as long as you want, but I will catch you eventually." She stopped swaying and frowned, and he couldn't believe it when she stuck out her bottom lip. "Are you pouting?"

"You won't play with me," she said, exaggerating the lip, and batting her eyelashes. Porter dropped his arms and strode towards her, keeping his eyes on hers. He could see her eyes soften, and her pouted lips turned into a smile, as she saw him getting closer. Her eyes stayed on his, and when he was right in front of her she lifted her face to his. He grazed his thumb along her jaw and then he slowly lowered his mouth to hers, gently kissing her. The kiss grew quickly into a fast and frenzied storm of a kiss. He couldn't stop his hands from pulling her closer, sealing their bodies to one another. He could feel her heart pounding, and she was breathing just as quickly and frantically as he was. He pulled away, moving his hands to the sides of her face, leaning his head against hers.

"You want to play games, Ella?" She answered him with a playful kiss in the affirmative. A big smile spread across his face. "You better run then," he growled. Her eyes opened wide in shock, realizing his intentions. She shrieked and bolted around him. He let her go, knowing it would be more exciting if she had a head start. Once she hit the stairs, however, he figured she was fair game. He took off after her, and once she could hear his footsteps pounding after her, she started squealing with nervous laughter. As he came around the stairs he saw her just reaching the top, so he took the stairs two at a time, and the exhilaration of the chase was making his heart trample through his veins. She kept up with her loud fits of giggle-shrieks, and the closer he got to her, the more frenzied they became.

He followed the sounds of her footsteps, and she had gone back into the bedroom. He found her in the middle of the room, and she was breathing heavy, with a half grin on her face. They both looked at each other for a moment, gauging the situation. Then, at the same time, they dove for each other, the excitement of their game spurring on the frantic need to be near one another. Their bodies collided in a jumble of arms and legs seeking out the other, and his mouth crashed down on hers. He grabbed the back of her thighs, picked her up, and moved to the wall, pinning her against it. His hands slid back and forth along her thighs as he used his hips to hold her against the wall. His mouth was in heaven, tasting her lips, her neck, her shoulder. All the while he felt her hands urgently gripping and rubbing him wherever they could grasp, trying to not only keep herself wrapped around him, but also in a need to get close to him. It seemed that they could never get close enough to each other, and he felt it, too. He could pull and hug and hold her to him all night and it was never close enough.

He grabbed her shirt and pulled up on it, and a thrill went through him when he realized she was bare underneath his shirt. He would need to remember which shirt she had on, because it had just been upgraded to his favorite. After he got the shirt over her head he went back to work on her mouth while his hands found her breasts. There was nothing about her body that didn't turn him on. He'd already realized her neck was going to be a huge distraction for him, but her breasts were amazing. He snaked one hand around her back to hold her steady and palmed one of her breasts. He used his thumb and finger to roll her nipple back and forth. She pulled her face from his to lean it back against the wall.

"Porter," she groaned.

"Feel good?" He asked, smiling and grinding his hips into her core. There was just two very thin pieces of cotton separating them, and he felt her tensing and grinding back against him.

"Oh God. Please Porter. Bed. Now." He didn't hesitate at her request. He grabbed her and walked to the bed laying her down right in the middle. He trailed his hands down her body starting at her shoulders, over the tight peaks of her breasts, glazing over her flat yet deliciously soft stomach, down the sides of her waist. He grabbed the boxers she was wearing and slid them off. He continued his trail from her hips, down her thighs to the bottom of her feet. She was watching him worship her body, grinning at him, and when his eyes returned to hers he saw he was under speculation. "You're still wearing your boxers," she said. He kept eye contact with her as he pulled his boxers down and kicked them across the room. "That's better," she smiled. He climbed onto the bed and came over her with his hands on either side of her head, with her legs cradling his hips.

"So, Ella," he asked, kissing her mouth for emphasis. "Who do you think is winning this game?" He nuzzled her neck making her squeak a feminine noise, high pitched, laced with laughter.

"Um," she drew out the word, mocking his question with an over-exaggerated contemplation, adding a finger to her lips for dramatic effect, "technically, Porter, I don't think either one of us has won just yet."

"Is that right?" He laughed, and made her laugh as he tickled her sides lightly.

"Yea, but I think I could give you a head start." Before he knew what was happening, she grabbed him from between her thighs and started to gently stroke him up and down. He was taken by surprise, and the feeling of her hands on him was spectacular. He leaned his forehead down on to hers, and could feel his breathing become more ragged as she continued to draw her hand up and down him. She was letting out little whimpers again, and he could tell that holding him in her hands was affecting her, too.

"Ella, that feels amazing. You're amazing," he said as he kissed her mouth that was already swollen from all the roughness he had inflicted on it that night. He felt her shifting under him, so he rolled on to his back. She stayed next to him, draped over his side, still grasping him. He reached for her neck to pull her to him, kissing her again and again, gently caressing her all over, trying to focus on the feeling of her hands on him.

She pulled away from him and reached into his

nightstand drawer as he had earlier. He watched her pull out a condom, rip it open, and roll it down him. She locked her eyes on his, straddled him, and then took a moment to lean down and kiss him, gently pulling on his bottom lip with her mouth. He growled at her as the sensations took him over. He felt her lift off of him slightly, position herself over him, and slide down onto him incredibly slowly. This time, their moans of pleasure mirrored each other. He watched as she reached to her messy braid, and pulled out the band, and then shook her hair loose so that is was framing her face is crazy waves.

He was paralyzed by the sight of her sitting atop him, the feeling of her enveloping him entirely and deeply, by the hitched sounds of her breathing while she took him all in. Everything about her at this moment left him incapacitated. And then she started to move.

Anything he'd experienced before this, and anything after, would never compare to the sight of Ella, naked, with wild and abandoned hair, losing herself on him. Her eyes were closed, her mouth slightly open letting our small gasps and miniscule moans, her hands glued to his chest using him as an anchor for the rocking and grinding she was assaulting him with. He tried to close his eyes, tried to get lost in the immense feelings of pleasure, but he couldn't take his eyes off of her.

"Ella, baby," he said quietly.

"Hmm?" She answered still in her far away state of wantonness.

"Come back to me."

She stilled immediately and opened her eyes. She looked down at him momentarily, and then lowered her mouth to him again. This kiss was reverent, and sweet, and was so full of wanting and longing. They were connected again, and she began her assault once more, slowly taking him deeper with every roll of her hips. Once he was in tune to her rhythm, he used his hips to drive into her, adding even more pressure to their melting bodies. He was driving up and pulling down on her arms, and she was quickening her thrusts.

"Porter, I'm close," she cried.

"I know, baby. I'm right here with you," he answered.

And that was all she needed. She continued to ride him, quickening her pace, strengthening her grasp on him, searching for the right combination to send her over the edge. He felt her core start to tighten around him and heard her cry out, and he followed her. He felt himself fall, and it reminded him of water draining from a tub. Swirling, out of control, wrapped up in something so much bigger than himself. No matter what, he was along for the ride.

She collapsed on top of him, breathing hard. He wrapped his hand around the back of her neck with on hand, and used the other to trail his fingers up and down her back. He closed his eyes, and breathed her in, and knew it was over.

He would follow her anywhere.

Chapter Twelve
Ella

This time, when Ella woke it was definitely morning. Dull light shone through the enormous window of Porter's room. She looked out the window and could only see grey sky and the tips of some green trees stretching up to find the hiding sunlight. She stretched her arms out and was surprised to find that she could stretch out her entire person and still not disturb Porter who was still asleep on the other side of the huge bed. She gave herself a small smile to see him sleeping. He was lying on his stomach, face turned towards her, with his arms under his pillows. She could see his beautiful face and took a minute to study it while she could.

He had a day's worth of stubble and it looked astoundingly sexy on him. His floppy hair looked as rumpled as it usually did and she remembered running her fingers through it the night before. Her eyes began to drift down his back and it was all she could do to keep herself from reaching out and running her hand along his hard muscles. They were everywhere. One tight muscle ran right into another and they all intermingled, forming one seriously sexy man. She smiled again, thinking that she should consider herself lucky to have had him. Then her smile grew wider, thinking he was pretty lucky, too.

She rolled to the edge of the bed and saw the tee shirt he'd given her to wear laying on the floor near the door. She quietly snuck out of the bed to grab it and swiftly put it on. She couldn't help but notice the Porter scent that wafted over her as she pulled it over her head. It smelled of aftershave and wood. She inhaled deeply trying to soak the sexy scent in. She looked down at the shirt, noticing the words "Lincoln City" written right over her heart. It looked as though the shirt was once a dull blue, but had now faded to a grey color. It was obviously well-worn and soft from being washed so much.

Once she was clothed, she walked softly around the bed over to the picture window to admire the view. All she could see were trees and ocean, forever. Greens and browns melded into the gray-blue of the sea. Waves were rolling in and out and a few boats speckled the surface of the water.

"That is definitely my new favorite shirt."

She heard Porter's voice and turned around. He was lying on his side, looking at her. She looked down at the shirt she was wearing.

"This one?"

"Yeah, that one. I'll never forget the way you look wearing it."

"Hmm. It's a little short," she smiled.

"Yeah. I know," he grinned. She walked over to him and sat down on the very edge of the bed. He brought his arms around her waist, with his head in her lap. She looked down at him and ran her fingers through his hair. He closed his eyes and leaned into her hand. They sat that way, quiet and content, for a few minutes. Finally, she leaned down, kissed him gently on the mouth and then stood up to find her dress. "What time does your sister come in today?" He asked from the bed as she started to gather her things.

"Well, she's driving out after her morning class, so maybe like eleven? I'm not really sure but I should probably get back to the house." She had found all the pieces to her outfit from the night before, so she went to the bathroom to change. She had put herself back together and then caught a glimpse of herself in the mirror. She was smiling. She hadn't even realized it.

She looked like she had just spent a very satisfying night with a man. Her hair was crazy, her make-up was long gone, and she would be leaving his house in the light of the early morning wearing a pretty fancy cocktail dress. She had never done the walk of shame in college but she was pretty sure this was a good comparable experience. But she was still smiling. She thought about how she had agreed to more than just last night; she wouldn't write this experience off to just a rebound. Porter could be pretty convincing when he wanted to be. He had shown her a new level of intimacy she hadn't really believed existed and now, the dreaded morning after when she should feel awkward and removed, she felt confident, cherished, and still a little bit sexy.

She pulled her crazy hair up into a less crazy, but still out of control, bun. She walked out of the bathroom and saw him leaning up against the door frame of the bedroom waiting for her. He had gotten dressed and looked just fantastic in a simple pair of jeans and a tee shirt. Ella smiled as she thought about how unfair it was that he looked normal while if anyone saw her, it would be obvious how she had spent her evening. She embraced her new found confidence by walking over to him and leaning up to place a gentle peck on his kissable mouth. He smiled as she pulled away.

"See, now aren't you glad you didn't bolt on me last night?" He asked.

"Mmm, yes, for multiple reasons. Thank you for talking some sense into me."

Porter laughed, "Damn, I thought I had sexed some sense into you."

"Well, that, too," Ella smiled. She leaned up again to kiss him again, but this kiss went much deeper than gentle. He wrapped his arms around her waist and pulled her to him as she did the same around his neck. He pulled away and leaned his forehead against hers.

"How long is your sister in town for?" He breathed.

"Just for the night."

"So, I can have you back tomorrow?"

The answer was simple, "Yes."

They left Porter's house and she found herself daydreaming as she watched the ocean through the window of his truck. Small snapshots of their night kept flashing through her mind. Even though most of them were totally hot, more than a few were sweet and tender. The times she remembered him stroking her face or looking into her eyes. Goosebumps rose up on her arms and she glanced over at Porter curiously. He caught her looking, smiled, and reached over to hold her hand. She looked down at their linked fingers and there was something floating around in her brain that kept nagging her. Everything felt so effortless. Being with him was so easy. There were butterflies, but no apprehension. There was excitement, but no nervousness. There was certainty, because there was no doubt. How long could this last? She thought perhaps she should continue down her path of carefree abandon and let things happen as they happen without letting expectations muddle everything up.

After they pulled up to her house, she smiled as he got out of the truck and came to open her door. She was beginning to really appreciate some of his chivalrous tendencies. She hopped down from his truck and they continued up her porch. She unlocked the door and turned to him.

"Thank you again for such a beautiful dinner and the amazing cheesecake," she said as she leaned into him, placing her hands on his chest.

"My pleasure," he said as he placed a very small and sweet kiss on her lips. "Mind of I text you later?"

A smile crept across her face although she tried her best to hide it, "Sure. Have a good day at work." He kissed her one last time and then turned towards his truck. She watched him get in and drive away before she went inside.

A few hours later, she had showered and felt much more

like herself. She had on a comfy pair of jeans and a dark blue tee shirt. She was downstairs straightening up the living room when she heard a knock on the door. When she opened it, she was accosted by her sister's loud and forceful greeting.

"Fella!" Her sister threw her arms around her in a giant hug. No matter how many years passed, or how old Megan was, she had always called her 'Fella'. Ella gave herself a smirk, knowing she'd kept her nickname from Porter, but she figured he'd find out about it eventually.

"Hey, Megs. How was the drive?"

"Pretty predictable. City. Fields. Trees. Beach. Same drive, different day." Ella and her family were no strangers to the beach and it was true that the drive was pretty boring. "This is a cute house."

"Yeah, it's kind of big for just one person, but since I was expecting two..." Ella trailed off, not really knowing where to go from here.

"Ella, I am so sorry about Kyle. Have you talked to him?"

"No, not since we officially broke up." Megan looked like she wanted to say something but was holding back. She was twirling her hair around her finger which was her nervous habit. "What's going on, Megan?"

"What? Nothing. I'm fine," she said full of guilt.

"You're a terrible liar. Tell me what's going on." Megan exhaled loudly and then walked over to the couch and sat down.

"Don't be mad at me."

"Megan, just tell me what you did."

"I spoke with him."

"Ok," the word crawled out slowly. "What did you talk about?"

"You, of course."

"Oh my gosh, Megan," she said, exasperated. "What specifically did you talk about?"

"Well, you told me to text him about the bed and I did that for you, but about 5 minutes later he called me. Ella, he sounded really torn up about everything. He sounded like he had been crying. I felt really bad for him."

Ella knew she probably looked ridiculous; her face was scrunched up in confusion. She was a little taken aback that Megan had spoken to Kyle about their issues, but was a little more confused by the fact that Megan sounded like she was taking his side.

"Megan, of course he was upset. He got caught – really red handed – cheating on me, and we broke up. We spent four years together. I would expect anyone to be upset about it."

"You don't look too upset about it," Megan said, coldly. Ella snapped her head up to look at her sister.

"Listen, Megan, I don't have to justify my feelings to you," she said calmly. "It is too bad that Kyle is taking the break up hard, but I was upset too. I had my own breakdown. But it's probably different for me. I left him, Megan. He probably didn't anticipate getting caught and now he has to deal with it. But I'm not going to let you make me feel guilty for breaking up with him after I caught him in a sweaty romp session with another woman, got it?"

Megan looked at the floor, and then back at Ella. "I'm sorry. I just thought when I came here I'd find you a little more upset and I thought maybe I could get you back together with Kyle. You guys were together for so long. Aren't you sad?" Ella walked over to where her sister was sitting on the couch and sat down next to her.

"It turns out, I've been sad for a really long time. I just wasn't really admitting it to myself, or anyone else." Ella took in a deep breath and then let it out. "Kyle and I weren't happy, Megs, and we hadn't been for a while. I think we were just together because it was what was comfortable for us."

"But don't you love him?" Ella thought for a moment,

trying to understand why her sister was so invested in her and Kyle's relationship.

"Of course I love him. I spent four years with him and shared a lot of my life with him, but I'm not in love with him anymore. Both he and I deserve better than that. I deserve to be in a relationship with someone who cares about me enough not to sleep with some bimbo." Megan wouldn't look her in the eye and kept her own eyes down.

Finally, in a voice so low and so shallow Ella could hardly hear her, Megan asked, "How did you know the difference between just loving him and being in love with him?"

"Megan, what's going on?" Megan continued to look down at the ground with her elbows on her knees and placed her head in her hands. She was really starting to worry Ella; she'd never seen her sister act this way. "Is everything ok with you and Patrick?" Megan looked up from her hands.

"Yes. Everything is fine with Patrick right now. All of this trouble with Kyle is really freaking me out though. If you and Kyle can have this many problems and break up, what if that happens with Patrick and me?" All of a sudden it became very clear to Ella what the real issue was. Ella wrapped her arm around Megan's shoulders and looked her in the eyes.

"Megan, what happened between Kyle and I won't happen to you and Patrick. Kyle and I didn't do the work we needed to stay together. We felt ourselves drifting apart and we waited too long to fix it. We should have worked harder at being together and making each other happy. And he shouldn't have cheated. We shouldn't have taken our relationship for granted. There are so many things that went wrong that were preventable or fixable, but we both just got too focused on our jobs, or life, and just assumed that the other would always be around. That's all."

Megan looked at her with tears welled in her eyes.

"But you guys were perfect for each other."

"If we were perfect for each other then he wouldn't have cheated on me. Trust me on this, Megs. Kyle and I are better off this way. We weren't giving each other what we needed. Now we both have a chance to find someone who gives us everything. If you don't want to end up like us, just make sure that you love Patrick more than anything. Try every day to make your relationship better, even on the bad days make sure you're always moving forward with each other." Ella paused for a minute to let her sister soak up everything she was saying. She smoothed down Megan's hair, trying to comfort her. "Megan, are you in love with Patrick?"

Megan sniffled a little. "Yes. I love him more than anything," she said as she looked back up at Ella.

"I know Patrick feels the same way about you. He is head over heels in love with you. Just make sure he always knows you feel the same way about him. Don't let life get in the way of making him your first priority."

Ella felt an ache in her chest for her sister and didn't want to see her worried about her own relationship just because she and Kyle couldn't keep theirs together. She hadn't even considered the possibility that her sister would be so affected by her failed relationship. It hurt her heart tremendously. She continued to hug her sister until she had calmed down, and seemed to be feeling a little less distressed. It was obvious they were both in need of some serious sister time. For the next twenty-four hours she would make sure her sister was having a good time and not worrying herself sick over love.

"Come on, Megs. Let's get out of here. It's a predictably chilly day at the beach. Let's go get some lunch and then we can go walk around the shops at the waterfront." Megan wiped the residual wetness from below her eyes and smiled up at Ella.

"That sounds awesome. I will go freshen up a little."

"Ok. You can have the room at the top of the stairs to the left." She watched Megan go up the stairs and then she exhaled loudly. She hadn't expected her sister to have a mild breakdown and it was emotionally taxing to watch her go through it.

She decided that while she had a few minutes she would call her store, just to check in and make sure everything was going well. She dialed the number and someone answered on the first ring.

"Thanks for calling Poppy. How can I help you?"

"Hey, Brittany. It's Ella."

"Oh, hi Ella. How's the beach trip?"

"It's going well. How is the store holding up?"

"We're doing great here, no issues. It's been pretty steady but nothing Sarah and I can't handle." Ella released a small breath she wasn't aware she was holding. She knew her staff was capable but she likened it to leaving your child with someone for an extended period of time. She just needed to check in to make sure the place hadn't burned to the ground.

"Great. Just remember that tomorrow the freight will come in, so make sure you – "

"Sort it, tag it and stock it. Yes, Ella, we've got it. I don't want you to worry about the store. Enjoy your vacation. If anything comes up and we need you, we will call," she said sweetly. Ella was a little surprised about how Brittany had put her in her place. Maybe the girls deserved a raise. It was something she'd look at next week when she got back to the store.

"You're right, Brittany. Thank you so much for being there for the store while I'm away. Thank Sarah for me too. Don't work too hard."

"No problem, Ella. See you next week!" As Brittany disconnected the call Megan came down the stairs.

"Ready to go?" Megan looked fresh and not anything like the teary girl who had been on the couch not ten minutes ago.

"I'm ready if you are," Ella answered.

"Sweet, let's get out of here."

It was a beautiful afternoon on the Oregon coast. The sun was trying to poke out from behind the clouds, but the wind was blowing making it chilly still. It was almost like a mandatory uniform on the beach for people to wear hoodies or sweatshirts displaying their favorite beach town. Everywhere you looked someone's shirt said 'Seaside', 'Newport', or 'Lincoln City'. No matter how cold it was, if the sun was out people were on the beach. A few hardy souls braved the water, which was never warmer than frigid even at the height of summer. Children could be seen digging in the sand, building sand castles, erecting tunnels, or burying each other to their necks. Kites were everywhere. You could see anything from a small child flying a Mickey Mouse kite, to a troop of professional trick kite flyers, entertaining everyone on the beach. Oregonians took their kites very seriously.

Megan and Ella had enjoyed lunch together, chatting about Megan's wedding plans and school. The depressing thoughts from their earlier conversation forgotten, which was typical for Megan. She was quick to get upset over something, but could dismiss it just as quickly. They had gone to the waterfront where there were cute little shops that lined the main road right along the harbor. Most of the stores sold silly souvenirs, but you could always find really beautiful artwork and jewelry in the higher end stores. And of course, there was no shortage of salt water taffy which Megan would live off of if allowed. The candy store painted a bright pink color had been their first stop and now Ella was stuck listening to her sister chew the taffy.

"Megan, please. You sound like a cow. Close your mouth."

"Sorry," Megan giggled. They had left a little shop and

were walking down the sidewalk when Ella saw a very familiar set of broad shoulders walking towards her. Porter noticed her just a second or two after she saw him and she couldn't miss the heart dropping, stomach churning smile that graced his face.

"Ella, hi," Porter said smoothly. "I wasn't expecting to see you around today." Ella blushed a little, mainly because she couldn't look at him without thinking about him naked.

"Hello, Porter. What a nice surprise." Ella heard her sister clear her throat and then Megan nudged her with her elbow. Remembering her manners, Ella turned to motion towards her sister. "Porter, this is my sister, Megan. Megan, this is Porter."

"Well, hello Porter. Nice to meet you." Megan looked back and forth between Ella and Porter. Ella was fully aware of the awkwardness surrounding them but she couldn't help the smile plastered on her face. "How do you two know each other?"

Ella gave Porter a sly smile, "Um. Well…"

"I rescued Ella Friday night," he said with uncompromising confidence.

"Rescued is a bit of an exaggeration, Porter," Ella teased, shooting one of her eyebrows up at him.

"I don't think so. Who knows where you'd be right now if it weren't for me. Sitting on the porch of your dark house, probably." Porter was still looking Ella right in the eyes and she was staring right back at him.

"Ok, well that sounds exciting. Ella, what is he talking about?" Megan asked, breaking Ella's trance.

"Oh, well, it's kind of a long story. My car battery died Friday night outside of his mother's bar, and he gave me a ride to the house and then helped me get situated," Ella blushed a little, knowing she was leaving out so much. "He was just a kind stranger who helped me out." She was dying inside. She could feel her cheeks turning red as she looked back at Porter who was obviously enjoying her uncomfortable explanation.

"Well, aren't you just a regular gentleman," Megan said, smiling at him.

"You bet," Porter winked.

"We were just heading to the next shop. It was nice running into you, Porter," Ella said as she started to head down the sidewalk.

"It was nice to meet you, Porter," Megan said.

"You too. Enjoy your afternoon."

Ella and Megan started to walk away, but as Porter passed Ella he gently held her elbow and whispered in her ear, "You are absolutely beautiful when you blush." Before she even had a chance to register what he said, he continued on his way. She was left standing in shock on the sidewalk. Her heart was racing. Just a few words from him could leave her breathless. Megan, who had made it to the door of the next shop, impatiently yelled for her to hurry up.

"What's wrong, Fella? You look all flushed."

"I'm fine. Let's go," Ella said, trying to shake her sister off.

"That Porter guy is seriously one hot man. He seems to be the reason God invented blue jeans."

Ella laughed at her sister's observation. "Yes, he is definitely good looking."

"You've been blinded by 4 years of monogamy. He's sex on legs, Sister."

"What the hell, Megs! You've been monogamous for just as long as I have."

"Yes, but I've always been more appreciative of the male form than you have."

"Whatever, Megan. Let's go in this store." Ella couldn't help but laugh. Her sister had no idea just how much she had already admired Porter's male form. "And keep your eyes to yourself."

Chapter Thirteen
Ella

"Hurry up, Megan! I am starving," Ella shouted up the stairs.

"Coming!" Megan yelled in response. The sisters had spent the rest of the afternoon shopping and walking on the beach. They had brought big beach towels out to the sand and sat together talking about everything and nothing. Megan spent a good portion of their time together trying to convince Ella that she should tell their parents about the breakup. Ella insisted that she wanted to tell them in person and planned to do so after she returned to Portland. There was no need to worry them and it wasn't an over-the-phone conversation anyway.

Ella took one more look in the mirror by the front door making sure she was presentable. She had found a dress while they were out shopping today and, even though she wouldn't admit it, she knew she was wearing it because there was a small chance Porter would be at the bar when they went to dinner. Looking at her reflection, she liked the way the purple and blue flowers brought out the creamy color of her skin, as well as enhanced the blue of her eyes. She loved the halter top of the dress, but covered it with a white cardigan because she knew it would be cold outside.

"Oh, yes, Fella. That dress was made for you. It looks amazing. You ready?"

"Thank you. And yes, let's go."

When they walked into the restaurant Ella immediately made eye contact with Tilly behind the bar. Tilly waved and then made her way towards the girls. Tilly wrapped Ella in a warm hug and even though she was taken by surprise by the friendly gesture, she was also glad that Tilly seemed to like her. It seemed to make the situation between her and Porter just a little easier.

"Hi, Tilly. I'd like you to meet my sister, Megan."

"Well, it is certainly nice to meet you, Megan. If you're half as sweet as your sister here, you're ok in my book."

"Tilly is Porter's mom and she was here the night my car broke down. She calmed me down and made Porter drive me home."

"Oh, Honey, I didn't make him do anything. Driving you home as the best decision he's made in months." Tilly winked at Ella and she hoped Megan didn't see it.

"Well, we'd really like to have dinner here tonight. I heard the menu is awesome."

"Sure thing. Pick a table and one of the girls will be over real soon."

Ella and Megan walked over to a booth that was tucked in the back corner of the restaurant. They took a seat and a friendly waitress gave them menus. They were looking over the menus and Ella could feel the air change in the room. She looked up and saw Porter walking through the bar. He didn't notice her when he came in and she tried to keep the menu up, covering her face, if only to allow her to watch him unnoticed for a few minutes more. He walked up to his mother behind the bar and gave her a quick peck on the cheek, which couldn't have been any sweeter and only added to the ever growing list of cute things Porter did. If he wasn't so damn sexy he might have been irritatingly adorable. She watched him chat with his mother for a few more moments and then he walked through the double doors behind the bar towards the back of the restaurant.

Ella released the breath she'd been holding and tried to focus on the menu again. She had narrowed her choices down when she heard her phone vibrating in her purse. She pulled it out and saw a text message from Porter.

Tell your sister you'll be back and head towards the restrooms.

Ella looked around the restaurant but didn't see him anywhere. She was a little confused and could feel her eyebrows furrowing.

I'm sorry, you want me to meet you in the bathroom?

No, I want you to go down the hallway towards the bathroom. What's the matter? You don't trust me?

She smiled at the last text and decided to follow his instructions. "I'll be right back, Megs. I'm going to head to the restroom real quick." She got out of the booth and walked towards the hallway as instructed. Once she was about halfway down she felt an arm grab around her waist and she was being yanked to the side. The room she found herself in was dark. She heard the door close and then she was being pushed up against it by his strong body. His hips were pinned against hers and his hands were framing her face. Her breaths were shallow and fast; just his touch was making her crazy.

"You can't even begin to imagine how many times I found myself thinking about you today," Porter said as he trailed his thumb over her lips. "It can be very distracting, especially when I'm trying to use power tools." She felt a hand snake around her waist, pulling her even closer. She ran her hands up his arms, still massively turned on by his muscular shoulders. His finger on her lips was making it even more difficult to breath.

"Porter?"

"Yes, Ella?"

"Did you drag me into what I can only hope is a supply closet just to talk?" He feathered his lips across hers barely making contact, driving her crazy, and then his hands moved into her hair.

"No," he moved his face into her neck and whispered, "I just needed to be close to you."

The profound warmth she felt pulsing through her body at his words was making her dizzy. He was making her dizzy. She didn't know what was going to happen tomorrow, or a week from now, but she did know that at this very moment she needed to be close to him too. She found his lips, pouring all the longing and need she was feeling into a kiss. How long could this possibly last? She found her mind drifting to him all day, pondering silly things that made her feel giddy like a teenager with her first boyfriend. Was he thinking about her? Did he miss her? Would he call her? It was almost all consuming. She enjoyed the feeling of his body pressed against hers for a moment more and then pulled away gently.

"How did you even know I was here?" She asked him, as he continued to nuzzle and trail soft kisses along her neck.

"As soon as I walked in I could feel you," he said simply, and she knew what he meant because she could feel his presence as well. "Also, your car is parked out front." She giggled.

"Ah. You're powers of deduction are impressive, sir." She leaned against his chest, enjoying just being with him. "We are in a supply closet, aren't we?"

"Indeed. The location choices for a romantic interlude are limited here." She could feel his fingers playing with hair and his breath feathered across her skin making every nerve in her body stand at attention. "You should probably get back to your sister," he said and kissed her forehead.

"Do you want to join us?" she asked hopefully.

"I would love nothing more than to sit and look at you all night, but I don't want to interfere with your time with your sister. But I call dibs on you for dinner tomorrow night."

It touched Ella that he was considerate enough to let her and her sister have dinner alone, although a very selfish part of her wished he would join them. Obviously, it would cause nothing but confusion for Megan to have Porter eat with them. There was no way Ella could sit across from him all night and not have Megan pick up on something going on between them. It was better that he leave to keep their situation under wraps, but her body was already feeling his absence.

"Deal. Want to come to my place? I could cook," Ella offered.

"That sounds great."

Ella smiled. Then she sighed as she took a small step back, trying to concoct a plan to exit the closet.

"Ok, I'm going to go back out. Wait a minute or two before you come out so no one gets suspicious."

He framed her face with his hands again and gave her a sweet and simmering kiss.

"See you later," he whispered. She reached behind her and pulled the door open. She walked back to the table where Megan was waiting for her, taking deep breaths to calm herself and trying to pull the blush from her face she knew was there. "Decided what you want yet?" She asked Megan as she sat down.

"Yes, salad with the shrimp."

"Sounds good. I'll have the same." The waitress came back, and as Megan was ordering she saw Porter come out of the hallway and it was all she could do to hide her smirk. He headed back behind the bar and through the double swinging doors. When the waitress asked her what she wanted to order, she told her she'd have the same thing. Megan and Ella both ordered a beer, as there was nowhere else in the country with better beer than the Pacific Northwest. After a few minutes Tilly came to their table carrying their beers.

"Here you go, girls," she said as she set down their drinks. "Did you find the bathroom ok, Honey?" Tilly asked with a smile that told Ella she knew about the secret supply closet rendezvous. Ella blushed, stumbled over her words a little, and finally managed to mumble, "Yes, thank you."

"Oh no, dear," Tilly said very seriously. "Thank you." Then Tilly put an arm around Ella and gave her a sideways half hug, rubbing her hand up and down her arm. Tilly gave a satisfied sigh and walked away.

"Uh, that was a little weird," Megan said, watching Tilly walk away.

"So, what do you want to do tonight? Watch movies?" Ella said trying desperately to change the subject.

"Sure, sounds like fun, but no romances. Let's rent a comedy or a horror flick! Hey," Megan sounded confused all of a sudden and pointed towards the bar. "Isn't that the sexy guy from the waterfront today? Porter?"

Ella looked up just in time to see him walking towards the door. He looked over at her as he passed by and then he gave her a wink. Before she could even stop herself, she winked back and smiled. She looked back at Megan, whose mouth was hanging wide open, her eyes darting back and forth from Ella to Porter.

"Ella, what the hell is going on?" Megan was looking at her waiting for a response and Ella was absolutely drawing a blank at what she was supposed to say. How could she explain without seeming like she'd slept with the first man to show any interest? Well, obviously she'd slept with the first man who showed any interest, but it was more than that. How could she make Megan understand when she wasn't sure she even full understood?

"What are you taking about?" Ella said, aiming for mild confusion and nonchalance, but in reality delivered high-pitched nervousness.

Megan pointed at the door he had just exited from, "Porter just winked and you and then you winked back. You both had the same look on your faces which, by the way, was completely obvious. You both looked like you were picturing the other naked. What the hell is going on?"

Ella dropped her head into her hands realizing it was going to be useless to try and deny anything was going on between them.

"Did you cheat on Kyle with him?" Megan asked completely shocked and appalled.

"No! I would never cheat on anyone, Megs. Jesus."

"Well, something is happening. Spill."

"Fine!" Ella said louder than she had intended. She took a calming breath and decided that honesty would be a welcomed addition to her life at the moment. "Everything I've told you so far is true. I stopped at Tilly's on my way to the house Friday night. Between my sobbing and the terrible rain, I couldn't see anything. When I came in for a drink, I accidentally left my lights on in my car. My battery died and Porter drove me home. The next day he took me back to my car and jumped it for me." Ella paused, thinking about how to explain how everything else had taken place without making it sound seedy or cheap.

"Keep going, Ella," Megan said irritated.

"That night I met Porter here for a drink. It was innocent. He was really nice to me. I didn't think there was anything wrong with meeting a man out for drinks. I was single at that point. No big deal. Well, he said he wanted to take me out for an official date." Ella paused again, remembering how he'd been so sweet that night asking her out. "I can't really explain this without sounding ridiculously girly, so I am just going to say it. He makes me feel amazing. He's so sweet, and kind, and a complete gentleman. He took me on the most romantic date. We talked all night and I had the best time." She was rambling now trying to explain thoroughly how exactly she felt about him. How should she explain to her little sister that she'd slept with a virtual stranger, and that it was the most exciting, fulfilling and satisfying sex she'd ever had? That what she was starting to feel for him made her question things she'd never thought about before?

"So, you broke up with Kyle on Friday and by Saturday you were having drinks with Porter? Ella, don't you think that's a little soon?" Ella sighed loudly. This is what she was afraid of, the judgment. She could tell Megan thought it was too soon and, by all socially acceptable timetables, 48 hours was too soon to go on a date after a breakup.

"I know it seems rushed."

"Uh, a little," Megan said sarcastically.

"But my break up with Kyle has nothing to do with Porter. It's hard to describe the finality I felt with Kyle. It was over. I was upset, sure, but I didn't feel the level of devastation you would expect. I think I was checked out of that relationship a while ago. That sounds terrible." This wasn't going well.

"Yeah, ok. So you're saying that this wasn't just a rebound? You didn't go out with Porter just because you were feeling sorry for yourself?"

"Exactly. I went out with Porter, at first, because I thought I was entitled to go out if I wanted to. I had no attachments. But I can't really explain what happened. It turned into something more."

"How much more?"

Ella cringed.

"You slept with him!" Megan practically shouted.

"Hush! His mom is here!" Ella looked around, but she didn't see Tilly and she let out a relieved breath.

"Oh my god, Ella! I can't believe you slept with him already!"

"I didn't plan on it. I mean, honestly, you saw him, right? What woman wouldn't want to sleep with him? Besides, it was special circumstances."

"Uh huh. Special circumstances, my ass! This is all very scandalous, Ella," she said as she crossed her arms in front of her chest.

Ella frowned. She didn't feel like it was scandalous. She

felt like it was exciting, warm, romantic, and totally hot.

"I don't know what to tell you. He and I are both adults and we want to see each other regardless of when my last relationship ended. It's not as sordid as you'd imagine."

Megan was quiet for a few moments and seemed to gain a little composure. Ella could almost see the wheels spinning in her head. "Was it weird being with someone other than Kyle?"

The question caught Ella off guard and she gave in to a little blush. She tried her best to maintain a cool and collected composure, but it was difficult with all the sexy images running through her mind. "It was different."

"Oh, come on, Ella. We're supposed to be bonding here. Give up the details, Woman."

"Ok, ok. Well," Ella began, "it wasn't weird. I mean, it was a little nerve-wracking at first. I had been with Kyle forever and I was so use to the way we had sex." Ella looked around again and made sure her voice was low. She did not need Tilly overhearing this conversation. "When Kyle and I were together, it was never really about being together. It was mostly about him. I was fine with that because, well, I guess I figured that was what it was supposed to be like. I haven't been with a whole lot of men, but they were all pretty much the same. They did obligatory things, you know, to get me going, but then it was just about them." Ella paused and got caught up in another memory of their night together, the way he seemed so focused on her and how he seemed to enjoy having sex with her, not just having sex. "He just seemed so into me, that's all. It was really sexy."

"Do you think he's, like, into you into you?" Ella laughed at how all of a sudden they both sounded like hormone driven teenagers.

"I think it's fair to say that he's interested. I mean, he just dragged me into that broom closet over there to make out with him," she said with a huge grin, gesturing towards the bathroom hallway.

"What? When? You little sneak. You're naughty, Ella." Ella laughed at her sister's reaction just as Tilly set down their salads on the table.

"You girls sure do seem to be enjoying yourselves. What's got you laughing so much?" Megan almost did a spit-take with her beer and Ella managed to maintain control enough to answer Tilly with the first lie that came to mind.

"Oh, we were just talking about this funny movie we love." Tilly put her hand on Ella's shoulder and gave it a little rub.

"It's so good to see two sisters getting along with each other and laughing. You enjoy your dinner now and let us know if you need anything else, Honey."

"Thanks, Tilly."

They spent the rest of their dinner talking mostly about Porter. Ella was glad that her sister seemed to get past the fact that there was no turnaround time between men. She loved Megan, but she was done justifying her actions to her or to anyone. She wanted to continue to see Porter and just go wherever she was lead.

Dinner was great. Porter was right when he said the blackberry cobbler was amazing. Ella hadn't remembered anything tasting that good. She and Megan had a few more beers, then decided to go rent some movies and head back to the house to begin the movie marathon. When they walked in the door, Ella headed up the stairs to change into some comfy pajamas.

"Megan, pick a movie and I will pop some popcorn after I change." Ella put on her favorite pair of pajama shorts and a strappy tank top. She headed to the bathroom to take off her makeup, and heard her phone vibrating in her purse. When she finally found her phone, she saw she had a text from Porter. She immediately smiled and sat down on the edge of her bed.

I hope you made it home alright from the bar.

We did. Thank you for your concern. What are you up to?

Not much. Out in the shop working on the boat, trying to keep my mind occupied. I seem to be having a hard time controlling my thoughts today. They just keep wandering back to you.

Ella didn't have a ton of dating experience, but she was pretty sure that men weren't usually this forthcoming when it came to their feelings. He seemed totally sincere. She believed he was being truthful about his feelings for her, but it was hardwired in her to play hard to get. Isn't that how it was supposed to go? He was supposed to be removed and aloof, and she was supposed to be coy and somewhat unavailable. Instead he was sweet and present, without being overbearing. He was just the right amount of everything.

Well, the feeling is mutual. Trust me. By the way, the cat is out of the bag with my sister. She saw us eyeing each other when you left and, it turns out, I am a terrible liar.

How do you feel about her knowing? What did she have to say about everything?

I am fine with it. In fact, I was glad to be able to talk to her about it. She was a little concerned at first, for obvious reasons, but I just asked her not to tell our parents. I haven't told them about Kyle yet, and I really don't want them to find out about everything over the phone.

Ella sent the text, and hoped he wouldn't feel like she

was ashamed of their seeing each other. She was put in a really tricky situation and was doing her best to deal with it in a way that satisfied everyone's needs. But she knew telling her parents over the phone that she had broken up with her boyfriend of four years and started seeing someone new in the span of two days wasn't a great idea.

I understand. Are you still feeling comfortable with everything going on between us?

Ella sighed and smiled. Of course Porter would be more concerned with her feelings than anything else.

Yes. I am very comfortable, thank you. I had better get back to my sister. I will see you tomorrow.

Goodnight Ella.

Porter

Porter came in the back door and headed straight for the fridge to grab a beer. He had spent the majority of the evening working in his shop and he was covered in dust from his electric sander. He had been happy for the distraction, as most of his thoughts today had been straying to Ella and the night they'd spent together. He'd admit that running into her and her sister at the waterfront was a coincidence, but he had a feeling she would go to the bar for dinner and couldn't stop himself from trying to see her there as well. It was almost painful when he couldn't touch her at the waterfront. He knew she would be uncomfortable with that in front of her sister, so he'd respected her boundaries. When he saw her in the bar, however, there was no question that he needed to feel her in his arms, and was glad that she had wanted to be near him too. Even a situation less than romantic, and sort of comical, he felt like everything was simply better when they were together.

He looked at his watch and thought that maybe she had made it home from the bar. He felt the urge to make sure she'd arrived home safely. He decided to text her just to be sure.

I hope you made it home alright from the bar.

We did. Thank you for your concern. What are you up to?

Not much. Out in the shop working on the boat, trying to keep my mind occupied. I seem to be having a hard time controlling my thoughts today. They just keep wandering back to you.

**Well, the feeling is mutual. Trust me. By the way, the

cat is out of the bag with my sister. She saw us eyeing each other when you left and, it turns out, I am a terrible liar.**

It didn't matter to Porter who knew that they were together. Although, if his mother found out it would be more annoying than upsetting, only because she would never let up on him about Ella.

How do you feel about her knowing? What did she have to say about everything?

I am fine with it. In fact, I was glad to be able to talk to her about it. She was a little concerned at first, for obvious reasons, but I just asked her not to tell our parents. I haven't told them about Kyle yet, and I really don't want them to find out about everything over the phone.

Porter knew that Ella was having a hard time making sense of what was happening between them, trying to rationalize jumping into another relationship so quickly. Porter felt the transition for him had been easy. He felt a pull towards Ella and besides her hesitation, there were no obstacles for him. He had wanted her, and luckily for him, she seemed to reciprocate. But he could appreciate that it would be difficult for her to explain everything to her parents, and even her sister. He wanted to make sure Ella knew that he wasn't pushing her into anything and that he could wait as long as she needed for her to explain things to her family. It was a non-issue. The last thing he wanted was her feeling uneasy about something he viewed as so trivial and unimportant.

I understand. Are you still feeling comfortable with everything going on between us?

**Yes. I am very comfortable, thank you. I had better get

back to my sister. I will see you tomorrow.**

Goodnight Ella.

He took another pull from his beer. The thought of going back up to his bedroom and trying to sleep in his bed without Ella in it made him grumpy, but there was nothing to be done about it. He decided he should shower to wash the dirt and grime from the day away. He also decided it should be a cold shower, if only to make it easier to sleep in an empty bed that, undoubtedly, still smelled like vanilla and Ella.

Chapter Fourteen

Ella

Megan and Ella had spent the night in true sisterly-bonding fashion, painting their nails and doing homemade facials made from ingredients from the refrigerator. They watched horror movies and screamed at the scary parts, ate entirely too much junk food, and got more than a little tipsy on cheap girly wine. When they had finally made it to bed, it was past two a.m. Ella was still a little drunk and found herself wondering what Porter was doing. She thought he was probably sleeping, but decided that she wanted to tell him sweet dreams.

She sat up in her bed groping around on the bedside table for her phone. When she found it she looked through her contacts until she found Porter's name. She took just a moment to wonder if this could possibly be a bad idea, but her slushy mind told her it was totally cool, so she hit send. The phone started ringing on the other end and she almost hung up, but thought maybe she could leave a message if he didn't pick up.

Just as she'd flopped back down on her pillows, she heard the other line pick up. She heard a man grumble something but she couldn't really understand him. It made her giggle a little to think of Porter answering his phone while still sleeping.

"Ella? Is that you? Are you ok?" She smiled thinking Porter was worried about her.

"I'm more than ok, Porter. I just felt like calling you to say goodnight and sweet dreams. Were you sleeping?"

"Mmmm. I was. But I am more than happy to wake up and talk to you." She could hear him groaning, imagining him stretching in his bed. She wondered if he had a shirt on. "Did you have a good night with your sister?"

"Yes, sir, we did. We watched scary movies and ate too

much. It was awesome."

"Scary movies? Aren't girls supposed to watch romantic comedies at sleepovers?"

"Traditionally, yes, but we decided I've got too much romantic drama going on and that we should stay away from those. Besides, I've gotten enough romance out of you in the last two days; I don't need to watch any girly movies."

"Glad I could be of service," he laughed. "Have you been drinking?"

"What kind of sister would I be if I didn't provide the wine?"

"I'm not sure. I've never had a sister. So what are you doing now?"

"I am just lying in bed, thinking about you." She smacked her hand over her mouth, embarrassed that the filter between her brain and her mouth was drunk too.

"Well, this conversation just got a lot more interesting," he said and she could hear his smirk.

"What I meant to say was that I was going to bed and I wanted to tell you goodnight and sweet dreams."

"Damn, I liked the first version better."

"Well, how fair would it be if I was sitting here thinking of you in bed and you weren't thinking about me? I am an equal opportunity fantasizer." The last word of her sentence came out a little slurred and she giggled again.

"If you had called me two hours ago, we'd have been on the same page, Babe. But I don't have anything going on right now, if you'd like to arrange something." His voice was low and gravelly, and ridiculously sexy.

"What is it you're trying to suggest, Babe?" She emphasized "Babe", hoping he would pick up on the fact that she really liked it when he called her that.

"I'm simply suggesting that if you wanted to have a conversation with me that involved fantasies, I'm game." Ella was shy all of a sudden, not really sure she was sober enough for this conversation.

"Have you had fantasies about me, Porter?" she asked quietly.

"Ella, since the first night I met you I've had nothing but fantasies about you," he paused and she smiled breathing in slowly, feeling the familiar cinching of the muscles in her core. "But nothing I've imagined even comes close to what it was like actually making love to you." The dizzy feeling she had become accustomed to whenever Porter was involved began to take over. He had a way of saying the most romantic things that caught her completely off guard. She was usually so busy recovering from whatever sweetness he'd said to her she never had a chance to tell him how she was feeling.

"I didn't want you to go," she whispered.

"What?" He asked, sounding confused.

"Earlier tonight, at the bar, I didn't want you to go. I wanted you to stay. I wanted you to stay with me. I know I needed to be with my sister and spend some time with her, but I really just wanted to be with you."

"Well, that makes two of us, but it wouldn't have been fair to Megan. We can see each other tomorrow, just the two of us."

"Ok. What would you like for dinner?"

"Hmm. Are you on the menu?"

"Smooth, Porter," she said sardonically.

"Hey, they can't all be winners. Seriously though, I'm not picky."

"Fine, I will surprise you."

"You already surprise me, Ella," Porter said, suddenly quiet and soft. It made her heart rate spike all over again. "You show up out of nowhere, literally storming into my life, and all of a sudden everything is different, better. Do you know how miraculous that is?"

"I feel it too, the better part. You make everything better," Ella giggled softly. "Besides literally fixing everything for me, I feel happier than I can ever remember."

"I guess I should let you go to bed. I am going to have a hell of a time trying to fall back asleep after this," he laughed.

"I'm sorry. I promise I won't drunk dial you again."

"Yes, you will, and I will gladly answer the phone every time. Goodnight, Ella, sweet dreams."

"Goodnight, Porter, see you tomorrow." She heard his end of the line go dead. She smiled and gave herself a satisfied squeeze. He was so damn cute. She felt the wine start to take her under and she fell asleep smiling, thinking about Porter.

The next morning, after doling out doses of Advil for both herself and Megan to combat their hangovers, she helped Megan load her car. She stood next to the driver's side door and Megan turned back to her.

"Thank you for driving all the way out here to see me."

"That's what sisters are for. Although, I thought I would be here to help dry your tears, but you seem to be doing ok," she said as she raised one eyebrow.

"Yes, I will be just fine."

"Well, here are my younger, fresher words of wisdom. Don't start something with Porter just because you're both available. I totally understand why you don't want to be with Kyle anymore, and it's valid, but you don't have to be with anyone right now."

"I know that, Megs. Besides, I'm not with him. We're just seeing each other. I haven't made any promises or commitments. He's really sweet and fun to be around, amongst other things," she said and immediately started blushing.

"Oh my gosh, Ella," Megan said rolling her eyes. "That's totally my cue to leave. Enjoy the rest of your week having amazing sex with Porter!" She quickly slid into the car, started the engine, and pulled out onto the driveway. As she drove away Ella could see a hand waving to her out of the window. Ella smiled and waved back. Even with all the uncomfortable Kyle conversations and Porter confessions, she was still really glad to have spent the evening with her sister. They didn't spend nearly enough time together. That was something she would rectify when she got back to Portland.

The morning passed quickly into the afternoon, and Ella spent her time relaxing on the couch reading and napping. She had very little opportunity to be lazy at home, working crazy hours at her store. So even though it felt amazing to be doing nothing, she also felt a little guilty. Not guilty enough, however, to do anything about it. Eventually she got a text from Porter, which was like riding an express train right back in to her excited reality.

What time should I head over tonight?

Whenever works for you. I've got absolutely nothing going on right now and I love it.

6:30 sound good?

Sounds great!

Can't wait to see you.

A few hours later Ella had found the motivation to head to the store to buy supplies to make Porter grilled chicken alfredo. She loved Italian food and hoped he did too. By the time Porter arrived she had dinner under control and was just lighting the few candles she had purchased to set out around the table. She heard his knock and there was no denying her excitement by the smile that spread across her face.

She walked to the front door stopping at the mirror to smooth out her sheer blue blouse she had put over a navy camisole. Her hair was down and wavy, and still maintaining its smoothness despite the cooking going on in the kitchen. Satisfied with her reflection, she pulled the front door open and nearly gasped. Porter stood on her porch looking almost edible. He had on another pair of dark blue jeans that accentuated his glorious legs, and for a shirt, he was wearing her sexual kryptonite: a white baseball shirt with blue sleeves. Ever since high school she had a very unusual, yet strong, attraction to men in baseball shirts. The only sight greater than Porter standing in front of her, unintentionally fulfilling one of her long standing sexual fantasies, would be the sight of his bare chest as she peeled it off of him. Her mouth was still slightly agape as he took a step into her house.

"Hey," he said and stood in front of her, cupping her face with his hand. He bent down and laid a light kiss on her mouth, lingering for a few seconds. "I've been thinking about doing that all day," he said with a smile. She was still having a hard time finding any words.

"Nice shirt," was all she could manage. He cocked his head to the side slightly, looking amused.

"Thanks."

She opened the door wider and stepped to the side to let him in. "I hope you like Italian."

"I do. Whatever you've been cooking smells amazing." She shut the door and headed back towards the kitchen, purposefully taking deep calming breaths.

"Dinner is pretty much ready, if you want to sit at the table. Would you like a glass of wine?"

"Sure, sounds great."

"White ok?"

"Definitely."

She brought two glasses of wine to the table setting one

in front of him. She headed back into the kitchen and returned with their plates.

"This looks amazing. Thank you for cooking dinner. I'd like to say I'd return the favor, but we've already covered the fact that I cannot cook."

"Well, you haven't tasted it yet, so don't jump the gun." They both dug into their meal and she was gifted the sound of an appreciative groan from Porter.

"My god, this is fantastic," he said. She smiled, glad he was enjoying his meal.

"So what did you do at work today?" she asked.

"Well," he took his napkin to wipe his mouth. "The storm on Friday took down a pretty large tree. It fell on a house and pretty much demolished the garage. Luckily, no one was in the garage at the time so no one was hurt. Anyway, my team and I went over there today to start rebuilding. It took them a few days to get the tree removed so there was a lot of water damage from rain water getting in over the weekend."

"Wow, how lucky it was just their garage and not part of the house."

"Yes. How was your day? You sounded pretty tipsy last night."

Ella blushed, remembering their conversation from her drunken phone call to him the night before.

"Sorry about that, by the way."

"You've got nothing to be sorry about; I very much enjoyed our chat," he said grinning at her.

"Well, I spent the day trying to recover from all the wine and did a whole lot of nothing." She took a sip of her wine, enjoying the cool crispness of the white wine on her tongue. It paired really well with the pasta. "I can't remember the last time I spent a whole day doing nothing. It's a rarity and I don't take it for granted."

"Your store keeps you pretty busy, huh?"

"Well, at this point, I could hire someone to do what I do,

but I have a hard time picturing myself doing that. The store is my baby and the only way I could see myself spending time away from it would be if I were to open another one."

"That's what you want, right? To expand?"

"Yes and no. I want to open more stores and build a bigger name for myself, but it's a really big step and it's a little scary. I would hate to neglect Poppy to open another store, have that store fail, and in the end lose Poppy because I wasn't around to keep an eye on it. It's a slippery slope."

"Well, it sounds like you just need a little confidence. If you go into it thinking you're going to fail, then you will. It's always a little scary doing something new and different, but scary can sometimes be exciting if you just change your perspective." She blinked at him, a little surprised by the sound and somewhat philosophical advice he offered.

"You make it sound so easy," she paused. "I guess it is easy. I'm the one making it more difficult and complicated by over-thinking it. I really just need to dive in head first."

"Exactly. You've done it once before and you know what you're doing. Trust yourself."

Ella picked up her wine glass and took another drink, peering at him over the rim. "You sure have a lot of faith in me, which is surprising seeing as how we hardly know each other," she said as she took another bite. Porter gasped in mock insult.

"Hardly know each other? You crush me, Ella." She giggled at his playfulness. "But seriously, what would you like to know? I don't know everything about you, but I know enough to figure out that the rest doesn't matter. I know that you're smart and funny. You're proud, yet humble. You don't like confrontation, even when you're right. You care a lot about your family and what they think about you." Ella was frozen, completely lost just staring at him, with their eyes locked. "I know that when the wind blows through your hair it dances around your face and I know that the crook of your neck smells like vanilla. I also know that when you're turned on your make the sexiest little whimpering sounds I've ever heard." Ella was trying to remember how to breathe. She couldn't seem to get enough air in her lungs and every time she took a breath, it was panted back out immediately. He paused a moment to take another drink of his wine. "I know you, Ella. I know the important stuff. I hope to spend a lot of time learning the rest. But at this point, it's just noise."

Ella managed to grab her glass to take a sip of her wine. She closed her eyes and tried to calm her breathing. When she opened them he was still looking at her expectantly, waiting for her to respond.

"Do you want to go sit on the porch for a little while? It shouldn't be too cold out yet," she asked quietly. She didn't wait for a response, but got up from the table and headed towards the back door. She heard him get out of his chair so she knew he was following her outside. She walked out the door, went to the edge of the porch, and leaned against the railing. Porter didn't touch her, but he came to stand right behind her. She could feel the heat from him. Ella took in the scenery around her. The sun had already set, but the light was still fading behind the horizon. The sky still had some pink and orange hues fighting against the dark midnight blue that was slowly taking over. In the back of her mind she thought that she was sad she'd missed the sunset and would have to make a point to see one before she left the beach for good. Her breathing had finally returned to normal, but her mind was still racing a mile a minute trying to process all the thoughts and emotions that were coming at her. After a few minutes of silence, he finally spoke.

"I didn't mean to upset you," Porter said gently. Ella sighed trying to put some words together to respond to him.

"I'm not upset. I'm moved, touched, and a little freaked

out, but I'm not upset," she said shaking her head at the ocean.

"Ok, well, can you tell me which parts of what I said you liked and which you didn't?" he asked hopefully.

"Not really. I loved everything you said."

"But?"

"It scares me. Ever since we met, you've done nothing but say all the right things and do everything in your power to make me feel special and taken care of. You're such a gentleman and you're constantly surprising me with how capable you are. And then there are your words." She turned around to face Porter and saw the confusion painted across his face. "You say things to me that make my heart stop beating and sometimes I forget how to breathe. When you say these things, I can't tell if I'm falling for you or your words. Then I feel guilty that I'm falling at all." She was starting to lose her breath again and she felt a panic coming over her. She looked at the ground and felt Porter's hands come up and grasp her shoulders. He pulled her close to him and rested his lips against her forehead. He ran his hands down her arms and then wrapped them around her waist clasping his hands together behind her back.

"Is this all happening too fast?" She looked up at him as she asked the question.

"Not for me, it's not." Porter sighed and pulled her in closer to him. "I didn't know it, but I've been waiting a long time for you to get here, for your car to breakdown at my mom's bar so I could drive you home. I didn't know I was missing you. But then you showed up and now I'm convinced that it all happened for a reason. It's too coincidental to be a mistake. However," he said slowly, "it isn't up to me at this point. I'm not the one dealing with the guilt." Ella nodded her head because she knew he was right. He reached up to brush a lock of wayward hair off her face. "I'm not going anywhere Ella. I will be here for you, waiting for you to catch up with me, for as long as you need."

"You know I feel that way too, right? I feel safe and protected with you. I feel sexy and beautiful with you. I love how much you adore your mother and how hard you have worked to take care of her. I love that you worry about me and check up on me." Ella was starting to calm down and even felt a smile come across her face as she listed the things she loved about Porter. "I love that when you touch me I come alive. I love that even though there's no way you could have possibly known, you showed up to my house wearing a baseball shirt which just happens to be one of my most favorite, sexy things for men to wear." She grinned up at him and moved her hands around the back of his neck.

Porter laughed, "Oh really? Well, then, the fates are really pushing us together."

"So it would seem," she smiled and then reached up to kiss him. As her lips met his she felt his hands pulling her towards him. She wrapped her arms around his neck, molding her body to his, fitting herself up against him as close as possible. His hands moved from her back, gliding down to grab her ass, then continue their journey up her waist, then up to her shoulders. She pulled away and smiled up at him. "You know what I really want to do right now?"

"Hmm?" He said as he kissed the tip of her nose.

"I want to sit on this swing with you and drink a glass of wine," she laughed because she knew that wasn't what he wanted to hear. He looked down at her and smiled.

"Sounds like a plan."

"Great. You wait here and I will go get us wine." She walked back into the house, poured two more glasses of wine, and then headed outside. "Here, I'll be right back," she said as she handed him the glasses. She went back inside and grabbed the big throw blanket off the back of the couch. When she made it back to Porter, she held the blanket up and said, "It's getting chilly out."

He was already sitting on one side of the swing, so she sat down next to him with her legs curled under her and snuggled into his side. He handed her the wine then put his arm behind her pulling her into him. She used her one free hand to spread the blanket out over the both of them. Once they were finally settled, Ella let out a content sigh and relaxed further into him. They sat together, swinging gently, watching the final light of the day drift below the horizon for quite some time. Eventually, darkness surrounded them and the only sounds heard were those of the sea, gentle waves kissing the beach, coming back again and again for more.

They sat in comfortable silence for a very long time, listening to the ocean, listening to each other breathing. She felt chills run along her spine when he started softly running his fingers up and down her shoulder, the sheer fabric of her shirt doing nothing to lessen the friction and impact his touch had on her. Eventually she had drank all her wine, so she put her glass down on the ground then wrapped her arms fully around his waist, her face cozily snuggled into his chest. She didn't try to hide the smile that came over her face when she noticed his baseball shirt again. His broad shoulders and strong arms looked delicious in that style of shirt and she couldn't stop herself when her hand reached up to graze his bicep.

"You really do like this shirt, don't you?"

"You have no idea. It's almost silly how much I am attracted to these shirts. I think it has something to do with the fact that they accentuate the arms, which is my favorite part of the male body."

"Arms?" He asked, laughing at her.

"Yes, arms. Why is that funny?"

"I don't know. I guess I've just never heard of anyone being attracted to arms before," he laughed even more.

"Well, it's not like I'm attracted to all arms, just really well built ones. It's not a magical shirt. It only works on men who are in shape."

"And you think I fit that description?"

She leaned back to look up at him and smiled, "Are we fishing for compliments now?"

"Hey, guys need confidence boosts every now and then too," he joked.

"Oh no, is someone feeling insecure? Let's see here," she said as she sat up to look him right in the eye. "You have an incredible body, Porter. There isn't one thing about you I would change. And yes, your arms are my favorite part. They are strong, sexy, capable, and I feel safe wrapped inside of them. I also really love your dark hair, unruly as it is, and your beautiful brown eyes. Physically, you are quite the catch. I cannot tell you how shocked I am that none of the women in this town have camped out in your yard vying for the chance to catch your eye."

"None of them would stand a chance against you, Ella," he said as he gently rubbed his thumb across her bottom lip. As usual when Porter touched her, her breath stole away and she was left to survive off the heat he gave her as his eyes traveled from her eyes down to the lip he was fingering. She watched him lean towards her and bring his mouth down to her. The instant his lips touched hers, it was explosive. The quiet and serene time they had spent on the swing gave way to frenzied and frantic grasping and clawing.

Ella pulled away, breaths panting, "Can we go upstairs?" Porter didn't answer her. He just stood up letting the blanket fall to the ground and grabbed her hand, pulling her inside making her giggle. He led the way through the living room, all the way up the stairs, and then stalled, looking left and then right. "All the way at the end," Ella said helping him locate the bedroom. He continued forward finding her bedroom. Once they were inside he led her to the bed and he sat down keeping her in front of him, holding her waist. She ran her hands through his hair, smiling. He pulled her belly against his chest and she leaned down to kiss his lips. His tongue gently teased her lips, asking to deepen the kiss. She opened for him, inhaling sharply as he grabbed and pulled on her ass while he attacked her mouth with his. She pulled her knees up on the bed to sit astride him, putting her face level with his. Her hands were all over him, touching and rubbing. She leaned back breaking their contact.

"As much as I love this shirt, I think it's time to take it off." She smiled as she lifted his shirt up over his head. Once he was bare chested she leaned back and took a moment to admire him. She gently pushed him down so he was lying on the bed. She leaned down and trailed kissed up his stomach. He had the sexiest patch of hair that started at his bellybutton and went down past the waistband of his pants. It was soft to kiss. As she traveled farther up, she stopped to place light nibbles along the way, paying special attention to his nipples. A groan escaped from him making her smile. She felt his hands sliding up her back pushing her shirt up so he was touching her skin, causing her breath to catch in her throat. Her mouth reached his jaw and she gave him small kisses all along his jawline and chin, loving the feel of his stubble against her lips. He grabbed the hem of her shirt and camisole and pulled it off of her in between her kisses. She looked down at him and heard him breathing heavy.

"Damn Ella, you wear the sexiest things under your clothes." She looked down at her bra and laughed a little. It was a dark blue lace that was practically see-thru and not made for modesty. This was the second time he'd commented on her lingerie. She would have to remember his fondness for fancy things.

She gave him a naughty smile, "My panties match." His eyes shot wide open and he quickly maneuvered them in a slick roll so that he was on top and went to work on the button of her jeans. Within seconds he had them unfastened and was pulling them down her thighs. He stood up to pull them completely off her. Once she was in just her bra and panties, he stood in front of her gazing down at her.

"You are so beautiful, Ella. You do crazy things to me, just by laying there. I want to look at you forever."

His words caught her off guard, but melted her heart. He wasn't delivering a line or trying to sweeten her up. He was being completely sincere. She sat up and reached for the button on his jeans. She never broke eye contact as he slid his pants and boxers down his legs and he stepped out of them. She slid back on the bed, laying back into the pillows, and crooked a finger at him. He climbed on the bed and crawled over her, his hands on either side of her head. He peered down into her eyes and was looking like he wanted to say something.

"What is it?" she asked him, placing her hands on the sides of his face.

"I don't want to scare you," he stopped and shook his head.

"Porter, tell me. It's ok."

He leaned down and kissed her with so much gentleness and passion it broke her heart a little. He broke the kiss but only moved back far enough to speak, so his lips still brushed hers with his words.

"I just can't imagine going back to a life without you in it." They stayed there, frozen, mouths barely touching, breathing in each other's shaky breaths, looking into each other's eyes.

"Then don't," she whispered. He searched her eyes for a few seconds more. Then his mouth was on hers again, only this time it was a starving kiss, like he needed her to breathe or survive. He was kissing her like it was all he knew how to do.

His hands started to move on her body, softly he trailed a

hand down over her breast, stopping to palm it, making her whimper slightly into his mouth. He pulled away from her suddenly.

"There are those sexy sounds you make. They drive me crazy. Don't ever stop making them." She didn't have time to respond before he put his mouth on her nipple over the lace of her bra, his teeth teasing her.

"Oh god," she cried. He pulled the lace down and took her whole nipple in his mouth, sucking and kissing. She was writhing beneath him, her hands grasping at the sheets beneath her. She wanted him inside of her. Then she remembered something that startled her. "Porter!"

He quickly abandoned her breast, "What's wrong? Are you ok?" Ella laughed a little and put her hands over her face.

"Oh my god, Porter. You're going to kill me."

"Unlikely. What the heck is going on?"

"I don't have any condoms. I'm sorry. I didn't bring any with me to the beach and it never occurred to me to buy any," she was looking at him through the slots between her fingers, waiting for him to become frustrated.

He laughed a little and cocked his head to the side. "Would it have been presumptuous of me to bring some?"

"What? You thought I was a sure thing?" She asked smiling.

"A guy can hope," he said and resumed his attention at her breast.

"You're like a boy scout, always prepared," she giggled. Porter stilled and then looked up at her.

"For future reference, when I am trying my hardest to turn you on, please refrain from using the term 'boy' to describe me."

"I'm sorry. Did I insult your manhood?" She asked with a smile.

"Hmm. My manhood is fine, thank you very much."

"Yes, I can tell," she said suggestively, wiggling

underneath him. He groaned at the friction she caused and then he did another ninja roll. She ended up sitting on his lap, as he sat in the middle of the bed, her legs wrapped around his waist. Nose to nose, he tucked her hair behind her ears and then reached behind her to unclasp her bra. He pulled it down her arms and tossed it on the floor. He began kissing her again, as one hand found her now naked breast. He used his fingers to roll and pull her nipple. She groaned and arched her back, lost in his touch. His free hand moved from her waist and cupped her over her panties, using his palm to grind into her. Electricity shot through her body at his touch and the combination of all he was doing to her was taking her higher and higher.

"Sorry about your underwear," he said in a gravelly voice. Ella was confused, but didn't have time to voice it before she felt him grab her pretty blue lace panties and tear them off of her, completely demolishing them.

"Holy shit, Porter," she breathed, more turned on now than ever. Then she felt him gently tease her opening, running one finger slowly up and down. She was relishing in the moment and the sheer intimacy of it. They were so close, looking in each other's eyes and he lazily stroked her. He continued to look right at her as he slowly sank two fingers into her and she let out another whimper. He massaged her from the inside and she was rolling her hips against him, urging him along, begging for more. His thumb found her clit and she was unable to keep her head up, dropping it on his shoulder, moaning and looking for relief.

"Oh, please..." she panted.

"We're almost there, Baby," he whispered. He quickened the pace, going from a slow leisurely caress to a more vigorous and firm stroke. She could feel the ball of pressure building in her core and the muscles in her legs tensing. It was all she could do to hold her breath until the relief came. "You feel so good around my fingers, Ella."

"Yes. Please don't stop," she panted on his neck.

He continued his assault on her and with a detonation she felt crash through her body, she came around his fingers.

"Oh god," she moaned and leaned her head backwards, delighting in the warmth that was flowing through her.

"I will never tire of watching you come, Ella. You are stunning."

She looked back at him and placed a light and lingering kiss on his mouth. He slowly placed her back on the bed, and after a moment pulled back from her mouth. He turned to the side of the bed and reached to the floor. Digging around for a few seconds he came back to Ella with a condom. She watched as he opened it and put it on. He crawled back over her, kissing his way back up her body. When he got to her neck, he nuzzled in and inhaled deeply.

"Mmmm, vanilla," he said quietly and she smiled at his sweetness. He used his hands to push her hair off her face, and they were nose to nose again, his body draped over hers. He looked directly into her eyes.

"I want you to be mine, Ella," he said as he slowly entered her.

"Porter," she breathed his name, shivering from the intense intimacy she felt with him inside her.

Once he was fully engulfed in her, he stilled and let her feel him.

"You don't have to answer me now and I am not trying to pressure you," he pulled out slowly. "I just want you to know what you mean to me and how much I want you for myself," and he pushed back in with a gloriously slow thrust. Ella felt tears forming behind her lashes. Never had a man moved her in such a romantic and intimate way. Even though her gut was telling her to never let him go, her brain was yelling at her about moving too fast and broken hearts. She wanted to lose herself in Porter and let him lead her into whatever he had waiting for her, but she was too scared to lose control.

"Porter," his name was a prayer.

"Ella?"

"Please make love to me," she cried silently.

"Always."

His hips continued to move in slow and sinuous circles, taking his time, slowly building the wall she would eventually fall over. Breath by breath, and thrust by thrust, he was slowly lifting her again. The higher she got, she knew the more devastating the fall would be. His mouth found all the places on her body that were begging for attention. He kissed her neck, ran his lips along her collarbone, nibbled on earlobe. All the while his hands were worshiping her, softly caressing her breasts, grazing over her stomach, cradling her face.

Eventually, his thrusts became deeper and fractionally quicker, alerting to her that he was just as close as she was. She helped them along by meeting his thrusts allowing him to feel her deeper. His mouth found hers again and this kiss was silently pleading with her. It was all she could do not to promise to be his forever. She knew promises made in the throes of ecstasy were impulsive and fickle, but it was tempting.

"Ella," Porter said as he went over the edge. It was the love and affection with which he said her name that finally pushed her over as well.

Chapter Fifteen
Porter

Porter woke up and wasn't sure at first where he was. All he saw at first were white billowy curtains hanging around the bed and unfamiliar walls. Then he felt movement on the bed and looked over to see Ella asleep. She was curled towards him, lying on her stomach, with her hair fanned out on her pillow. The comforter they were using had been pulled down low and he could see the length of her back and the swell of her backside. She was the most breathtakingly beautiful woman he had ever seen and he was going to do anything he could to convince her to be with him.

He took a look at his watch, cursing the time, and figured if he left now he would have enough time to go home and shower before heading to work. He slowly rolled over and climbed out of bed, trying hard not to disturb her. He found his clothes and headed to her bathroom. When he came out, she was still sound asleep. He didn't want to wake her, but he also didn't want to leave without letting her know. He gently rubbed her bare back, trying to rouse her from sleep.

"Ella," he whispered.

"Hmm?"

"Ella, I have to go to work, I wanted to say goodbye." She rolled over to look at him taking the comforter with her to cover herself.

"What time is it?" She asked sleepily.

"Early, I'm sorry. I just didn't want you to think I ran out on you," he said looking down at her, captivated by her early morning beauty. He leaned down and placed a small kiss on her mouth. "Go back to sleep."

"Ok," she said and rolled back over.

He smiled as he walked out of the bedroom and down the

stairs. He found his keys on the hall tree by the door, and headed out the front door, making sure to lock it behind him. He was almost in his car when he heard Ella yelling his name behind him.

"Porter!"

He turned around and saw Ella running towards him wrapped only in the white comforter from her bed. "Ella, what happened?" She didn't answer him, she just continued running towards him. When she made it all the way to him she ran straight into him, pulling his face down to hers, and kissing him hard. He wrapped his arms around her waist, to feel her against him, but also to make sure she didn't lose her blanket. She held the blanket up with one hand, fisting it between her breasts, and used the other hand to thread her fingers through his unruly hair. Their tongues were dancing and she pulled his bottom lip between her teeth, making him groan into her mouth.

In his mind, he was logistically trying to figure out how he could spend the day in bed with Ella instead of going to work. Then she pushed those thoughts out of his head when she pulled away and moved on to his neck.

"Ella, you're practically naked," he groaned, liking the idea of her nakedness but unsure about their visibility.

"Mmm hmm," she garbled at him.

"Maybe we should go inside before someone sees something not intended for them." She pulled her mouth away from his neck and looked up at him.

"I thought you had to go to work," she said with a sly smile.

"I did. I do," he sighed, "but then you came running at me all sexy and I might be convinced to make poor, yet sexually satisfying, decisions."

"Oh, I didn't come out here to get you to stay with me," she said with a completely straight face.

"You didn't?" His eyebrows furrowed with confusion.

"No. I just wanted to make sure you remembered to call

me later," she winked at him.

"You play dirty, Babe. Now I've got to go to work like this, all hot and bothered. You should be ashamed of yourself." He tried to sound like he was upset but the giant smile on his face gave him away immediately. Ella lifted onto her tip toes and kissed him quickly before turning to saunter back to the house.

Halfway there she said over her shoulder, "I never promised to play fair, Porter. Have a good day at work and call me later."

He watched her go inside and was shaking his head as he got into his truck. He was glad he had already planned to take a shower, because there was no way he was going to make it to work in this state and be safe to handle powered equipment. She was a firecracker that was for sure.

He managed to make it through half the work day without seriously maiming himself or any of his workers, although, not for lack of his mind wandering. Again, he spent his day thinking about her, picturing her as she was the night before, tangled around him making those seductive whimpers that make his blood boil through his veins. It was his lunch break, so he pulled out his cell phone to call her.

"Having a good day at work?" Her voice was smooth and lazy, and he pictured her still lying in her white shrouded bed.

"I am distracted again and I blame you."

"You like my distractions," she teased.

"Yes, well, that may be true but it doesn't do anything to ease my mind. I've got the image of you asleep in bed, just barely covered by the blanket. Tell me your still in bed," he said hopefully.

"I don't think that would help you and your distractions any, and I need you in one piece. Tell me, what are working on? Still the demolished garage?"

"Yes, partly. That's where my team is, but after lunch I am headed to do an estimate on a rebuild."

"What's a rebuild?"

"Well, a lot of the beachfront houses here are older, so when people buy the houses they usually are just interested in the land. So they hire someone to tear down the existing house and build a new one. People are looking for modern houses and it's cheaper and faster to just build it yourself."

"That sounds like a big job."

"It can be. If they like my bid and I win, this job could keep my team busy through January."

"January? That's a long time from now." He detected a shift in her mood; she sounded almost sad.

"Well, that's the idea, Babe. So on Wednesdays, my mom has the day off and I usually take her out for dinner. I was wondering if you would like to go out with us tonight."

"You want me to go to dinner with you and your mom?" She asked with a hint of frustration.

"I was hoping," he said hesitantly, not sure why she sounded upset. "Is everything ok? You sound like something is bothering you."

"I'm fine, Porter," he heard her sigh. "I'd love to have dinner with you and your mom. When and where?" He was confused by her ambivalence.

"I can pick you up at six," he answered.

"Perfect. I will be waiting. Have a good rest of your day, Porter."

"Are you ok, Ella? You'd tell me if something was wrong, wouldn't you?"

"Yes, of course. I'm fine. I will see you at six." He heard the line go dead. Despite her words, he felt like she was holding something back. He ran his hand through his hair in frustration. He wanted to go to her and make her talk to him, but knew it probably wouldn't do any good. He resigned himself to making sure he had a moment to talk to her tonight and he would try to get her to open up to him.

He arrived at her house right at six o'clock and knocked gently on the door. She opened the door and he couldn't help but sweep his eyes up and down her. He wasn't really in tune to fashion in any way, but there was no denying that Ella was a very well-dressed woman and that she took a lot of pride in the way she looked. It made sense that she owned a boutique. She wore a pair of jeans and a cream colored shirt that looked incredibly soft that had lace draped delicately from the collar. She wore a small jacket that tied with a bow that made her look young and feminine. The part of her ensemble that took his breath away was her hair. It had been pulled up to make a neat and tidy bun and all his mind could see was her delectable neck. It was going to be a long night of trying not to touch or kiss her neck while his mother was around.

"You look amazing, as usual," he said with a gentle smile, leaning in to kiss her. She accepted his kiss but didn't deepen it and pulled away quicker than he would have liked. He looked at her quizzically for a moment. "Are you ready?"

"Yes. Let's go." She pulled the door shut behind her and locked it. He walked her to his truck and opened her door for her. Once he got in the driver's seat, he looked at her before he started the engine. She kept her eyes at the front of the truck, never looking his way. The drive to the restaurant was brutal; she wasn't talking and when he asked her questions she'd answer him in monosyllables.

"Do you like Mexican food?"

"Yes."

"My mom loves Mexican food, so we usually go to the same place every Wednesday."

"Great," she replied with a strained smile. He grew frustrated.

"Ella, please tell me what's bothering you. I can tell

you're upset about something. Just talk to me about it."
She looked over at him and smiled, but the smile did
nothing to light up her face or make the tiny crinkles by her
eyes he'd grown to love. She was placating him.

"There's nothing wrong, Porter. I swear. I'm just tired."
She turned her head to continue looking out of her window.
He reached over to hold her hand and when his fingers
intertwined with hers, she looked down at their hands. He
saw her eyes close briefly and when they opened he saw
sadness in them. She resumed looking out of her window.

When they parked at the restaurant, he went around the
truck to open her door. As she got out, he let his hands
slide up over her hips and rest on her waist.

"I wish you'd let me into that pretty head of yours. I
know something is bothering you."

Ella shook her head, looking down at the pavement.

"Later," she whispered. He feathered a kiss on her
forehead and took her hand leading her towards the
restaurant. It would drive him crazy through dinner
wondering what was on her mind. It was obvious she was
upset about something and until she told him his
imagination would run wild. Tilly was already inside
sitting at a table. When they came in, she stood up to greet
them.

"Hello, Favorite Son," she said with a loving smile as she
gave him a hug. "And Ella, I am so glad you could come to
dinner with us," and she gave Ella a big hug as well.

"It's nice to see you again, Tilly," Ella said with a tight
smile. They gave their drink orders to the waiter and
settled into their booth. Tilly was on one side and Porter
motioned for Ella to slide into the other side of the booth
and slid in next to her. He wanted to put his arm around
her shoulders or place his hand on her knee under the table,
but he didn't want to make her uncomfortable. His need to
sooth and touch her was like an itch he couldn't scratch.

"How did the estimate go on that rebuild you were telling

me about?" Tilly asked.

"I think it went well. They have a few other contractors bidding, so we will see how it all shakes out. However, I did some work on the owner's brother's house last summer, so I think I have an edge up."

"That's great, Honey. That would be so good for you and your team to have that steady work to look forward to. You always take good care of your team, so I'm sure they aren't worried, but construction can be so unpredictable."

"Do you usually have a hard time getting steady jobs?" Ella asked.

"Not usually, but there is always the chance that when one job ends it could be a while before something else comes along."

"That must be stressful for you and I'm sure the men on your team probably get stressed about it too," Ella said, her voice soft.

"Yes, this is why it would be nice to be able to guarantee some work for the guys through the New Year. In fact, it's such a big job I would probably even have to bring on someone else just to keep up." Tilly's face lit up and he knew exactly what was coming next. He almost rolled his eyes at her but was smart enough not to.

"I'm so proud of you, Porter. Your dad would have been proud too." Tilly reached across the table to pat him on the hand. She always got sentimental whenever things were going well for him. "And he would have loved you, Ella," Tilly added quietly, still trying to maintain her composure.

He looked over at Ella and saw her give his mom an uncomfortable smile. Yes, he was sure his dad would have really loved Ella. But hearing this from his mom had really made her squirm. The woman sitting next to him at the table was not the same one who had run out of her house this morning wrapped in nothing but a blanket just to kiss him senseless. This morning she had been happy and playful, but now she seemed distracted, distant, and sad even. His curiosity was slowly morphing into panic.

When their meals came, they ate while his mom told stories about customers at the bar and a few stories about him when he was younger. Luckily for him she didn't delve into any really embarrassing anecdotes, but it wouldn't have mattered anyway because although Ella was being polite and nodding her head at the right intervals, she was not engaged in the conversation. When his mother excused herself to the restroom, he decided to press the issue further.

"I don't understand why you said you would come to dinner if you were going to be miserable the entire time," he said without looking at her. She didn't respond at first, just continued to push her food around on her plate with her fork.

"You're right Porter. I shouldn't have come. I am sorry. I am not trying to be rude. Do you think you could take me home?"

"You want to go home?"

"I think that would be best, yes."

He just continued to stare at her, silently willing her to just tell him what was going on.

"If that's what you want." He motioned to the waiter to bring the check. He was busy signing it when his mom came back to the table.

"Mom, I am sorry, we are going to have to take off. Ella isn't feeling well," he said as he slid out of the booth. Ella slid out after him.

"Oh no, Honey, I am so sorry to hear that," she said as she gave Ella a quick squeeze. "Take her home and get her some tea," she said to Porter.

"I'm sorry to ruin your dinner. I would take myself home, but I rode here with Porter," Ella apologized.

"Don't you worry about dinner. Just go home and feel better."

"Thank you. Have a good night," Ella said as she walked

towards the door. Tilly grabbed Porter's arm before he could get too far.

"Whatever is bothering her, you need to make it right Porter," Tilly whispered to him urgently. "Don't let her sabotage what you have between you two. She's the best thing that's ever happened to you." He looked his mom right in the eyes.

"I know, Mom. I will see you tomorrow." He kissed her on the cheek and headed out after Ella.

As they rode back towards Ella's house, she was still silent and was giving no indication that she would be opening up soon.

"What happened between this morning and dinner, Ella? Why, all of a sudden, are you so unhappy?" She didn't answer right away. She kept looking out at the ocean. Finally, she turned towards Porter and he saw tears running down her cheeks.

"I am not unhappy. In fact, this is the happiest I think I've ever been," she said is whisper so quiet he almost didn't hear her. At her tears, he immediately pulled his truck over to the side of the road, threw the truck in park, and slid to her side of the seat. He cupped her face in his hands and looked at her, completely out of his element. He wasn't sure how to deal with this new side of her.

"Please tell me what is going on, Ella. I can't handle you crying. I'm am losing my mind here," he said as he wiped the tears off of her cheeks, a pointless task as more were rolling down even quicker than before. She griped his shirt with both of her hands and fisted them. She was taking deep breaths and he was waiting for her to calm down. Finally she looked back up at him.

"Last night was so special, Porter. I have never felt that connected to anyone before, ever," she sniffled a little, but continued. "We've been spending time together and I don't know if we've been naïve or just hopeful, but today after we talked on the phone, reality just sunk it. It hit me hard.

I can't get past the fact that in a few days I am going to leave here, leave you, leave all this behind. Your job is here and there are people who rely on you and your business to survive. You are tied here and I am tied to Portland. I will leave and we will be over."

"Ella," he said as he brushed a loose tendril of hair off her face and behind her ear, "it doesn't have to be that way. I don't want it to be that way at all. It's just two hours from here to Portland. Two hours is nothing. We can make this work." He was doing his best to soothe her by rubbing his thumbs over her cheeks gently. She was shaking her head.

"No. The distance is not something I can get past." Her voice was quiet again and she wouldn't look him in the eye. "What happens when we haven't seen each other in a while and another damsel in distress shows up in town and you fall in love with her? Can you honestly say you'd rather be with someone who lives so far away and you wouldn't be tempted by someone else? I don't think I could handle that." He couldn't believe what she was saying.

"You think I would cheat on you?" He asked angrily.

"Not intentionally, no. But I do think that if the right woman showed up and was more convenient for you, it would be hard for you to turn her down."

"That's bullshit, Ella. I'm not Kyle, I don't cheat on women. You can't give up on what we have based on some notion of an incident that hasn't happened."

"I don't expect you to understand," she said icily.

"Well, I don't understand. Besides, the threat of infidelity is something you risk in every relationship. You don't have to live far away to cheat on someone, Ella. I am not worried about you cheating on me because what I feel for you, how much I care, is stronger than any fear I might have about the future. Relationships are scary. So what? But if you throw a good one away before you give it a chance to grow, you've got no one to blame but yourself."

"There's no future for us, Porter!" she nearly screamed.

"You're here. Your mom is here, and your job is here. I can't be the reason you spend time away from Tilly. And what about your boat? All your free time would be tied to traveling and being out of town. I can't leave Portland; my business is there. It just wasn't meant to be."

"You think I care about a boat? Do you honestly think that I would rather spend time building a boat than building a life with you?" He asked, desperately pulling her face towards his. He was starving for her. He needed to look into her eyes and make sure she understood what he was saying. "I love you, Ella. Up until now I have just been waiting for you. You showed up and I loved you the instant I saw you. You were irritating, and stubborn, and smart, and sharp, and sexy as hell. You rattled my world this past week and I wouldn't change anything about it except this part, the part where you try to throw it all away because of fear."

Ella was looking at him with red rimmed eyes, tears still running down her cheeks. He willed her to say something with his mind, but the silence was palpable. She closed her eyes and leaned her forehead against his.

"I'd like for you to take me home now," was what she whispered to him, but what he heard was the sound of everything he never knew he wanted being torn away from him.

Ella

Breathe. Ella just needed to remind herself to breathe. She was near a total and complete meltdown but needed to hang on to her composure for just a little longer until she was safely alone in her rental house. She was reeling from how drastically her outlook had changed in just the last twelve hours. Twelve little hours were all it took for her hope of "happily ever after" to come crashing down around her, smashing into tiny little pieces, cutting her wide open, leaving her wounded and scarred.

This morning everything was nearly perfect. She was still basking in the glow of their lovemaking the night before, remembering the way he had told her he wanted her always, and how tempted she had been to agree. Even now, sitting in his truck, silently crying and trying to keep it together, she still wanted nothing more than to be with him. All it had taken to rip her happiness away from her was the one phone call from him, outlining how great he was doing here in Lincoln City. He was sharing with her how exciting the new job would be and how much all his men depended on him. All of a sudden it occurred to her that he was rooted here and she was rooted elsewhere. She couldn't ask him to leave and she had a good reason to stay .in Portland.

The obvious solution would have been to just deal with the distance, but distance was ever increasingly becoming her worst enemy. Distance, both emotionally and physically, drove a wedge between her and Kyle and she wasn't willing to purposefully set her or Porter up for another disaster. She couldn't resign herself to a relationship full of missing him and wondering when the other shoe was going to drop.

So she did the most selfish, but also self-preserving thing she could think of: she let him go. Now, sitting in his truck next to him as he drove her back to her house, she was feeling to ramifications of her decision. She knew he'd be upset, but she wasn't prepared for the anger he seemed to be simmering in. His knuckles were white from his grip on the steering wheel, and he hadn't said a single word in a while. Although, there wasn't much to say. She'd made it pretty clear her mind was made up. As he pulled onto her driveway and slowly came to a stop, she felt as though the panic might become too much for her to handle.

Porter turned the truck off, opened his door, and started to walk around the truck. When she realized that, even after everything she'd just done, he was still going to open her door for her, she lost her last thread of composure. Tears were flowing freely and she was trying her hardest to keep from making audible gasps as she transitioned into what could only be a really ugly cry.

He opened her door and stepped forward boxing her in, blocking her way out of the truck. She was turned so her legs were hanging out of the truck and he leaned down to put his hands on either side of her thighs. He wouldn't look at her. He was staring at the ground. She wanted to reach up to hold his face in her hands, take everything back, and tell him that they would find a way to make it work. But she wasn't willing to put either one of them in that position. She waited patiently for Porter to find whatever words he wanted to say to her. Finally, he raised his eyes to look at hers.

"You really want this to be over?" He asked her quietly.

How could she tell him the truth? How could she tell him that all she wanted was him with her? She was torn between what she desperately wanted, and what she thought was best.

"I think that is the best option, yes." Every word she said broke her heart.

"I think this is a mistake," he said through gritted teeth.

"I know you do," she answered through sobs she could no

longer keep at bay.

With no more words, he took a step back and walked to the back of the truck giving her to space she needed to get to the house. She slowly slid down from the truck, closed the door behind her, and walked towards the front door. Before she made it to the porch she heard Porter's door from his truck close and then he peeled out of her driveway, spewing gravel and dirt behind him.

She ran the rest of the way into the house and didn't stop until she hit the bed. In the back of her mind she was chastising herself for the way the week had turned out. Six days ago she had lain on this bed crying, mourning the end of one relationship. Today she was crying, mourning a relationship that never really made it off the ground. What hurt even more was that the depth of feelings she had for Porter made the way she felt about Kyle seem silly and insignificant. Still, she felt the loss twice.

She was stuck in this house, which now could only signify her inability to maintain any kind of relationship. She couldn't go home yet. She had told Kyle he had until the end of the week to move out. She didn't want to go back home and risk seeing him in the process of moving out. She felt doomed to spend the next three days reliving every moment she and Porter had shared in this damned house. She thought briefly about going to stay with her sister, but didn't want to intrude on her sister's house and life. She decided, however, to call Megan. She needed someone to talk to about everything happening and since Megan was the only one who knew about Porter, she seemed to be the obvious choice. Her sister answered on the third ring.

"Hey, Fella. How's it going?"

Ella couldn't bring herself to say a word because when she opened her mouth all that would come out was stifled sobs.

"Ella, what's wrong? Why are you crying? Is everything

ok?"

"No, everything's all fucked up," she managed.

"Are you hurt?"

"No, Megs, I'm not hurt."

"Ok, well that's good. What's going on?"

"I just ended everything with Porter."

"What the hell happened between yesterday and today? Yesterday you looked like you were on cloud nine anytime I even mentioned his name."

"I know, I know."

"Spill it, woman," Megan demanded.

"I just got to thinking about how we are both so settled in our lives and to be together would actually mean being apart."

"It's two hours, El," Megan said with softness.

"It's not just about that. I lived with Kyle and he still managed to find someone else right under my nose. Porter is an amazing man and soon some woman is going to realize that and I will be in a completely separate part of the state. Who do you think he's going to choose to be with? How could I expect him to sacrifice being happy with someone he can actually be with, just to be with me?"

"Wow, Ella. You are not giving Porter or yourself enough credit here. First of all, just because you wouldn't be around him all the time doesn't mean he would cheat on you and secondly, you are not everyone's back-up girlfriend. The problem with you and Kyle was Kyle. He's a dumbass and that trashy skank is his punishment for treating you poorly, not his prize. She's a dirty slut-bag, but she did you a favor."

"Would you purposefully start a relationship with someone who lived two hours away? Who was not in a position to move?"

"Well, you went and fell in love with him before you thought about logistics, so what does it matter now?"

"I never said I was in love with him," Ella stated

pointedly.

"Oh please, Ella. Give it up. You know you love him. Don't be obtuse."

"I hardly know him," she whispered.

"You know the important stuff," Megan said, mirroring Porter's words from the night before.

"That's what Porter said."

"He's a smart man, Fella."

Ella tried to catch up with the thoughts racing through her head. Love? She cared deeply about him and felt more for him than she had ever felt for anyone, but she couldn't love him. It had been six days. She wasn't one of those women who fell in and out of love so quickly. Everything her sister was saying was making her question herself. If she loved Porter, then what had she felt for Kyle? Why was it so confusing? She quickly felt exhausted.

"I think I'm going to let you go, Megan. I can't think about this anymore today."

"Ella, you cannot run away from him if the only reason you're running is because you're scared. The things in life that scare you sometimes turn out to be the best parts." Ella took a deep breath and mulled her sister's words over in her head.

"I'm not scared, Megs, and I'm not running. I am just trying to do the right thing."

"How about you do the thing that's going to make you the happiest and then let everything else fall into place?"

"Aren't you a little young to be so wise?" Ella asked snippily.

"Ok, well, if you're going to get crabby, I will let you go. I will call you tomorrow."

"Thanks, Meg, and don't worry about me. I will be fine. I always am."

"That's what I'm worried about," Megan said with sadness.

Chapter Sixteen

Ella

The next day was like an exercise in controlled, prolonged, acute, self-imposed heartache. Ella wasn't even sure she slept. All she knew for sure was that she felt like shit. Her head was pounding and her throat was raw, a product of the crying she had done overnight, no question. Every time she closed her eyes she saw Porter's face, close to hers, his brown eyes searching hers for answers she simply didn't have. When he wasn't peering into her eyes, he was touching her and the imprints of his hands on her skin felt like they had been burned or branded on her. She was familiar with the emotional turmoil but hadn't been expecting the physical pain that accompanied his absence.

Had he really told her he loved her? Was it even possible? Regardless of how she felt about him, it seemed improbable that he could fall in love with her in so short of a time. Things like this didn't happen to her. It seemed as though she couldn't win, no matter how she proceeded with him. Either she chose to leave him and then would have to find a way to mend the hole that seemed to be growing larger and more immense by the minute, swallowing every breath she took and tear she cried, or she could choose to be with him, assuming he still wanted her, and perhaps end up broken in the end anyway.

She figured a shower was in order. If anything, she needed the hot water to remind her that she was human. She always felt better after a shower anyway. She rolled off the bed refusing to stop and smell the pillows Porter had used again. Her mind knew they still held his scent hostage, torturing her endlessly throughout the night. At one point she almost removed them from the bed completely, but eventually came to the conclusion that, as pathetic and stupid as it made her feel, she couldn't bear any more separation from him. She gave herself the consolation of smelling him on her pillows as she cried.

Every muscle ached as she walked to the bathroom as if her body was actually protesting being away from him. She couldn't let herself wonder whether or not he was feeling the same way. If she started thinking about him at all, she didn't know is she would be able to stop herself from contacting him. Calling him and telling him to come back to her, to kiss her, to touch her. All she needed was for him to breathe some life back into her and she knew the choice to be with him or not wouldn't be in her control anymore. Her own body would betray her and demand him to hold her, and there wouldn't be anything she could do about it.

As she hobbled to the bathroom and turned the water on for her shower, she removed her nightgown and looked at herself in the mirror. She was seeing her same reflection, albeit, she looked like a train wreck. Her eyes were puffy and bloodshot. She had dark circles under eyes which only accentuated the bags that had formed there. Her hair resembled a bird's nest with crazy tendrils of blonde sticking out every which way. Beyond all the effects of her night of crying, she could still see the body Porter had admired. She ran a fingertip down from her chin to her collarbone, remembering his mouth there. She did the same motion from her ear down the side of her neck; that was Porter's favorite spot. Her hand ran smoothly, yet tentatively, down over her bare breast, bringing fresh new tears to her eyes. His admiration of her body had given her a confidence she hadn't ever felt before and even though she could still see the body he had loved so thoroughly and fully, it meant nothing to her now that his hands would never roam over her skin again.

She walked over and turned off the lights. She would rather shower in the dark and not have to look at the body that would remind her only of his absence. She stepped into the shower and let the hot water run in tiny streams along her body. The touch of the water on her skin was the most contact her body had felt all night and the sensation made her weep, salty tears mixing with shower water and soap.

This was too much. Her breaths came quicker and with a more frantic, thudding need. Panic was setting in and she was unaccustomed to this new feeling. She slid down the wall of the shower and continued to try and breathe as she sat on the floor, water pelting the top of her head, beads of water flying out of her mouth as she managed to keep the air flowing in and out. It occurred to her that being here, in this house, in this city, was more damaging than she could have ever imagined. She would have to leave. Perhaps it was time to go to her parents, explain what had happened, and stay with them for a while.

After a few minutes, her breathing returned to a somewhat normal rhythm and her heart rate was back to the familiar pace. She shut the water off wondering if she'd remembered all the steps of washing and conditioning her hair, but not caring enough to backtrack in her mind. As she dried her hair and body with a scratchy towel, she heard a knocking on the door.

She halted, mid-scrunch, towel in hand, drying her hair. Was someone really knocking on her door? Who? Why? Then she heard it again, the unmistakable sound of knocking. She quickly threw on a tee shirt and shorts and was going down the stairs when the knocking became more hurried and insistent. She pulled on the door handle and was immediately shocked.

"Tilly. What are you doing here?" Ella's mind was running through a million scenarios that would bring Tilly to her door and most of them involved Porter being injured. "Is Porter all right?" She asked in a panicked voice.

"He definitely isn't ok, Ella. But he's not hurt, no." Ella breathed a sigh of relief.

"Then why are you here?"

"To talk some damn sense into you. Can I come in?" Ella backed up and opened the door to Tilly, letting her slide past her into the living room, caught off-guard by her swearing. Manners took over and Ella was offering something to drink.

"No, I am fine. Come sit down, Ella," Tilly commanded. Ella found herself sitting next to her on the couch, looking at her blankly, completely at a loss for words. "Ella, why are you doing this?"

"Doing what?"

"Torturing yourself. Torturing Porter." Ella looked away from Tilly and stared at the floor.

"I'm not trying to torture anyone. I am sorry if he's hurting, but he's not the only one. This wasn't easy for me either."

"Then why are you doing it?"

Ella exhaled loudly with irritation. Why did she have to explain this to everyone? Porter was the only one she felt needed an explanation. Now she was getting frustrated that he had told his mother and that she was here making pleas on his behalf. She rubbed her hands over her face, trying to remain calm.

"Tilly, I understand you are trying to protect Porter, but what happened between us is private. I don't really want to talk about it."

"I'm here to protect you as much as I am him, Honey." Ella felt Tilly's hand on her shoulder as she gave it a gentle squeeze. "Porter didn't tell me what happened. All I needed was to see his face to know what was going on. It was obvious at dinner last night that something was bothering you. This morning when he came to the bar, I just knew."

"I can't talk about this," Ella said as she rose from the couch.

"Neither one of you deserve to hurt this way, Ella. He's

never felt this way about anyone, Honey. He loves you and you love him."

"Why does everyone keep saying that to me? I don't know if I love him," Ella whispered.

"Of course you do. Why else would you put yourself through this? If you didn't love him, you wouldn't have a problem seeing him on the weekends or letting him rearrange his life for you. I understand the fear that comes with loving someone, but I also understand the heartache of losing that love. I can't understand, for the life of me, why you would give up his love willingly."

More tears, even though she was sure she'd used them all up, came pouring down her face.

"It would never work, Tilly, him and me. There's no way for us to be together," she said through loud, racking sobs. Tilly came to stand in front of her placing her hands on her shoulders and looking her in the eyes.

"Let him figure that out, Ella. Give him your heart and let him figure out how to keep it, how to protect it. It's what he needs. He needs you to surrender, to stop fighting him, and then he will move heaven and earth to make sure you feel nothing but love and happiness."

"To ask Porter to be with me is asking him to give up too much."

"No, my dear girl, asking him to be with you is giving him the best gift anyone could ever give him."

Ella wanted that to be true so badly.

"Did you ever ask him what he wanted, Ella?"

She thought for a moment and shook her head.

"I knew he would give up everything if I asked him to."

"Hmm," Tilly said softly in understanding and agreement. "And that scares you?" Ella nodded. "I assume, based on what I know of your last relationship, that you are not use to feeling like a priority."

"I suppose not," she answered quietly.

"Porter is a simple man, Ella. What you see is what you

get. He wants to be there for you, but he won't force you."

"I know." As Ella said the words she heard the vibration of her cell phone against the hard surface of the counter in the kitchen. She picked up the phone and saw she had a text message from Porter. Her heart stopped and any attempts to breathe were halted as well. She unlocked the screen and his message appeared.

Ella, I never knew I could feel this wrecked just from missing someone. It's like I am missing a piece of myself. Please, let's talk about this again.

"Is that from Porter?" Tilly asked.
Ella nodded.
"I could tell from the way you stopped breathing." Tilly started walking towards Ella and stopped when she was in front of her. "Don't let your fear of being hurt stand in the way of your happiness, Ella. I would give that advice to anyone, not just the woman my son loves."

Ella watched as Tilly walked out of her front door, leaving her to contemplate what to do next. She was looking at her phone like the perfect response to his text message would type itself. Hoping for some inspiration as to what she was supposed to say to him next. She knew what would happen if she agreed to talk with him. She would crumble. She would undoubtedly be happy. But for how long? Was he worth the risk? Every fiber of her being was telling her yes.

Come to my house when you're off work. We'll talk.

Ella looked at the clock that said it was past one in the afternoon. The day had been lost while she was crying in her bed. She figured she had a few hours before Porter turned up. She didn't want to spend that time being anxious or nervous, but she feared she had no choice. She went back upstairs to finish getting ready for the day.

Ella started really watching the clock around six o'clock. She figured he would be there any minute and couldn't keep her hands from shaking when she tried to do mundane things like brush her hair or wipe down the counters. She tried to keep herself busy by sweeping the floor, making her bed, and loading the dishwasher. By seven o'clock she was starting to worry he wasn't coming.

At seven fifteen she heard a knock at the door and it felt like the floor had been pulled out from under her. She stared at the door for a few seconds, unsure if she would be able to move to answer it. Finally she regained use of her legs and walked towards the door. She stopped at the mirror to make sure she looked all right and gave herself a little laugh because she looked terrible. The dark bags hadn't gone away and she looked pale. There was nothing she could do about it, so she resigned herself to opening the door and letting him see what his absence had done to her physically.

She immediately made eye contact with him hoping that would give her the guise of being confident. What she saw stripped her raw. Once he saw the state she was in, she watched him flinch and move towards her, to hold her and soothe her, but he held back. She saw on his face the instant he remembered they weren't together and pulled his arms back to his side, fists gripping air so hard his knuckles were bulging and white. Watching him withhold himself from her hurt physically, caused her pain right in her gut.

"Do you want to come in, Porter?"

"No. I'd rather not." He said while still looking her directly in the eyes.

"Um, all right. Where would you like to talk?"

"Grab a sweatshirt and meet me on the beach," he said and then he turned and walked around the house towards the beach.

Ella stood in place for a few seconds trying to process what had just happened. He had looked more mad than upset, and the terse and abrupt way he'd spoken to her was unsettling. She sighed, went upstairs to grab her sweatshirt and then headed out the backdoor to the beach. She was resigned to accept whatever he had to say to her. Even if he was angry, she probably deserved it.

It was just after sunset and although she was sure the coloring of the sky would be gorgeous, a thick fog had rolled in and sat just off shore, creating a weirdly beautiful veil around the beach. She could see the sand and the waves crashing on the beach, but she couldn't see anything more than one hundred yards away. What she could see, however, was the outline of Porter, hidden in shadow, backlit by a roaring campfire.

As she got closer she could see a little more detail. He was facing her and he had his hands in his jean pockets. Closer still, she could see the firelight dancing off the sides of his face, illuminating the fact that his chocolate brown hair had very slight copper highlights. When she finally was close enough to see everything around him, she stopped mid-stride and instinctively placed her hand over her mouth to cover the sob and also the smile that had both sprung up on her. A blanket was laid out with some sleeping bags rolled up at one end, a picnic basket set out, and on the side of the basket was a bucket with ice, champagne, and two champagne flutes.

"What is this, Porter?" Ella asked as she approached him beside the licking flames of the fire he had built.

"Well, this is a picnic on the beach," he said motioning towards the blanket and basket. "But, it's going to get cold, so I built the fire and brought the sleeping bags." Ella fought the urge to roll her eyes at him.

"No, Porter, what is this? Why are you here?"

"Gonna go right for the jugular, are you?"

"I don't have the patience to waste any more time with

you, Porter. We've wasted enough time as it were."

"You've got a good point, Ella." Porter took in a deep breath, ran his hands through his hair, and then looked her right in the eyes. His gaze sent a shiver right through her whole body and all she wanted to do was close the gap between them. He was too far away. He was never close enough.

"Just say what you've got to say," she was dying from need to touch him and wanted him to get done saying whatever he had to say so she could fix everything between them. She saw him straighten his shoulders, seeming to brace himself to go into battle.

"I know it's only been a few days, Ella. But there's nothing you could say that would convince me that we're not meant for each other. Ever since I saw you sitting on that bar stool, my body has been tied to yours. I need to feel you in my arms and my body aches with need when you're not in them. I have never felt this inherent need to be with someone, and honestly, it's the best damn feeling in the world." She saw a little light leave his eyes and his shoulders slumped a little. "It was the best feeling, until last night when you pushed me away."

"Porter, I nev-"

"No, I listened to you last night and now you've got to listen to me," he demanded. Ella closed her mouth, her pulse racing from his commanding voice. Something inside her liquefied. Her resolve? Her last thread of resistance? Whatever it was, it was running like molten lava through her veins. She just continued to look at him, giving him the silent submission he was looking for.

"I have spent my entire life doing right by everyone else. I've done everything I could for my mom, making sure she was taken care of. I've been running my business just trying to make sure it was successful, working so hard almost because I didn't have anything else to do. None of it bothered me because I never thought I was missing anything. Then I found you, Ella. I wasn't even looking, but there you were." He stepped towards her, his hands reaching behind her waist, her arms instinctively looping around his neck, her fingers running through the hair at the nape of his neck.

"Please let me show you how good this could be. I know you're scared and I know I'm asking you to take a risk, but I promise you I will never make you feel like giving us a shot was a mistake. The thought of never kissing you again, never making love with you again, never feeling your smooth skin under my hands, it's more than I am willing to give up, Ella."

She felt another tear slide down her cheek and he reached up to wipe it away. His thumb gently stroked across her cheek and continued behind her ear. He continued to caress, all the while slowly pulling her lips closer to his. Her eyes were darting between his mouth and his eyes. She couldn't find any words, so she let her kiss do the talking.

She closed the distance between them, and nearly climbed up him with urgency. When their lips met it was almost as if their bodies both took a sigh into each other. He groaned, his hands moving all through her hair, while she was content to just hold his face. Their tongues we dancing slowly, lazily, enjoying each other while the memory of absence was still fresh. He was nipping at her bottom lip, sucking it into his mouth, shooting electric currents straight to her core.

"Porter," she said, interrupting the kiss that felt like it was breathing new life into her. His hands on her body were healing her, but they had more to discuss. "We need to finish talking." He pulled back and looked at her.

"Well, that was either one awesome make-up kiss or a really terrible goodbye," he said with a sigh. "The choice is up to you, Ella. But before you make your decision, understand that I will make this so easy for you. Whatever you need to feel secure, I will make sure it happens. I love you and I want you to be happy, but I hope you'll choose to be happy with me." He flicked her nose with his, as she had grown so accustomed to, and looked into her eyes waiting for her to speak.

Ella took a step back from him and reached out for his hand. He gave her a questioning look, but took her hand and followed her as she led them to sit on the blanket, already toasty from the fire. She motioned for him to sit down first and she sat in front of him between his legs. He wrapped his arms around her and she snuggled in to his chest.

"Did you know you're mom came to talk to me today?" She felt him tense around her.

"Um, no, I didn't," he said hesitantly. "Do I need to apologize for something she said?"

"No, of course not," she said lazily rubbing her hands up and down his forearms. "She just wanted to make sure I wasn't making a terrible mistake." Ella took a deep breath and let it out slowly. Then she turned slightly so that her face was looking up at Porter. She took just a moment to commit to memory how his chocolate brown eyes looked with the firelight dancing in them. They reminded her of caramel. He reached to tuck a piece of hair behind her ear, and she kept his hand on her cheek, leaning in and taking strength from him.

"She didn't say anything I didn't already know. She just made me consider your side."

"What did she tell you?"

"She said you loved me."

He leaned in and kissed her softly.

"She told me that if I gave my heart to you, you'd take care of it."

He kissed her again, longer this time and deeper, making her heart rate sky rocket.

"She said that you wouldn't force me to be with you, that you would take things slow, and make me a priority."

He went to kiss her again, but she put a finger up against his lips.

"Are all those things true, Porter? Will you take care of my heart? Will you make our relationship a priority? Because I don't want anything less and I will give everything right back to you. I promise to take care of you, cherish you, and make you the most important thing in my life. I cannot be in another relationship were I am alone in the dark. Does that make sense?"

Porter brought his strong hands to her face and pulled her in close, kissing her forehead.

"I will spend every day making sure you feel my love for you. That's all I can promise, Ella. It might get tough and we might have bad days, but you will never go to sleep questioning how I feel or what you mean to me. I love you, Ella."

She looked into his eyes and the love he was professing washed over her. It warmed her throughout, and she felt herself open up to him. She took in a sharp breath.

"I love you too, Porter."

His eyes grew wide with realization and she couldn't help the smile that spread across her face. He suddenly grabbed her by the waist and moved her to lay on the blanket as he draped himself over her. His mouth was on hers instantly and this kiss was different. This was the slowest, laziest, heaviest kiss she'd ever felt. He was in no hurry and she felt as if he was taking his time trying to savor every moment. The pace of the kiss was making her heart race but also making her sleepy all at the same time, making her drift into an other-worldly place where it was just the two of them, sharing their love with each other, basking in the intensity of what was passing between them. After what seemed like hours of intense, slow, mesmerizing kissing, finally Porter pulled away but only far enough to look in her eyes.

"I knew you loved me," he whispered.

"I knew I loved you too. I just needed a little time to acclimate myself to the idea of loving someone so deeply just days after meeting them. You can't deny that this, what's between us, is a little unconventional."

"I don't really care," he said firmly. She smiled at that, because it was exactly what she needed to hear.

"I guess I don't care anymore either." She gently moved some locks of his crazy hair from his forehead and spent a few moments admiring how ridiculously handsome he was, using her fingers to smooth over the features of his face. "Porter, I am sorry about last night. I never wanted to hurt you. More than anything, I was just trying to protect myself. I went about it the wrong way, though. I should trust you and myself for protection, because keeping myself away from you did more harm than good." He let out a loud sigh and rolled onto his back to look up at the sky. She hated that he pulled away from her, but knew he was working through something in his mind, and she wanted to give him the space he needed.

"Last night was possibly the worst night I've had since my father died. I was torn apart, Ella. I don't ever want to feel that way again." Ella looked over at him, his words slicing her open.

"I am so sorry, Porter."

He turned his head until their eyes met.

"I'd do it again, if it meant you'd come back to me. I'd do it a million times for you. But I'd rather not."

She rolled over slightly, hoping he'd hold her. He moved his arm out for her and she snuggled into his chest. The rhythmic rise and fall of his chest was soothing and let her relax for the first time that day. As she let herself unwind, she started to feel an emptiness in her stomach and realized she was starving.

"What's in the picnic basket?" She asked.

"Regular campfire fixings. Hot dogs, chips, stuff to make s'mores. Are you hungry?"

"Famished. I didn't eat today."

"Well, let's get the lady a hot dog then."

They sat up and she enjoyed watching him get everything set up as he handed her a stick with a hot dog on the end.

"I've never done this before," she said, a little embarrassed.

"With as much time as you've spent on this beach, you've never roasted hot dogs on a fire?"

"Nope."

"Ok, well, luckily for you I'm an expert hot dog roaster. Just hold the stick over the fire and when it locks done, stop."

Ella laughed. "Man, I'm not sure I can handle that level of culinary expertise," her words dripped with sarcasm.

"It's ok. I'll be here the whole time to supervise."

"My hero," she said with a smile.

After she'd had her fill of hot dogs and s'mores, Porter unrolled one of the sleeping bags, unzipping it all the way. He opened the champagne with a loud pop and poured them both a glass. He gave her both glasses and then sat down behind her wrapping them both in the sleeping bag. She gave him a glass and leaned back against his chest. She could feel his breath moving across her ear, eliciting shivers throughout her body. The need for him was coming on strong, causing an ache to form in her belly.

He lifted his glass a little above her head.

"A toast, Ella. To holding on to all things good, to love unexpected, and to finding something you never knew you were missing." He touched his glass to hers with a clink and she refused to cry again. She had a feeling that she would spend a good portion of their relationship simply trying to recover from his words. Instead, she took a drink of the champagne to try and force back the emotions he was pulling out of her.

The fog had thickened and moved inland even more creating a cloudy barrier around them. She could see the campfire, but she could no longer see anything past it. The waves could still be heard rolling and crashing onto the shore and they spent a few minutes in silence listening. Every now and again she took sips of the chilled champagne until her glass was empty. He took their empty glasses and put them in sand. She felt a chill come over her, most likely a product of the weather which was becoming more typically Oregon beach-ish by the minute, temperamental and cold. She shivered and he pulled the blanket around her tighter. She turned her head and looked up at his face, silently asking him for the contact she was desperately seeking. Of course, he understood exactly what she needed.

His lips came down slowly to meet hers. The kiss started slow, but quickly began picking up speed and intensity until finally Ella turned fully around to face him so she could feel him with her hands. She was on her knees holding his face between her hands and she felt his five o'clock shadow, the texture beneath her hands making her yearn to feel it all over her body. She felt his hands move from her waist to her ass, gently pulling her into him further, and she smiled into their kiss. She moved to sit astride him and pulled away for a moment.

"I am going to miss this when I go back to Portland," she said as she kissed the side of his jaw.

"Baby, I am not going to give you a chance to miss anything." He moved his mouth to the side of her neck, the spot that drove her crazy, partly from knowing how much he liked nuzzling her there. A slight moan escaped from her and she could tell it only fueled his urge to devour her. And she was more than willing to allow him to follow his urges.

"Porter, maybe we should go back to the house," she said breathily. He pulled away and looked around.

"We are surrounded by fog. No one can see us," he whispered and he went back to trailing kisses along her neck.

"Are you a closet exhibitionist?"

"Mmmm," he mumbled against her skin. "I am just not ready to stop kissing you, not even for a minute." Not even she could argue with that logic. She reached behind her, grabbing the sleeping bag, and pulled it over her shoulders. Then she used her mouth against his to push him down until he was lying on his back. He pulled the sleeping bag over her head to completely cover them. The guise of privacy they had created instantly ignited a fire between them.

Suddenly there was not enough. Not enough hands to feel him with. Not enough skin for her to kiss. Not enough time in the world to be with him and get her fill. It was imperative that she got as much from him in this moment as he had to give, because she knew what it felt like to go without.

His hands were roaming over her body. He trailed his fingers up her thighs until he reached her shorts, but continued past them, grasping at her skin. He was grabbing her ass beneath the fabric, pushing away the lace of her panties.

"I can't even see your underwear, but I can tell it's sexy." She giggled while kissing his throat.

"You have a serious obsession with lingerie, Mr. Masters."

"I have a serious obsession with you, Baby. And I love that you wear soft, sexy things under your clothes, things only I get to see," he said as he continued to massage under her shorts.

She crushed her mouth back down to his, his words creating a frenzy of lust and excitement in her. She felt his hands move from the back of her shorts, smoothly gliding over the tops of her thighs, and grazing the front coming ever so close to her panties covering her sex. In the back of her mind, all she could think was that they were on a public beach and anyone could happen upon them at any moment. She desperately wanted to shed their clothes, but she wasn't comfortable having sex on the beach, as turned on as she may be.

"Porter, please," she said through ragged breaths. "Let's go back inside."

"What's wrong, Ella? Don't you trust me?" He moved one of his hands to cup her sex and used his palm to grind into her over her shorts, causing her lungs to seize up. His other hand slid under her sweatshirt, found her breast, and began massaging. "I'm the only one who gets to see you like this. I wouldn't let anyone else watch you lose yourself to me," he said as he continued his ministrations on her most sensitive areas. Now it didn't matter where she was, all she could pay attention to was what he was doing to her body.

He pulled the cup of her bra down and her breast came free in his hand. He used his fingers to roll her nipple and pull and she was all but coming apart because of it.

"Oh God, Porter, you are so good at this," Ella whispered, unable to get enough air in her lungs to speak any louder.

"Feels good?" He asked. She could hear a smile in his voice.

"Mmm. Better than good, Baby." She could feel his arousal and she began to grind against him, partly to make him feel as good as she was, but also hoping to find some friction as she was desperate for release. Her hands snaked underneath his shirt and ran up along his masculine body, her fingers painting the picture of his muscular stomach. She pushed his shirt up as far as she could and laid wet kisses along his abs, smelling his scent of soap and wood and man.

Faintly, in the background, she registered the sound of drops hitting the outside of the sleeping bag. Within seconds the dropping sounds came quicker, and soon it was obvious they were caught in a downpour. Both of them halted their hands and mouths, listening to the rain.

"Porter?"

"Yeah, Baby?"

"Uh, I think our sexy picnic is getting rained out." He leaned up and kissed her hard.

"Race you to the house?" He asked. Even though there was very little light in their love tent, she could see the excitement in his eyes.

"You're on." In an instant he had grabbed her waist and rolled her over so she was on her back, kissing her hard, righting the cup of her bra he'd moved for access. He threw the sleeping bag off them, which allowed the fat, cold, wet raindrops to begin the quick work of soaking through her clothes. He quickly made it to his feet and she saw her chance to take off. She was up and running as quickly as she could through the sand. She chanced a look back at him and saw him frantically using the ice bucket to pour sand on the fire that had already been mostly extinguished by the rain. Then he was coming after her and seeing him chasing her down made her heart rate triple. She was rapidly being weighed down by her soaking sweatshirt and her dripping hair was plastered across her face. She was laughing. Loud, excited, screaming laughter.

Even though she'd obviously had the upper hand and a generous head start, she wasn't entirely surprised when, about ten yards from her porch, she felt him come behind her and lift her in his arms and carry her the rest of the way. She couldn't keep the laughter from spilling out of her, the happiness overwhelming her. He continued up the stairs and swung her legs around so her chest was up against his, pushing her back up against the outside of the house next to the sliding door.

The look in his eyes halted her laughter altogether. Playful Porter was gone, replaced with I'm Going to Do

Sexy Things to You Porter. She bit down on her bottom lip in anticipation and his eyes instantly went her lips. He raised his hand and used his thumb to pry her lip free, and then leaned in and sucked it into his mouth. She whimpered and he let out a sexy growl in response. His mouth moved over her cheek and back to her neck. Over his shoulder Ella could see the fog, so dense and thick, mirroring the wave of arousal she felt thickening in her body. She knew she should probably be cold, but felt nothing but the heat generated by their bodies and their love for each other.

She reached down and grabbed the hem of his shirt, lifting it over his head. He took the opportunity to free her from her sweatshirt as well, leaving her in her bra. Their skin, only separated by the thin material covering her breasts, met in a wet slap, and he lifted her legs to wrap around her waist, pushing her harder up against the wall. Using his hips to pin her in place his hands were free to roam over her body. Everywhere his hands touched her caught on fire. It was a burning she welcomed and felt the singeing low in her core. Ella leaned back against the wall with her shoulders, pushing the hotness between her legs up against his groin. She used her hands to push his shoulders back and he removed his mouth from hers neck with a reluctant groan.

She was looking into his eyes as she reached behind her to unclasp her bra and he watched her with wide and hungry eyes. She slid the straps down her arms and let it fall to the ground. He started to move towards her again but she put one hand on his stomach to keep him at a distance.

"Porter?" She said using the sexiest voice she could muster. He watched as she took her free hand and skimmed it up her stomach slowly, it came all the way up the center of her body, reached her neck and then headed down again and came to rest covering her breast. "Babe?"

she called to him again, secretly thrilled that she could distract him with her body.

"Yes?" His answer was a rush of air, nothing more.

"Do you see what I'm doing here? How I'm touching myself?" Her hand continued to massage her breast, stopping intermittently to tug on her nipple. She felt wanton and crazy sexy putting on this show for him out in the open on her porch.

"I see, yes," he growled, pushing his groin up against her.

"I want you to carry me inside and take over."

Chapter Seventeen
Porter

Porter was looking at quite possibly the hottest thing he's ever seen. Ella was wrapped around him, touching herself. She was writhing around, doing terribly sexy things, and she wanted him to take her inside. He didn't need to be told twice. He grabbed her around her middle and carried her in the house. He put her down once they were in the warmth of the living room, but wasted no time peeling the soaked shorts from her body. Leaving her just in her underwear, he picked her up again and carried her all the way up the stairs and to her bedroom.

He laid her down on the bed and crawled over her, scraping his nose all the way from the apex of her thighs, up her belly, between her breasts and up her throat. All along his journey he was smelling her and nuzzling her, trying to fill his senses with her. He stopped when he reached the crook between her shoulder and neck, breathing her in. He lifted his face to look her in the eye.

"I swear I am going to do everything I can to make you happy, Ella."

"I know you will, Baby," she said as she ran her hand down the side of his face.

"I love you," he said quietly.

"I know," she whispered. "Show me."

He stepped off the bed and took his pants and boxers off, making sure to grab the condoms from his wallet, very glad he'd decided to bet on reconciliation. He kneeled on the bed at her feet. He lifted one foot to his mouth and began trailing kisses from her toe all the way along her calf. She was watching him, her clear blue eyes hooded and asking him for more. His mouth continued its assault up her thigh, his hands worshiping her skin, squeezing and rubbing up and down her legs. She was so sexy, and so perfect. He couldn't keep the smile from his face knowing that she was his. The last twenty-four hours had been hell, wondering if he could ever convince her to trust herself enough to be with him. The depth of love he felt for her was earth shattering, and he was going to do his best to show her how he felt.

He ran his mouth along the crease between her thigh and her sex, nibbling a little along the way. He pulled her underwear down her legs, bent her knees up, and then let them drop to the sides, and then groaned at the sight of her, open and on display.

"Oh, Ella, you are one gorgeous woman," he said as he gently took a finger and teased her opening. He heard her breath catch, and watched as her eyes rolled back into her head. As he sank two fingers into her, he heard her whimper and he fought to keep his composure. He was determined to make this about her and give her everything he could. He began slowly pumping his fingers in and out, delighting in the fact that she was responding by meeting his thrusts.

"You're mine, Ella," he said through clamped teeth.

"Oh, yes," she breathed.

"Say it, tell me you're mine."

"I'm yours, Porter, only yours."

"I want what's mine, understand? I protect what's mine," he said as he was pumping into her faster, using his fingers to find her sweet spot.

"Yes." It was no longer an answer, but more of a long, loud, moaning affirmation. Her hands were twisted in the sheets as she grasped them at her sides. "Porter," she panted. "I need more, please," she pleaded.

He flattened his chest on the bed, resting between her legs, and while continuing to massage her with his hands, he lowered his mouth to her as well, his tongue lapping at her entrance. He found her clit and began to flick and suck on it.

"I will never get enough of you, Ella. Even the way you taste is addicting." He felt her legs begin to tense and knew he was bringing her closer. He quickened the pace of his tongue and his hand, listening to her, waiting for the sweet moment when she lost herself. Her moans were coming faster and closer together. Her hands found his hair and urged his mouth closer to her sex, grinding into him. The sounds she was making and the way she was gripping him was almost too much for him to handle. He never thought he would be able to get off by making a woman come, but he was close. Suddenly she let out a loud cry, her back arched off the bed, and her hands left his hair only to slam into the headboard behind her. He felt her pulse around his fingers, and knew she had found her peak. He slowly continued licking and sucking until he knew she had come all the way down.

"Holy hell, Porter," she said in a sleepy, sated way.

"You're amazing, Ella."

"I take no credit for that," she said smiling. He crawled up the bed and stopped when they were face to face. She placed her hands on his cheeks and pulled him down for a kiss. He pressed his chest into hers, and felt his tip at the entrance to her sex. She pushed her hips up towards him. "I want you inside me," she pleaded. He grabbed a condom, opened it, put it on in record time, and then returned to her.

He paused at her opening again, looking into her eyes. When he finally pushed into her, he wasn't prepared to feel all the air being forced form his lungs or the way being connected to her this way made him warm all over. He framed her face with his hands, content to just be inside of her for a moment, brushing the hair from her face. She ran her hands up his back, slowly caressing his skin, barely breathing herself.

"I love you, Porter," she whispered. She was looking up at him and in her eyes he saw something different than before. He was looking at his future. He didn't know how any of it had happened, or if he even deserved it, but she was his everything now. He would do anything to make sure she was with him always.

"It makes me so happy to hear you say that," he said as he nuzzled against her neck. "I want to hear you say it forever," he breathed into her neck. He came back to kiss her lightly on her lips, pushing into her again, deep and strong. "I love you too."

Then he began to move, rhythmically stroking in and out, constantly touching her. His hands were roaming her, finding her hips, her breasts, her thighs. She was so responsive, meeting him at every thrust, seeming to need the contact as much as he did. When she dug her nails into his back, it lit a fire in him and his motions became more forceful and passionate.

"Oh yes," she moaned, her eyes closed.

"You belong with me," he growled. "Open your eyes, Baby, I want to watch you come."

Her eyes darted open and with just a few more thrusts she came apart around him. He followed shortly after. He collapsed onto her, but wasted no time dusting light kisses from her mouth, down her cheek, to her neck. He slowly came down from his high and felt content to be wrapped around her, still inside of her, breathing in her scent. He might have fallen asleep for a few minutes, but was roused when he felt her move slightly. He saw her hand move across her face, leaving a trail of wetness.

"Baby, what's wrong? Are you crying?" He asked as he turned her chin towards him. She was definitely crying and the sight of it had his stomach in knots.

"It just makes me sad to think that I was almost stupid enough to let you go," she sniffled. He exhaled and then pressed a kiss to her temple.

"I understand that you were scared, Ella. I'm not saying that I wasn't scared either, but I don't want to you to get upset about it anymore. We're together now and that's all that matters."

"I was scared, Porter, and I still am. I won't lie to you about it. I am still terrified that come Sunday we'll go our separate ways and being so far away will tear us apart." Porter was gently running his hand down her hair, trying to sooth her.

"Ella, you are seriously mistaken if you think you will be going more than a few days without seeing me. Besides, do you think I could make it very long without you? I want to be with you all the time, but I know that's not healthy. It wouldn't do either of us any good to drop everything and move. We need to build a relationship, which means learning to trust each other and miss one another."

"Porter, I don't want that. I don't want you to drop everything and move. That's the last thing I want. From here on out I need to know that we are on equal footing here. Whatever decisions we make about our relationship need to be based on compromise. I don't want one of us giving up more than the other. I couldn't live with myself if I felt like I was tearing your life up from the roots. I want us to be in this together."

A smile spread across his face as he placed his hand on her cheek and moved it back to cradle her neck.

"I would love nothing more than to be in this together, with you." He placed a kiss on her mouth, pulling her closer to him, and he felt her smile against his lips.

The next morning when he woke up, he found her still wrapped around him and his arms were holding her in place. He realized he was still inside of her and the thought of spending a night connected to her like that had his heart racing. It was the most intimate scenario he could imagine and it made him love her even more.

"My beautiful Ella," he whispered against her temple. She stirred a little, eventually opening her eyes and blinking a few times.

"Hello there, Handsome," she smiled.

"I'm sorry to wake you, but I've got to go to work."

"Ok," she sighed.

"Can I see you tonight?"

"Of course," she smiled.

He kissed her lightly, and rolled away, dissolving their connection. After he'd righted himself and gotten dressed, he leaned down to the bed to kiss her again.

"Bye, Baby, I'll text you later." He laughed because she couldn't bother to open her eyes or kiss him back; she was almost asleep again.

"M'kay. Love you," she mumbled into her pillow and his heart nearly exploded out of his chest.

"Love you too," he said close to her ear and then headed for the door.

Ella

Ella woke a few hours after he had left, stretching, remembering the night before. Campfire. Kissing. Rain. Laughing. Loving. She rolled over and smiled to herself. She was so happy he had come over and wanted to be with her, officially. Her muscles were sore and she was a little slow to sit up in her bed. She had a whole day to fill before he was off work and she needed something to do. An idea occurred to her and she quickly grabbed her phone to type a text to her sister.

Hey, Megs. Are you free this afternoon?

My last class is over at noon. What's up?

Want to meet in Salem for lunch and shopping?

I've love to. Is everything ok?

Everything is fine. I'll fill you in when I see you at lunch. I need your help with a special project.

There is a cute little deli on Main Street. Want to meet there at one thirty?

Great, see you then!

Ella pulled up to the deli right on time and went in to find Megan already sitting at a table. They hugged and both ordered a sandwich from a polite waitress.

"Hey, Sis, thanks for meeting me. How was class?"

"Oh no, Ella. We didn't come here to small talk. What's happened now in the roller coaster that is your life?"

Ella frowned. "My life isn't a roller coaster," she pouted.

"Oh, yes it is and I love it. Now, tell me what's

happened."

Ella figured it was pointless to deny it; her life was a little crazy as of late.

"Well, the morning after we talked on the phone, Porter's mother came to my house." Megan's eyebrows shot up.

"Oh my. Was she in mamma bear mode?"

Ella cocked her head to the side, contemplating the question.

"Well, yes and no. At first I thought she was there to convince me to go back to him, or yell at me for hurting him. But eventually, she was a little more focused on me. She was trying to tell me that I shouldn't let my fear keep me from being happy."

"Smart woman."

"Yes, there are a few smart women in my life at the moment," Ella winked at her sister.

"So then what happened?"

"Well, coincidentally, Porter texted me while his mom was there and I agreed to see him last night. He showed up and told me to meet him on the beach. When I went out, Megan, he had set up a campfire with blankets and champagne." Megan smiled and placed a hand over her heart.

"Aw, he loves you, Fella!"

"Yes, I know. We talked, well, he talked. He basically wasn't taking no for an answer, which is good because my answer was yes."

"Yes?!"

"Yes."

"You're together?"

"Very much together," Ella smiled.

"I am so glad, Ella. You look so happy right now."

"I am, Megan. I feel amazing."

"Good sex, huh?"

"Oh my God, Megs, shut up." But Ella couldn't keep the smirk off of her face.

"I knew it. You slut," Megan laughed. "So what's the plan then? Are you guys going to do the long distance thing?"

"In the beginning, yes. He doesn't seem too worried about it, so I'm not going to worry about it. If I want to see him, I will just drive out and see him. Gas prices be damned."

Their sandwiches arrived and as they ate they spoke some more about Porter and a little about Megan and Patrick's graduation coming up.

"I can't believe my baby sister is graduating from college."

"Well, believe it. Now we've just got to find jobs."

An idea came to Ella's mind and she was immediately excited about it. It wasn't something to jump into though, so she would have to mull it over for a while. She pushed the thought to the back of her mind, saving it for later.

"That is sort of the next step," Ella replied.

"Well, speaking of next steps, what is this project you need help with?"

Ella smiled to herself, trying to hide the flush of embarrassment that washed over her.

"I was hoping you could come with me and help me pick something out."

"Ok, captain mysterious. What are we picking out?"

"Well, Porter sort of has an affinity for lingerie."

"What man doesn't?" Megan laughed.

"Yes, well, Porter seems to really like it. So I was hoping you wouldn't mind helping me pick something out. I would appreciate another girl's opinion."

"Sounds fun. I might pick something up for myself while we're at it," Megan waggled her eyebrows at her.

"Now who's the slut?" Ella laughed. Megan laughed with her, covering her mouth.

"Ok, let's get our slutty selves out of here and to the trashy lingerie store."

Ella was in a fitting room of a small boutique lingerie store, and she was a little overwhelmed by what she had in front of her. Megan had basically thrown piles and piles of lace and satin in her arms and shoved her in a dressing room. Ella went to sorting things out by style. One pile for nighties, one pile for bras and panties, and another pile for ridiculously perverted pieces of cloth that no respectable woman would wear. Ella held up a pair or neon green crotchless panties.

"Megan, I am not about to be in a porn movie. Don't bring me crotchless panties."

"Ella, don't be a prude. Crotchless panties aren't just for porn stars. They're pretty practical and men love them."

"Oh dear God, please stop talking. I will never be able to look at Patrick the same." She heard Megan giggle on the other side of the door. "I think we missed the mark, Megs. I'm looking for smoking hot, not totally trashy."

Megan groaned. "Those two things are not mutually exclusive, Fella."

"Ok, well, I need something softer, not so harsh. I want him to look at me and do a double take, not have a heart attack."

"Fine, wait a minute, I'll be right back," Megan said impatiently.

"He really likes lace," Ella yelled to Megan as she walked away.

A few minutes later Megan knocked on her door.

"This is as soft as it gets, Ella. Anything softer and you're going to have to go to a granny shop or something."

Ella cracked the door open and Megan handed in an indistinguishable pile of lace. As Ella untangled it, she immediately started smiling.

"Nice work, Megs. This is exactly what I was looking for."

"Glad to be of service."

Ella put on the navy blue corset, made of lace, with scalloped edging all alone the bottom. It came with matching lace boyshort panties. The corset pushed everything in and up and even Ella was approving of the image of her breasts hoisted up for display. The boyshorts were playful and sexy, and rode up just enough to accentuate the curve at the bottom of her ass. She was turning every which way, trying to catch all different angles. Finally, she opened the door just a little, and called for her sister. Once she was right outside the door, Ella opened up enough for her to see.

"Oh Ella, you're in trouble tonight," Megan said as her yes moved up and down the outfit.

"You like it?"

"Definitely, yes. Buy it. In all colors available."

Ella laughed. "It's missing something though. I need some fuck-me heels."

Megan laughed out loud. "Now we're talking!"

With her sister's help, she had found the perfect pair of heels to complete her outfit. They were walking to their cars in the parking lot.

"Thanks for meeting me and for helping me pick this stuff out."

"I live for lingerie shopping."

"Patrick's a lucky guy."

"Damn straight," Megan agreed, waving her own bag full of sexy purchases. "So is Porter. I am so glad you guys worked it out." Megan had a thoughtful look on her face. "You realize that Mom and Dad still think you're with Kyle, right? You've broken up with him and fallen in love with a completely different man whom they've never met, and you haven't told them any of it."

"Yes, I know," she exhaled loudly. "I just don't think I should tell them this over the phone. I will tell them next week when everything calms down a bit."

"Ok, well as long as you know what you're doing."

"I do."

"Ok, well, have fun tonight and I will see you next week when you get home." Megan gave Ella a big hug. "Love you, Sis."

"Love you back. Drive safe and thanks again." When she got into her car she checked her phone and saw she had a text from Porter.

Hey, Baby. What are you up to?

I met my sister in Salem for lunch and shopping. How is your day going?

My day is fine. I wish you would have told me you were going to Salem. You've got no jumper cables. I could have left you mine.

Ella smiled and rolled her eyes at his concern.

I'm sorry. Don't worry. I made it here fine and I am on my way home now. If I run into any trouble, I will let you know.

Okay, text me when you make it back to Lincoln City.

I will, promise. Have a good rest of your day.

Please be careful. I love you.

Love you too.

It was going to take some getting used to having someone so protective over her. Ella thought it was attractive the way he fussed over her; it made her feel safe. She had only one more stop to make before she put her master plan into action.

Ella pulled up to Tilly's, and took a deep breath before she got out of the car and headed towards the door. Once she was inside, she was reminded of how friendly and welcoming the bar was and it reminded her of its owner. She knew Tilly had just been protective of Porter and that was the driving force behind coming to confront her. She tried to remember how nice Tilly had been the night she first arrived and hoped that she hadn't permanently marred Tilly's opinion of her. It was important to her that she got along with Porter's mother.

She saw Tilly behind the bar, and when they met eyes, Tilly gave Ella a very big and genuine smile. Ella felt a little more comfortable approaching her, keeping her own smile plastered on her face.

"Hello, Tilly. It's nice to see you," Ella said, hoping she didn't sound too nervous. Tilly took a step from behind the bar and came to Ella and wrapped her in a big, warm hug.

"It's nice to see you too, Ella. I am so glad you're here." Tilly took a step back, her hands still resting on Ella's shoulders, eyes twinkling at her to compliment the smile she still wore. "Can I get you something? A drink?"

"You know? I would really like a beer," Ella decided.

"Coming up. Now why are you really here?" Tilly asked as she put a bottle in front of Ella.

"Well, I was hoping I could ask you for a favor. Have you spoken to Porter?"

"No, not since yesterday morning. Sometimes he stops in before work, but he didn't today. I'm hoping he was too busy," Tilly winked at her and Ella almost died of embarrassment as she felt a wave of heat from the blush that was most certainly crawling across her face.

"Well, regardless, I wanted to say thank you for coming to speak with me yesterday. I needed someone to help me see a different point of view and yours really helped. I just needed a little more perspective. I was hoping that you had a spare key to Porter's house that I could borrow."

"You want a key to his house?"

"Um, yes. I wanted to surprise him with dinner, so I thought if you had a key I could borrow it, just for the day."

"I am to assume, then, that you and my son have decided to give it another shot?" Ella looked down at her beer, unable to look Tilly in the eye because it was all a little too embarrassing.

"I was hoping he would have told you by now, but yes, we are together. He came by last night and we talked everything through." Ella finally looked up at Tilly, trying to overcome her discomfort, only to see wetness in Tilly's eyes. Ella's eyes became wide, realizing that Tilly was getting emotional. "Tilly, please don't cry. It's ok. Porter is fine. We worked everything out."

"Oh, Ella honey, I know he is fine," she said sniffling and grabbing a towel off the counter to wipe her nose. "You just don't understand. After his daddy died, Porter just sort of turned off emotionally. He has always been a good son and he's a hard worker, but he has been so disconnected. I was always so worried that he would spend his life alone." Tilly started crying harder now and Ella was compelled to go behind the bar to comfort her. As Ella approached Tilly, she hugged her hard again, silently crying onto Ella's shoulder.

"If it's any consolation, I feel like Porter is far from shut down in the emotional department," Ella said softly. "He is the most caring and sweet man I have ever known. He feels everything so deeply and he is so considerate. When I am with him I am blown away by how much he cares about me. He might have been shut down before, but he's doing fine now." Tilly cried a little harder with her words.

"I will thank the heavens every day that your car broke down in my parking lot," Tilly said as she pulled away, trying to wipe away her tears and get herself under control.

Ella couldn't agree more; if her car had started and she'd driven away, she might not have ever gotten to know Porter. The thought made her stomach bottom out and left her feeling queasy. A life without Porter? The thought was depressing.

"Well, luckily for all of us, I am a total airhead and left my lights on," she laughed a little.

"Ok," Tilly said with forced vigor. "You need keys to Porter's house and I've got a set." Tilly rummaged around in a compartment under the bar top and came out with her purse. She took a key off her key ring and handed it to Ella. "Have fun tonight and tell him to call his mother," she smiled.

"No problem and thanks for your help with this." Ella went back around the bar to sit down and finish her beer. As Ella nursed her beer, she thought it would be wise to check in with the store. She pulled out her phone and called.

"Poppy, how can I help you?"

"Brittany, it's me, Ella."

"Ella, great to hear from you! How's the beach?"

"Still beachy. How is the store going?"

"Just dandy over here, Ella. Really, no need to worry. Sarah and I have it under complete control. Although something pretty exciting happened yesterday."

"Oh?"

"Yea, so I guess they're filming some movie downtown and some of the crew came in. One of them was the wardrobe person and she really liked our stuff. She said she might be back to look more thoroughly and might buy some stuff for the movie."

"What? That's so exciting! I can't believe it!"

"Yes, so maybe they'll be back. It would be so cool to see clothes from your store in a movie."

"Wow, you made my day."

"Other than that, everything's been pretty normal. No

problems or debacles to speak of." Ella was now convinced the girls needed raises and vacations. It was nice to be able to leave the store for a week and have reliable competent people to run it.

"Great, well, I really appreciate you and Sarah taking care of everything. It means a lot to me. I will be back on Monday, so I will see you then."

"Take care, Ella, and enjoy the last few days of your vacation."

"I will. Bye." Ella ended the call and finished her beer. "Thanks for the beer, Tilly, and the key. I will get it back to you." Ella left a five dollar bill on the counter and left to prepare the rest of her surprise.

Chapter Eighteen
Porter

Porter had been in an exceptionally good mood all day, until Ella had told him she'd driven all the way to Salem. He immediately began to worry and it wasn't something he was used to. Later in the day when she had texted him that she'd made it safely to Lincoln City, he calmed down a bit, but was still restless to see her and feel her in his arms. If this was any indication of how it was going to be when she was in Portland, he was in for a long ride. Hopefully it would get easier to be away from her as time went by, but he wasn't betting on it. Sooner, rather than later, he assumed they were going to have to find a better solution than living two hours away from each other.

He was now off work and sitting in his truck. It had been a rough day at work and he was unusually sticky from sweat. He wanted to go to Ella's but needed to shower and change first. He picked up his phone to call her.

"Hey, Baby," Ella's voice swarmed his senses and made him smile immediately.

"Hey, yourself. What are you up to?"

"Um, I'm out. At a store," she said quickly.

"At a store? Any store in particular?" He asked, finding her answer a little strange.

"You know, one of those knick-knack stores on the waterfront. I don't know the name. I'm just out killing time, waiting for you."

"Oh, ok, well I was going to come over, but I need to go home first. Can I meet you at your house in about an hour? Maybe we can go get something to eat?"

"Sure. Sounds great! See you then!" He heard her hang up and thought she sounded rushed and a little nervous. He didn't know what was up with her, but he thought he had better hurry and get to her house to see if everything was all right.

When he pulled into his driveway he was confused by the sight of Ella's black Toyota in the driveway. Why was her car here? As he got out of his truck, he stared at her car, as if he wasn't sure it was real or not. He shook his head and walked towards his door. As he got on the porch and could see in his living room, he noticed there were small candles lit all around his house. He was still a little confused. He put his key in the lock and opened the door.

The smell of vanilla wafted into his nose and he had to admit, it smelled damned good. He looked around his living room and saw what must have been hundreds of tiny candles, on any and every surface. Ella had to be here, but his brain was still trying to put everything together.

"Hello, Handsome," he heard from behind him. When he turned to see Ella, his entire body froze and he absolutely forgot how to function. He wasn't breathing, his heart wasn't beating, his brain was fried. The only part of his body that was functioning was between his legs and beginning to make him uncomfortable.

"Jesus Christ, Ella," was all he could say. He gulped down one swallow, trying to jump start his body, trying to get his blood flowing.

Ella, his Ella, the woman he was lucky enough to have found and managed to hold onto, was in his house looking hot as hell.

She was leaning up against the wall wearing the sexiest goddamned thing he had ever seen a woman wear. It was blue. It was lacy. And it was making his heart pound out of his chest. The top part was tight and made her tits look amazing. They were almost spilling out of the top and all he wanted to do was put his mouth on them. Her underwear was another piece of lacy fabric that he would have no trouble shredding to pieces as soon as he got his hands on them. One of her legs was bent and her foot resting against the wall. She had on a pair of high heels that made her already fantastic legs so very long and sexy as hell. They were black leather, with a lot of straps, and he wanted to see them up in the air later.

"Ella," he said through deep and throaty breaths.

"Yes, Porter?" She replied sweetly with a grin that made it obvious she knew the effect she was having on him.

"I'm about five seconds away from coming over to you, ripping all that sexy lace off of your body, and fucking you, hard. If that is not what you want, you have three more seconds to tell me. Otherwise, it's game on."

She just stood there and gave Porter her sexy little grin.

"You asked for it," he said as he lunged at her.

He pressed his body up against her, his entire length flanking up against hers, pinning her against the wall. His hands found the spot in which they fit perfectly; thumbs on her cheeks, fingers splayed around her neck finding her hair. His mouth was so very close to hers. They were breathing in each other.

"You. Are. Fucking. Perfect." He almost growled at her, his words staccato. He was looking into her eyes and she was staring into his, giving everything back to him. Her breathing was ragged and with every breath she took in he could see her breasts rising, straining to be released. "This is a very sexy little outfit you have here, Ella," he said, trailing his nose along the soft swell of her breasts.

"I bought it just for you," she said quietly. He understood her meaning; this wasn't something she had worn previously for her ex. This was something she bought just for him and he was the only one to have seen her in it. That information alone made his dick harder. Looking down at her, he almost wanted to spare the sexy get-up, seeing as how she'd picked it out just for him. But right now, he really just wanted to see her bare.

He pulled her into him, crashing his mouth down onto hers. His tongue invaded her mouth and he swallowed a whimper she let out. He reached behind her, found the top of her outfit where there were tiny clasps holding her in, and with every ounce of strength he could muster, he ripped it right down the center.

Ella let out a startled shriek and then covered her mouth. He held the demolished garment out so that she could see it. He saw her eyes dart back and forth from her lacy top to him. He threw it on the floor, breathing heavily. She reached out and grabbed his shirt, and pulled him in close to her, her mouth finding his. They were starving for each other. His hands were palming her breasts, both at the same time. Her hands were tangled in his hair giving not so gentle tugs that were primal reactions to the tugs he was giving her nipples. Ella pulled away from him and leaned back up against the wall.

"I think you are wearing way too many clothes."

"Fix it." He saw Ella's eyes darken and he watched as she reached for his shirt. It had come untucked from his jeans, so she started working on the buttons. He watched her work the first two, but he grew impatient. He reached up, grabbed his shirt in the middle and ripped it open, buttons flying every which way.

"We're both going to need a new wardrobe if you keep this up, Porter," Ella laughed.

"Get the condom out of my wallet and take off my pants," he said with a smirk.

"Yes, sir." She took his wallet out and handed him the condom from inside. Without breaking eye contact he threw the condom over his shoulder and it landed on the floor near the living room. Ella unbuttoned his pants and grabbed the waistband of both his jeans and boxers. She slid them down his hips and as she took them lower, she went down with them. Expertly balancing on her sexy high heels, she pushed his pants all the way to the floor so he could step out of them. From below him, she looked up and into his eyes. He knew what she was thinking.

"You don't have to, Baby," he said sincerely.

"I know. I want to," she said as she wrapped her hand around his cock. She slowly moved her hand all the way down to the root and then back up to the head. His eyes closed and his head fell backwards. He felt her tongue lick small circles around his head, while her hand continued to glide up and down. Slowly, he felt her mouth slide around his entire tip, and she sucked him in.

"Oh my – Fuck," his words came out strangled and muffled, like he was grinding his teeth together. She was taking him all the way into her mouth and sucking him so hard. She had her hands on his thighs, no doubt to keep her balance on those shoes made for fucking. He felt her nails digging into his skin and he looked down at her. Their eyes met and he watched her pull his cock out of her mouth all the way to the tip, swirl her tongue around, and then take it all the way back down to the root.

"This is the hottest thing I've ever seen, Ella. You are so fucking beautiful. I love watching you put your mouth around me." She started bobbing faster at his words of encouragement and reached under him to cup his balls. The combination of sensations he was feeling were becoming too much. He eventually put a hand on her cheek and made her look up at him. "I want to kiss you, Ella."

She smiled at him and so very gracefully rose back up to meet his lips. While kissing her mouth, he turned her to walk her backwards into the living room. He maneuvered her to the arm of the couch, and when her legs backed up against it, he pulled his lips away from hers.

"Sit on the arms of the couch, Ella." She did as he said. "Now, I want you to lean back and lie on the couch, but keep your ass right here," he said patting the arm next to her. He watched her slowly lay down until her back rested on the couch. Once she was settled he took a moment to admire her. "You look so beautiful like this, Baby. I can't believe how lucky I am, that you're mine." He began to rub his hands down her thighs, needing to touch her.

"I think we're both pretty lucky, Porter. I never thought I could find this with anyone. You make me feel things I didn't know were possible."

He bent down and kissed her stomach, right below her belly button. He laid wet kisses along her skin and he felt her writhe beneath him. When his mouth touched lace, he smiled.

"I love how lace looks on your body, Ella," he said as he slowly ripped it from her body. He saw her move her hands to her hair, looking as though she needed something to do with her hands. "Touch yourself, Ella. I want to see how you touch yourself." He continued kisses down until he came to her sex. As his tongue found her clit, she began kneading her breasts, looking him directly in the eyes.

"Oh God, Porter," she moaned as he kept time on her clit with his tongue. He watched a blush of color start to spread up from her chest onto her neck. She was pulling and twisting her nipples as he was working on her. He took two fingers and teased her opening.

"You're wet, Ella."

"Yes, that's what you do to me," she answered with barely a voice, more of a whisper.

"Only me."

"Yes. Only you."

He slid his fingers inside of her and she moaned loudly, making his cock jerk.

"I love how you feel around me, Ella. So wet and warm. So sexy." He continued to lazily move his fingers in and out, gently stroking her from the inside, looking for the spot her knew would send her over the edge. When she jerked and yelped, he knew he'd found it.

"Is that it, Baby? Is this what you like?"

"Oh yes, please, Porter, make me come."

"My pleasure." He quickened his pace with his fingers and moved his mouth back over her clit. She was arching her back, shaking her head from one side to the other, saying nonsensical words, and he knew she was close. He thrust his hand further in, with a little more force and he felt her come around him. She cried out, her back completely lifted off the couch, gripping the cushions around her. He continued to lap at her opening until she had finished.

"Is that what you needed? What you wanted?" He asked her when she seemed to surface again.

"Mmm. Again, you've blown my world to pieces. I love you." He reached for her hands and when she gave them to him he pulled her up to stand in front of him. Then he turned her around so she was facing away from him. He reached around her body to palm her breasts as he kissed the side of her neck. Her head fell backwards onto his chest and she reached up to thread her hands through his hair. He moved her hair away from her ear and whispered to her.

"I'm going to bend you over this couch and fuck you hard, like I promised. I'm not going to be gentle, but I won't be rough. Please tell me if you want me to stop." He felt Ella nod her head and then he gently bent her to be face down on the couch. He quickly retrieved the condom from the floor and made quick work of rolling it down his shaft. He used his foot to spread her legs, and rubbed her back up and down her spine.

"You look incredibly sexy like this, Ella." She turned her head, facing away from the couch.

"Fuck me, Porter." He almost came just from her words.

"Jesus, Ella." He slammed into her once and she cried out. "Are you ok, Baby?"

"Yes, Porter. I'm fine. Don't worry about me."

"You'll tell me to stop."

"Yes. Fuck me."

With her words he slammed into her again, over and over. He heard her moaning and that spurred him on. Her cries became more frenzied and frantic.

"I'm close, Porter, please…"

He wanted desperately to give her what she needed, but wasn't sure if he could hold out long enough. He reached around her and found her clit with his fingers, rubbing it in quick circles.

"Oh yes, just like that…"

He was thrusting in and out, pumping into her hard, rubbing her clit and he couldn't take it anymore. He came hard and he heard her come along with him. He collapsed over her body. His sweat soaked body nearly slid right off her. She was breathing heavy, trying to speak, but couldn't make words come out. They lay like that for a few minutes until his legs got feeling in them again. Once he stood up, Ella rolled over on the couch and smiled up at him.

"I knew you had a thing for lingerie."

"So it would appear. Although, I feel like I have more of a thing for you." He held out his hands to her. "Let's go upstairs and take a shower." She reached out and let him pull her up to his chest. She wrapped her arms around his neck and looked into his eyes. He was running his hands down her back to rest on her ass.

"Porter, I'm not going to be able to have nice things if you keep shredding them."

"Don't pretend like that wasn't the exact response you were going for. You knew what you were getting into," he said with a smile.

"May be so, but it was still really sexy."

As they sat at dinner, Porter had his arm slung around the back of Ella's shoulders as they shared a booth at a little family owned Italian restaurant.

"I have an idea," he said between bites.

"What is it?"

"I think we should go back to your house, pack up all of your stuff, and you should spend your last two days with me at my house." Ella looked at him, and he was trying to read her mind.

"You want me to move in with you for two days?" She asked him suspiciously.

Porter laughed and gave her shoulder a light and gentle squeeze.

"Yes, I suppose that's what I'm asking."

"This is all so sudden, Porter," she said coyly.

"Ok, well, either you stay with me or I'm coming to stay with you. We've only got these last two days until you go back to Portland. I don't plan on spending much time away from you in the next 36 hours."

She leaned up and kissed him.

"I know, babe. I'm just kidding. I'd love to stay with you until I have to leave. What shall we do for the next 36 hours?"

"I don't really care what we do, Ella, I just want to be close to you."

The next day, after a day spent making love and walking on the beach, Porter had gone out to his shop to make sure everything was put away and locked up. When he came back into the house he didn't see Ella downstairs so he locked the doors and turned off the lights. Heading up the stair to the third floor he saw light coming out of his bedroom. When he entered the room he stopped at the doorway and took a moment to appreciate the sight.

Ella was lying on his bed, on top of the blankets, wearing the same shirt he'd given her the first night they'd been together. She was curled up on her side reading a book, twirling her hair around her finger. The t-shirt did nothing to hide her body from him, and even if it had, his imagination would have filled in the blanks. He had her body memorized. Every curve, every corner, every freckle. The t-shirt did, however, add an at home look to her that he was caught off-guard by.

"You look pretty sexy in my bed," he said, interrupting her reading. She looked over at him and gave him the same shy smile he hoped would melt his heart forever.

"You like my shirt?" she said, her smile indicating that she knew exactly how he felt about her choice of sleepwear.

"You weren't planning on stealing that, were you? That's my new favorite shirt."

"I think it's only fair that I get to take it back to my place. I will need a memento to remind me of you on nights when I am lonely. And it smells just like you," she said, almost pouting.

"And what will I have to remind me of you?" He walked slowly towards the bed. Ella put her book on the nightstand, and rose up onto her knees facing him.

"Whatever you want," she answered.

"Don't make promises you can't keep, Ella," he said with a smirk. "What if I want you?" He stopped at the edge of the bed and took her face in his hands. "Stay with me," he whispered.

Ella inhaled deeply and a pained look came across her face.

"I want to be with you, Porter. Nothing would make me happier than us, together, all the time. But I can't just uproot my life any more than you can yours." He saw her struggling with wanting to be with him and still maintain her life, and he understood how she felt. He rested his forehead up against hers.

"Baby, I'm sorry. I'm not trying to make you upset. I don't really expect you to just move here a week after we've met." He paused and kissed her forehead gently. "I guess I just need you to know that I want you that badly. That forever is where I am hoping this is heading. A t-shirt isn't going to make me feel any better when you're gone, and I don't know what I will do, or how I will deal with you being away from me."

"We'll get through it together. Lots of texting and phone calls," she said as she rubbed her hands up and down his arms, the contact soothing him.

"Lots of late night rendezvous is Salem?"

"Probably that, too," Ella laughed.

Porter pulled back and looked Ella in her eyes. "You can keep the shirt. I'd rather think about you wearing it than keep it here."

"A compromise, then. I will take the shirt with me, but in exchange I will send you pictures of myself wearing it." She grinned at him, obviously pleased with her idea. "Only, of course, to aide in your plans to imagine me in it."

"Ok," Porter said, as he rubbed his chin in mock contemplation. "Visual aids might be useful."

"It might also be useful, you know, in terms of memory, to get a visual of me not wearing the shirt. In case that is something you'd like to visualize when we're apart." Ella reached down to grab the hem of the shirt and pulled it up over her head. He was surprised and pleased to see she had nothing on under the shirt. He was a sucker for lingerie, but seeing her bare under his shirt sent shocks of arousal throughout his body. Instantly he was hard and getting harder by the second. Porter ran his hands down the front of her body. Starting from the top of her shoulders he gently grazed his hands down her chest, over her breasts, continued along her stomach, and down her thighs. He watched her eyes change from crystal clear blue, to a darker and deeper shade, alluding to the effects he was having on her body. His hands circled to the back of her legs and came up to rest on her ass, pulling her into him.

"Now that you're already naked, I should tell you that I didn't need a visual. There is no part of your body that I haven't used my body to memorize." His mouth slowly descended on hers, and she opened for him instantly. His hands came up to wrap around her waist and held her close. With every sweep of his tongue he was trying to convey his need and his love for her. His mouth moved over her jaw, down to her neck.

"My mouth knows the slope of your neck," he said as he trailed kisses along the tender curve. He heard her whimper breathily, knowing fully what his mouth on her neck did to her. He felt her body tense slightly as her back arched from the pleasure. He brought his hands up to cup her breasts, using his fingers to pinch and tug her nipples. "My hands know your breasts, Ella. I know how they feel when you're turned on, when you want me." His mouth took one of her breasts in his mouth, swirling his tongue around her nipple, feeling it harden between his lips. "I know how you taste, babe, and nothing tastes sweeter than you."

"How will I ever survive a day without your words, Porter?" Ella said as her fingers threaded through his hair. "I will miss your words almost as much as I'll miss your touch."

"Not a single day will go by without you hearing how much I love you, how much I miss you, or how much I need you." His mouth came back to hers and he used their kiss to lower her back onto the bed. He peeled his shirt off of his back and took off his pants and boxers before climbing onto the bed and resting over her, coming back to her mouth. His hands were slowly wandering her entire body, paying every inch of her skin attention, hoping that the memories of his hands on her would keep loneliness at bay for both of them once she was back home.

Ella's hands were exploring as well, and when they found him hard and waiting a quiet growl escaped from him, vibrating against her mouth. She was stroking him up and down, synchronizing the sweeps of her tongue through his mouth with the silky passes of her hand on his cock.

"Ella," he said against her mouth, mid-kiss. "You're driving me crazy."

"Good," she said. "The feeling's mutual." She suddenly

pulled away from him and placed her hands on his shoulders, pushing him onto his back. She straddled him, giving him the sexiest, sly grin he'd ever seen. "Relax, babe," she said. "I've got you." He placed his hands behind his head, prepared to enjoy whatever she had planned. He watched her head dip low and start to kiss down his chest. Slowly she made her way down past his belly button and when her breath hit his cock he smiled as she looked him right in the eyes and tasted him.

Her tongue moved all the way from the base to the tip, up and down, and where her tongue wasn't, her hand was sliding and rubbing and coaxing him into oblivion. Finally she took the head of his penis in her mouth and in slow motion sucked him all the way down. Her mouth was like hot velvet, and she took him in and out, over and over. He couldn't watch anymore as the pleasure took over his body. His eyes closed and his head fell back. He was consumed by her.

"My God, Ella…" He was quickly reaching his breaking point.

"You like this, Porter?" She said between gulping him down and pumping him with her hand. "You like it when I put my mouth on you?"

"I love it, baby."

She moaned around him and the vibrations sent a whole new sensation through his veins and he couldn't take much more.

"Ella, get a condom from the drawer." She sat up fully and smiled down at Porter, and by the look on her face she knew he was on the edge. She opened up a condom and pulled it down around him. Without breaking eye contact, she climbed up over him, and with an expertly maneuvered roll of her hips she captured him and took him all the way inside the depth of her. She paused once he was buried in her and her head fell back.

"Oh Jesus, Porter. I love how you feel inside me." He

reached up and placed his hand on her hips, urging her to move. Eventually, at her own pace, she started rocking back and forth. He never lost sight of her face, and she kept her eyes on his, only breaking the spell to lean down and kiss him between slowly torturing him with her grinding hips. She was looking for release, and enjoying the journey, and he was happy to help her along the way. As she continued to use his body to find her orgasm, he brought his thumb to her clit and slowly circled it.

"Oh God, yes. Porter, just like that…" She let out a series of moans, each one louder than the last, until she stilled and her nails sunk into the flesh on his chest. He watched her ride the wave and could feel her tighten around him. She eventually sank back down onto his chest, slightly out of breath. He let her rest for a moment and then rolled her over so that he was blanketed over her. He flicked his nose on the tip of hers and smiled down at her.

"You're the sexiest woman I've ever seen," he said as he nuzzled into her neck and pushed into her slowly.

"You'd be wise to remember that, seeing as how you're in me right now," she giggled. The sensation of her laughing, her muscles clenching around him, kicked his arousal to the next level, and his mouth crushed into hers. Thrust for thrust she met him, spurring him on.

"There will never be anyone but you, Ella. And there will be no one else for you but me," he said.

"I'm all yours, Porter."

Her words triggered his lust and he pumped in and out until he found his release inside her. After they had both caught their breath, and cleaned up, Ella lay in Porter's arms. They were in the dark, breathing each other in.

"I don't want tomorrow to come," she said quietly.

"It's ok," he said as he placed a kiss on her temple. "We have a whole lifetime of tomorrows."

Ella

"So you'll text me as soon as you get to your apartment, right?

"Yes, Porter, I promise I will text you when I get there."

They were standing on his porch and his arms were wrapped tightly around her waist and hers around his neck. They had spent the last two days in each other's arms one way or another, and it was causing her a near panic attack to know she'd have to drive away from him in just a few minutes.

He gently flicked his nose against hers and gave her a small, sweet kiss.

"I bought you a present," he said.

"What? Why? I don't need a present."

"Well, actually, you do. This isn't a typical gift a man would get a woman, but I think it's fitting." He winked at her and then took her hand and led her to her car. "Open the trunk, Babe."

Ella looked up at him with a questioning glare. As soon as she opened the trunk, she let out a loud laugh and covered her mouth. Sitting in her trunk, wrapped with a big red bow, was a box of jumper cables.

"Everyone should have jumper cables in their trunk. Now, you've got no excuse."

"You just don't want some other responsible man to come to my rescue. Joke's on you, Babe. I will still need someone to jump me."

Porter spun her around to face him and brought his mouth down to hers, stopping right before they met, teasing her with his breath.

"I'm the only one who gets to jump you, Ella." His mouth closed in on hers and she fell into the kiss, giving him every ounce of longing she felt down in her core. She longed to be by his side, to stay tucked under his arm and feel the warmth of his body wrapped around her. Getting in her car and driving away wasn't going to be easy, but she was determined to put on a brave face. She didn't want to be the weeping woman. She wanted to be the funny, sexy, and strong woman that she felt like when she was around him. That's how she wanted him to think of her when she was far away. She savored the kiss for a few minutes, trying to be present in every moment of it, so she could relive it in her mind whenever she needed to. Finally, she pulled away.

"I have a present for you, too."

"Oh yeah?"

"Yes. It's upstairs on your bed. But you have to promise me you won't open it today." He gave her a questioning look and raised an eyebrow at her. "You have to wait until you miss me so much you can't take it anymore. When you feel like I might slip away from you and all you want to do is hold me in your arms. Then, and only then, can you open it. It's my insurance policy," she said with a smile.

"What are you trying to insure?"

"That you'll still want me when I'm not here." He framed her face with his large hands and drew it close to his, looking into her eyes.

"Are you still confused about what's happening to us? I'll miss you every second you're away. I'll ache every morning to wake up in an empty bed without you. But I'll never want you again, Ella. You can't want for something that you already have. I have you. Don't I, Ella? You're mine." A single tear slid down her cheek, the lone evidence of the river of tears she wished she could cry at his words. His words that always seemed to be the salve to heal her heart, offered her reassurance when she needed it most. He wiped away the tear trail with his lips.

"I'm yours, if you're mine," she laid her forehead against his cheek.

"I've never belonged to anyone but you," he whispered. They stayed like that, breathing each other in for a few minutes.

"I should probably get going. I don't want to drive in the dark."

Porter exhaled loudly and stepped back.

"Promise me you'll pull over if it starts raining too hard. Call me if you have any problems." Ella smiled as his protective nature came out, loving the fact that he worried about her.

"I will. I promise. Don't worry. I've made this drive plenty of times. And I only pick up hitchhikers who look friendly."

"Very funny," he said, as he slapped her ass. She started to walk towards the door of her car, trying hard to keep her thoughts off of their separation. She was running through a grocery list in her head, thinking about things she wanted to do at her store when she went back to work the next day. Anything to keep her mind from thinking about the man who was keeping a large part of her heart here with him, from thinking about the fact that she would spend the next five nights alone without his touch or his voice. She reached out for the door handle putting on the bravest face she could muster. She felt his hand grip her arm gently and twist her around. His arm wrapped around her waist and his other hand held the back of her neck. He walked her backwards until her back was pressed against the car.

"You forgot one thing," he said as he traced his mouth from her temple down the side of her face and landing finally on her neck.

"What's that?" She whispered, unable to find her voice.

"You forgot to tell me that you love me, and that you'll think of me all the way home. You forgot to tell me that being without me is going to be the hardest thing you'll ever have to do." She reached up to caress his face and made him look her in the eyes.

"I love you, Porter. You're the best thing that's ever happened to me. It's taking everything I have to leave you here. You'll see how hard it is next weekend when the roles are reversed. But until then, please believe me when I tell you that there isn't anything in this world I wouldn't do for you or for us."

"I love you too, Ella, so much. I'm going to love you forever."

Ella laughed.

"Ok, I'm going to hold you to that."

"I fully expect you to." He pressed his lips to hers and they rested there. She was absorbing him, waiting for him to inevitably pull away. But he didn't. He pushed her back harder against her car and pressed her lips open with his. His tongue swirled around hers, inviting her into his mouth. They were lost in each other and everything she was dreading floated away. This kiss was the reminder she needed. He would need her forever.

Their kiss ended but their breathing needed a minute to calm down. She rubbed her hands up and down his arms leaning against his chest. He laid feather-light kisses against her hair, his hands on her hips.

"I'll text you in a few hours, ok?" She said as she pulled away.

"I love you," he said quietly.

"I love you too, Porter." She quickly kissed him on the lips and then turned and got into her car. Her hands shook as she put the keys in the ignition, put the car in gear, and started down his driveway. She tried really hard not to look in the rear view mirror, but had no self-control and was blessed with the image of her ruggedly handsome man standing on the sturdy porch attached to the breathtaking house he'd built with his own hands. That was a picture she'd keep in her mind for a while and pull cut every now and then when she missed him.

The road and weather was kind to her, getting her back to

her apartment in the usual two hours. She pulled in to the parking lot of her apartment and found her reserved spot. The sun was going down and the light was fading quickly from the sky. She pulled out her phone and sent a text to Porter.

Made it home safe and sound. The hitchhikers were very appreciative of the ride and were very good travel buddies

   She waited for his response. She knew he was waiting to hear from her, so she figured she wouldn't have to wait long. She was right.

I am glad you made it home safely. Perhaps along with the jumper cables I should have also gotten you a shotgun or a hunting knife for protection.

She grinned at his response and then a small frown came across her face as she typed her response.

I miss you.

I know. I miss you too. Everything will be ok. I promise. Call me tonight before you go to bed.

Ok. I love you.

I love you too, Baby.

   She made it all the way to her door with her bags, a small smile across her face as she thought about all the sweet things Porter had said to her before she left his house. She put her bags on the ground to search for her keys. She didn't know what her apartment would look like when she walked in. She had no idea what Kyle had taken with him or where she would even sleep that night. Hopefully, he left the couch. She finally found her keys and as she put them in the lock, she felt the door shake and watched as the doorknob turned from the inside. Her eyes darted up as the door opened and she looked right into Kyle's eyes.

Chapter Nineteen
Ella

"Kyle?" Ella nearly shouted his name, she was so shocked to see him inside their apartment.

"Ella, come in. Here, let me get your bags," Kyle reached for her bags and took them into the living room, setting them against the far wall. Ella looked around the apartment as she slowly took a few steps in. Nothing had changed, not one single thing. His golfing magazines were still stacked on the coffee table. His shoes were still in the basket by the door. His keys were still hanging on the hook on the hall tree. She couldn't even get words out of her mouth; she just kept opening it and closing it, like a fish. "Ella, I know you were expecting me to have moved out by now," he said cautiously, treading lightly to gauge her reaction.

"Yes, I was expecting to you be gone. Why aren't you gone?" She looked at him and her confusion was slowly turning into anger.

"We need to talk about this, face-to-face, sweetie. We have been together for four years; we can't break up over the phone. I wanted to give you the week to cool down and get some perspective. I made us dinner. Babe, let's just sit down and talk about everything."

It made Ella sick to hear him call her "babe". Her eyes roamed around the living room and dining room. The table was set, complete with lit candles. She looked down the hallway towards the bedroom where she had walked in on him fucking someone else.

"There's nothing to talk about Kyle. I don't understand where you got the impression that we could fix anything. There's nothing left to fix."

"Don't say that, El," he came right up to her and put his hand on her face, the same place Porter had his hands just hours ago. "I love you and you cannot just walk away from this."

"I didn't just walk away from you, Kyle!" She pushed him away from her. "You FUCKED someone else in our bed! I didn't put the nail in this coffin. You did." She was breathing heavy and seeing red. "You don't have any right to be here! You agreed you would leave and I believed you! I can't be here with you. Either you leave or I leave, Kyle."

"You're being unreasonable. Come sit down and eat."

"No."

Kyle ran his fingers through his hair, obviously becoming frustrated with her.

"Why are you resisting this? It's just dinner."

"This isn't just dinner," she said, motioning towards his attempt at a romantic meal. "This is you trying to convince me to come back to you and that's not ever going to happen. I'm not trying to be rude here, but I feel like you lied to me on purpose about moving out just so that you could get me alone with you. I'm not comfortable here with you." She grabbed her purse off the coffee table.

"What do you mean come back to me? It's been a week, Ella. We've barely been apart. Why are you uncomfortable? I'm the same person I have been for the past four years."

"No, Kyle, you're wrong. We're farther apart now than we ever were and I am not the same person who left this apartment last week. I have to go." She headed towards her bags near the door but felt him grip her arms and spin her around.

"What happened at the beach, Ella? Why are you so quick to let our relationship slip through your fingers?" His face was close to hers and she could feel his panting on her skin. She thought she smelled alcohol on his breath.

"Those are two separate questions. I'm willing to let you slip through my fingers because I don't want the kind of relationship we had any longer. I don't want to be in the dark anymore, hoping things will change one day. I don't want to have to worry about my boyfriend sleeping with some Gumby-Slut. And what happened at the beach doesn't concern you." Her eyes darted down to his hand that still tightly gripped her. "Let go of my arm."

"Not until you tell me what's really going on. Did you sleep with someone at the beach?" Ella tried to keep her face as stone-like as possible, not wanting to give him any satisfaction or ammunition. "Who did you fuck, Ella?"

"Let go of me, Kyle. Please just let me go." She started to feel the fear permeate through the anger that had been running through her blood. Kyle had never gotten physical with her before and this new side of him was as frightening as it was unexpected.

"You did," he chuckled. "You slept with somebody." He laughed to himself, let go of her arm and started pacing up and down the length of the living room. Ella watched him pace for a few seconds and then realized that now was her time to get away from him. She bolted for the door and as soon as she grabbed the door handle and pulled it open, it slammed closed again. His hand came from behind her and he leaned over the back of her, breathing into her ear furious fast air that made her hair blow past her cheek. Her heart pounded so hard that she could hardly hear over it. She felt him grab her shoulders and spin her around, pinning her back up against the door. His grip on her was painful and her eyes were tightly closed, trying to block out what was happening.

"You're a dirty slut, Ella," he said. Hot, sour breath invaded her nostrils and she tried to turn her face away from it, but his hand came up and gripped her jaw and squeezed. A cry escaped her mouth and fear now coursed through her blood. "Did you put this mouth on him, Ella? You probably did all kinds of things to him that I haven't gotten in years." He laughed again and his hand moved from her shoulder and slid down to cover her breast. She tried to let out a whimper, but his fingers crushed her jaw so hard it made it difficult to make any sounds.

"That was most of the appeal of Tiffany. She was willing to do all kinds of things in the bedroom that you would have snubbed your nose at. When did you get so boring, Ella? And who did you find at the beach who even wants you?"

She couldn't help but cry and tears were coming down her face, running over his hand still clamped at her jaw. She could taste metal in her mouth and figured her teeth were cutting into her cheeks and she was probably bleeding. His hand gripped her breast and pain radiated across her chest. His hand suddenly reached up to the neck of her shirt and pulled down, ripping the front of her shirt down the middle. He looked down at her bared chest and she saw his distraction as her opportunity.

She swiftly brought her knee up and met right with the target of his balls. He folded immediately, bending at the waist, grasping at his crotch. She wasted no time. She used all her anger and fear and took her other foot and kicked him right in the face. He crumpled to the ground with a thud, unconscious, and she watched him sprawl out on the ground. Blood was rushing out of his nose, and she could see it start to pool behind his head. She was frozen, afraid that if she moved he would come to and resume his assault. After a few seconds, a voice inside her head told her to run.

She reached behind her and opened the door and quietly shut it, hoping not to disturb the man she thought she once loved lying unconscious on the other side. The closer she got to her car, the more she fell apart. She pulled her shirt closed around her, trying to simply get to her car without falling to the ground in a messy heap. She needed to get away. She made it to the car and got in, locking the doors immediately. She looked back towards the alcove which her apartment was in, and didn't see any disturbance. She didn't know how long she had until he came to, but she wanted to be long gone before then.

She found her keys in her purse but it took her many tries to get the key in the ignition. She heard crazed cries and sobs coming from somewhere in the car. Deep in the back of her mind she realized it was her who was screaming, but she focused on getting the car started. Finally, she heard the car come to life and managed to navigate her way out of the apartment complex.

She didn't know where she was going, but auto pilot had her headed towards Poppy. Once she had pulled up in front of the dark store, she finally let herself break down. She cried out of fear and she cried from the pain. How had she spent four years with that monster? She hadn't. That wasn't the Kyle she had shared a life with. Something had happened to him in the last couple months. She cried for him too. She cried until she didn't have any tears left and then she was just gasping for regular breaths.

With a new panic, she found her cell phone and dialed Porter's number.

"Hey, Babe, are you going to bed already?" He sounded happy and relaxed, and she began to cry all over again. "Ella? What's wrong? Are you ok?" She tried to answer him, but only sobs came out again. "Damn it, Ella, what the hell is going on?"

"Kyle," she managed to half whisper, half cry.

"Kyle? What about Kyle? Are you hurt? Did he hurt you?" He sounded panicked and angry and on the edge of hysterics.

"He wouldn't let me leave, Porter. I tried to leave and he wouldn't let me go. I think I'm ok, but he hurt my jaw. He started to -" she tried to reign in her sobs.

"Where are you now? Did you get away?"

"Yes. I'm outside my store. I'm going to go inside and clean up. Will you please come here, Porter? I don't want to be by myself."

"Baby, I'm already in my car. I'm on my way. Can you call your sister? Can you go to her house? I don't want you to be alone until I get there."

"I don't want to bring her into this. I will be fine here. There's an alarm system and a security guard does laps every half hour. Please, just hurry."

She heard Porter let out a loud breath.

"Ok. I'll be there as soon as I can. Can you text me the address?"

"Yes, as soon as we hang up."

"Are you sure you'll be ok until I get there?"

"Yes. Please, just hurry. The store is closed so you'll just have to knock and I will let you in."

"Call me if anything else happens."

"Ok, I will."

"I love you. I will be there soon."

"I love you too" she said, trying to hold back more cries. "Please just hurry." She texted him the address and then got out of her car and walked to the door of her boutique. She used her keys to let herself in and then made sure to set the alarm after she was inside. She mentally patted herself on the back for never giving Kyle a key or the passcode to the alarm system.

The store was dark, but she went straight back to the employee bathroom to try to clean herself up. When she made it to the bathroom and turned on the harsh fluorescent lights she was startled by her reflection in the mirror.

Her eyes were red, puffy, and swollen. It would be obvious to anyone that she had been crying. Her hair was a disaster, a halo of blonde craziness that she would have been concerned about if it weren't for the other alarming things she saw in her reflection. There were purple marks in the shapes of fingers cradling her jaw. He had squeezed her jaw so hard he had left bruises. On the sides of her mouth there were traces of dried blood from the cuts she could feel on the inside of her cheeks. Her left breast was also tender, but she couldn't bring herself to look to see if there were bruises there.

Ella cringed when she thought of what Porter's reaction would be when he saw her and the state she was in. He would lose his mind; she was sure. He would do anything to get his hands on Kyle, but she would have to talk him down. She didn't need any more trouble with Kyle and the less contact they had with him, the better.

She looked down at her torn shirt and a wave of nausea came over her. The thought of what might have happened if she hadn't managed to get away in time had her running to the toilet where she battled dry heaves. Once her body finally calmed down and she was steady again, she stood up and splashed cold water on her face. She looked in the mirror one last time and was saddened by her reflection. She went into the office space in the back of the store and found one of the University of Oregon sweatshirts she kept in the back for cold inventory nights. She took off her torn shirt and threw it in the garbage. She pulled the sweatshirt over her head and left the hood up trying to cover as much of her body as possible.

Suddenly, she felt exhausted. She laid down on the love seat in the back of the office, curled her knees up to her chest, and pulled her arms inside her sweatshirt. She managed to drift off to sleep quickly, hoping Porter would help her figure out her next move.

She woke up to loud banging on the glass of the front door. She glanced at the clock. It had only been an hour and a half since she called Porter. He must have been hauling ass to get here that early. She righted her sweatshirt and headed to the door to let him in. As she came around a large rack of clothing, she saw the person outside of the store, but it wasn't Porter. The man was wearing a dark hoodie and had the hood pulled down far enough that she couldn't see his face. She came to an abrupt stop once she saw him, and her first instinct was to turn back around, but he saw her.

"Ma'am? Do you have any spare change?"

Ella exhaled loudly. Transients were part of the territory in Portland. There were people begging for money on most busy streets and as a Portlander you just learned how to deal with it. She took a step closer to the glass door and shouted to him.

"I don't have any money. I'm sorry."

"Do you have any food? I'm hungry."

"No, I'm sorry. There isn't any food here." The man started looking from side to side. He finally raised his head far enough up that she could see his face. Before she could get a good look at him though, he pulled something out of his pocket and pointed it at her. She heard glass shattering and something pushed her shoulder back with brutal force. She was stumbling backwards and then she felt herself falling. Then everything went black.

Porter

Porter drove as fast as his truck could carry him safely. He managed to make it more than halfway and he started to calm down a little. He was no longer shaking and his heart rate seemed to be back to normal. But his thoughts kept wandering to Ella and he knew the closer he got to her, the more worried he was going to get.

He saw the sky scrapers of the Portland skyline come into view and he knew he was getting close. He was able to shave about twenty minutes off the commute just by driving way too fast. His GPS gave him direct instructions to her store, but he was still a little confused by all the one-way streets. It was obvious that his big construction truck wasn't made to navigate the streets of downtown Portland.

He came upon the last turn until he reached her store, but there were barricades up and police men redirecting traffic. He continued down the street while the GPS recalculated his directions and it led him to the same street, just a few blocks down. Again, when he came up to the street he was supposed to turn on, it was blocked off by police. He suddenly got a terrible feeling in his gut. He pulled off to the side of the road, not really caring if he was parked in a legitimate spot or not. He got out his phone and dialed Ella. It rang a few times and then went to her voicemail. He heard her sweet voice asking him to leave a message.

"Hey, Babe, I'm trying to get to your store, but all the streets are blocked off. I don't know what's going on, but I can't get to you and it's making me nervous. Call me when you get this. Love you."

Just as he finished his message he saw an ambulance pull through the barricades, sirens blaring. Something in him snapped. He got out of his truck and jogged towards the police officer manning the barricade.

"Sir, this street's blocked off right now. No vehicle or pedestrian traffic allowed through."

"Listen, Officer, I'm supposed to pick up my girlfriend at her store just down this street. Can I just walk there? We'll leave right away. I just want to go get her."

"Which store is she at?" The officer asked.

"Poppy. It should be just up one block on the left." The cop turned around to look down the block and when he turned around his face had gone from all business to regretful.

"Listen, Sir. We had a robbery down this block about twenty minutes ago. A suspect broke into a place of business and the owner was present. She suffered some injuries and she is being taken to the hospital right now."

Porter heard the words he had said, but couldn't understand what they meant. He shook his head a few times and looked past the officer towards where most of the commotion was happening. There were at least seven police cars parked along the street, another ambulance and a fire truck. Police officers were scattered around the street.

"What do you mean? Which store was robbed?"

"I'm sorry to tell you it was Poppy."

Porter stumbled back a step.

"No," Porter demanded, hoping the officer was mistaken.

"I'm terribly sorry. They took her to the hospital just a few minutes ago."

"What happened to her?!"

"Sir, I'm really sorry but I cannot give you any specific information. I can tell you she was taken to OHSU up on the hill." The officer pointed behind Porter and vaguely motioned towards a foothill on the other side of the sky scrapers.

"Was she hurt? Are you sure it was Ella?"

"Sir, there was only one person there, a female, about thirty years old. I can't give you any more information."

Porter turned around and made his way back to the truck. Once he got in he picked up his phone and tried to plug the hospital name into his GPS. His fingers were shaky and he kept hitting the wrong key.

"Shit!" he yelled as he threw his phone down on his seat. He breathed heavy and his hands shook. He raked his hands through his hair and forced himself to take deep breaths in through his nose and out of his mouth. With his eyes closed, he tried to picture Ella as he last saw her. She was up against her car with her arms wrapped around his neck, smiling up at him with more love in her eyes than he ever hoped he would see reflected back at him. He was so close to losing his mind but he needed to get to Ella. He would find time to process these feelings later. Right now he needed to find this elusive hospital "on the hill".

As he pulled into the emergency room parking lot, he prayed he wouldn't have to find his way here again because it would be useless. He threw the truck in park and made his way to the admittance desk at the emergency room. A woman behind the desk smiled politely at him.

"Can I help you, Sir?"

"Yes. My girlfriend was brought here by ambulance a few minutes ago. I need to see her. Can you tell me where she is?"

"What is her name?"

"Ella. Ella Sinclair." The woman behind the desk typed furiously, and when she stopped typing, she looked back up at him with strained eyes.

"Ok, Miss Sinclair was taken into emergency surgery. You can take the elevator up to level 8 and you will see the surgical waiting room. Wait there and I will notate that she has visitors waiting. The surgeon will update you when they get a chance."

"Surgery? What happened to her? What are her injuries?"

"Sir, I cannot tell you any more information. You will have to wait until the doctor updates you. I am sorry."

Porter felt like a mouse in a maze. All he wanted was to

get to Ella, but every road was a dead end. His hands gripped the woman's desk so hard he began to feel tingling in his fingers. He bent down so that his head level with the counter, trying to reign in the frustration that was slowly taking over. He took a few deep breaths and then pushed off the desk and headed towards the elevators.

Once he was in the waiting room, he couldn't sit still. The room was empty but for some chairs and a few magazines. A television was hanging from the ceiling in the corner of the room, but it was turned down low and Porter couldn't concentrate on anything except watching the door, waiting for someone to come and tell him that Ella would be fine. That she would be released shortly and that her injuries were minimal. He would go to see her and she would smile at him and he would kiss her forehead and hold her hand while she slept.

He heard the door open and his head snapped up hoping to talk to a doctor about Ella, but the only person who came in the room was another man who was obviously waiting for someone as well. He looked like he'd had better days. His nose looked broken and Porter assumed he'd been in some sort of car accident and was waiting for someone, just like he was. The two men made eye contact and exchanged small smiles of commiseration.

Porter sat until he felt like he was going to explode. He started to pace around the room but nothing seemed to help. All he kept thinking about was how he might be losing Ella that very moment and how he would never be able to tell her he loved her again, or feel the warmth of her hand in his. He would give anything just to hold her and know everything was going to be ok.

Suddenly, the door opened again and Porter hopefully looked towards the door and let out a sigh when he saw Megan come through the doors. Megan looked at him with a confused look. Then her eyes moved to the other man in the room and he saw a panic come over her.

"Porter? What are you doing here?" Megan walked towards him.

"Ella called me and asked me to pick her up from her store, but when I got there the police told me she had been taken here."

Megan's eyes darted to the other man in the room again. He was sitting in his chair watching Porter and Megan.

"Have you heard anything about her condition?" Porter asked Megan.

"How do you know Ella?" The man asked as he slowly stood from his chair. Porter turned towards the man.

"Excuse me?"

"I said," his voice sounding serious all of a sudden, "How you know Ella?"

Porter didn't exactly know how to answer that question. He told the woman at the admittance desk that Ella was his girlfriend, but the labels of boyfriend and girlfriend seemed to pale in significance for what he felt towards her. He hated to cheapen their relationship by calling her a girlfriend when he felt like she mattered so much more than the word implied.

"She's my girlfriend."

"Oh, really?" The man said with a smile on his face that looked more menacing than friendly.

"Kyle, calm down," Megan said. "Why are you even here?"

"I'm Ella's in-case-of-emergency person. The hospital called me when she was brought in."

Realization dawned on Porter and he saw red. He lunged across the room at Kyle and his fist instantly connected with his jaw. Kyle reeled backwards from the blow but stayed on his feet. He heard Megan scream in the back of his mind, but continued towards Kyle. He wrapped both of his hands around his neck and slammed his head up against the wall, bringing his face just inches from Kyle's.

"What the hell did you do to her?" Kyle sputtered and

coughed, not able to get enough air into his system to speak clearly. "I'll kill you for putting your hands on her," Porter growled. He removed one hand from Kyle's neck and slammed his fist into his stomach. Kyle fell to his knees, one hand one the ground the other hand clenching his stomach. He raised his head and looked at Porter.

"You must be the rebound fuck Ella found at the beach," Kyle said, spitting blood onto the floor. "I didn't do this to Ella. She was fine when she left the apartment. I don't know what happened after she left, but I had nothing to do with it."

"Kyle, you better get the hell out of here before security comes and before Porter kicks your ass," Megan said.

"I'm going to kick his ass regardless of whether or not he leaves. But if he leaves now I might let his nose heal before I break it again," Porter said, then pulled a foot back and plowed it into Kyle's stomach. Kyle let out a groan when Porter's booted foot connected with his stomach and he rolled onto his side.

"Fuck you and fuck her, man. She isn't even worth this shit," Kyle mumbled from the floor. "You can have her."

Porter lost every ounce of restraint he was holding on to and leapt at him again, but was stopped cold when Megan stepped in between them and placed her hands on Porter's shoulders trying to hold him back. Megan was no match for Porter and she couldn't have held him back if she tried, but Porter wasn't about to hurt Megan to get to Kyle; that wasn't his style.

"Porter, you have to calm down. They're going to kick you out of here and then who will be here for Ella? She needs you to be here when she gets out of surgery." Porter took a few deep breaths and knew Megan was right. Porter looked at Kyle over Megan's shoulder.

"Take your sorry ass out of this hospital right now. Go back to Ella's house and pack up. You have twelve hours to move your shit out of her apartment and then you will never see her again. Do you understand me? If you ever so much as speak her name I will find you and beat the living shit out of you. Are we clear?"

"Fuck you."

"Kyle, shut the hell up and go," Megan intervened. "I will call on the cops on both of you if you don't leave. Now." Kyle struggled to get to his feet, but eventually made his way towards the door. He opened the door but before he walked through it he turned his head towards Porter.

"Have fun with that frigid bitch. She's as cold as they come, and you'd be smart to just walk away now," Kyle spat the words out.

"Get. The. Fuck. Out. Now." Porter's body shook and did everything he could to hold himself together. Kyle left the waiting room and Porter remained standing in front of Megan. She left her hands on his shoulders and looked as though she was afraid that if she removed them he'd go running after Kyle to finish what he'd started. Porter took a deep breath in and it came out in a rush and he felt a wave of tension flow through him and finally leave his body. He was suddenly very tired and really wanted to sit down.

"I'm fine now, Megan. Thank you for stepping in and stopping me. I'm not sure I would have stopped on my own." Porter ran his hands through his hair as he collapsed into a chair.

"I suggest you pull yourself together. My parents are on their way here and I'm sure they'll be surprised to meet you under these circumstances."

Porter stood up and left the room. He walked down the hall until he found a restroom. He shoved the door open with so much force it bounced back against the wall. He walked to the sink and splashed water on his face, trying to bring himself out of the haze of rage. Fighting was not something he was used to and it wasn't something he enjoyed doing. But knowing that Kyle had caused the panic he heard in Ella's voice the last time he spoke to her was more than enough ammunition to kick his deep-rooted protector role into action. Kyle's hateful words about her only pushed him farther past the point of no return. Porter rested his face in his hands and tried taking deep breaths, but the adrenaline was coursing through his system and making breathing regularly a chore.

Suddenly his heaving breaths were joined by hot tears in his eyes. The stress of not knowing what was wrong with Ella was bottoming out his soul. He remembered how devastated he had felt when they hadn't spoken for a day. He'd gladly go back, never speak to her or hold her again, never kiss her lips or tuck her golden hair behind her ear, if only he could know she was going to be ok. He fisted his hair, pulled on the roots, and hoped to alleviate the aching pain in his chest through distraction. He took a few minutes to continue to calm himself. He would be no use to anyone if he couldn't keep his emotions in check.

After he finally felt like he could control himself, he walked back to the waiting room. When he entered the room he saw Megan sitting next to a man who looked to be about her age. He held her hand and she rested her head on his shoulder. Next to her sat the two people he assumed were Ella's parents. Her dad sat silently with one arm crossed over his chest while his other hand cupped his jaw. Her mom stood next to the window looking out at the Portland skyline, wiping tears from her eyes every few seconds. She was exactly what Porter imagined Ella would look like in twenty five years. Megan lifted her head to look at her mother and gestured towards Porter.

"Mom, Dad, this is Porter. He's here to see Ella too." Porter took a few steps towards them with his hand out.

"Mr. Sinclair, Mrs. Sinclair. I am glad to meet you, although these circumstances are a less than what I was hoping for."

"I'm sure Ella will be thankful to have the support of her

friends," Mr. Sinclair said as he shook Porter's hand.

"Nice to meet you," Mrs. Sinclair all but whispered.

He turned to Megan. "Have you heard anything yet?" Megan didn't bother answering she just shook her head.

"Megan, I thought you said Kyle called to tell you about Ella. Where is he? Has he been here yet? How is he holding up?" Ella's mom looked at Megan with confusion. Megan let out a loud breath and Porter knew she was bracing herself for the onslaught of questions she would have to answer once she revealed everything that had transpired in the last week. She stood and walked over to where her mother was standing, placing a cautious hand on her shoulder.

"Mom, I know this is going to be hard for you to understand, but I need you to listen to me carefully. Last week, Ella caught Kyle cheating on her." Porter watched as Mrs. Sinclair's hand flew to her mouth and she started crying harder. Megan told her the entire story, as Ella had relayed it to her throughout the week. Her parent's eyes both darted back and forth between him and Megan.

As Porter listened to her explain their situation, it only made his memory torture him with flashbacks of the time they'd spent together over the last week. He remembered how wet and irritated she looked the first time he saw her at the bar. He remembered the dress she wore on their first date. He remembered when she'd kissed him for the first time. He wanted more kisses with Ella and not knowing if she was ok was killing him. Porter came out of his memories and was back in the waiting room.

"Mom, Ella really loves Porter. She would want him here and she would want you to know how much she cares about him."

Just then a man in a white coat came into the waiting room.

"I'm Dr. Andrews. Are you all waiting for Ella Sinclair?"

"Yes," Ella's father stepped forward. "Is she ok?"

"Ella is in recovery. She made it through the surgery." A collective sigh waved through the room and Ella's mother let out a cry as the emotions of learning Ella was still alive took her over. Porter stepped towards the doctor.

"What happened to her? What are her injuries?"

"She had a gunshot to the shoulder when she was brought to the hospital. She also had a head injury. It would seem that when the bullet hit her in the shoulder it caused her to fall and the back of her head came into contact with some hard surface. Whether that was the floor or something else, I cannot be sure. It really doesn't matter. While the gunshot is a serious injury, it luckily was a simple, clean, wound. The bullet went in the front and out the back without damaging any major arteries or muscles. She was lucky in that regard." Porter saw the doctor stop and take a breath, and he knew the worst news was yet to come.

"Unfortunately, the head injury is what we are most worried about. It seems that she hit her head hard enough to cause a major concussion, which has cause a little bit of bleeding and a significant amount of swelling."

"What does that mean?" Porter asked.

"Well, it means that we had to cut into her skull to relieve some of the pressure the swelling was causing. We were able to stop the bleeding, but we are still concerned about the swelling. Until we see the swelling come down we are going to keep her in a medically induced coma."

"A coma?" Ella's mother practically shrieked with her hand covering her mouth. Her father pulled her into a hug and wrapped his arms around her, cradling her head and smoothing down her hair.

"Will she be ok?" Megan asked quietly.

"It is too early to be sure about prognosis, but the next 24 to 48 hours will critical. We are doing everything we can to bring the swelling down, but it really is out of our hands at this point. Ella is in the ICU, and you may go see her, but only two people at a time."

"Thank you doctor," Ella's father said.

"You're very welcome. I will take good care of her." Dr. Andrews turned and walked out of the waiting room.

Porter watched as Megan turned to Patrick and found her comfort in his embrace. Ella's parents were quietly crying into each other's arms. He was painfully aware of the fact that at that very moment the only person he wanted in his arms was somewhere in this hospital fighting for her life. He had never felt more alone in his life, but he was determined to stay strong for Ella.

Chapter Twenty
Porter

He could see her in his mind. Sleeping. Peaceful. Angelic, even. She was asleep on her stomach, her arms tucked under her pillow, her golden hair fanned out behind her. Her mouth was slightly open and when she breathed he could hear the gentle swoosh of the air moving in and out, reminding him of the sound of the ocean. She wasn't wearing any clothes; he had stripped her of those many hours ago in an attempt to rid them of any barriers between them. He had needed to feel her skin on his.

The blanket was covering her from the waist down. His eyes roamed over the curve of her spine, trailing from her shoulders down to the swell of her hips. Her skin was flawless, freckled, and perfect. He ached to run his hand down the ravine her spine created, but didn't want to wake her. He was mesmerized by the sight of her and wanted to stay in the moment as long as possible.

Even though the bed was big, and she could very well be at the other side, she was snuggled up next to him, as close to him as possible. That was what it was like to be around her. She was missing from him even when she was with him, she was giving him everything even though he still longed for more, and she was as close to him as possible but it was never close enough.

She stirred and turned her head so she was facing away from him. The familiar scent of vanilla wafted to him as her hair fanned out next to his face. He silently groaned, wrapped his arms around her middle pulling her into his chest, and nuzzled into the crook of her neck. She reached up to run her fingers through his hair and gently caressed him as he cherished her. Her hand fell away and found his as she lazily twined her fingers around his as he held her close.

"I love you," he whispered into her neck.

"I love you too," she sighed. "Let's go back to sleep."

"Porter." Megan's voice pulled him out of the memory of Ella asleep in his bed just that morning.

"Yes?"

"My parents are done visiting her for now. Patrick and I are going to go get some coffee. You can go in and see her if you'd like." Porter rubbed his hands over his face, trying to bring himself fully back into reality.

A hospital volunteer had brought the five of them to the ICU waiting room a few hours ago. Ella's parents had gone in to see her first and when they came out Porter saw the overwhelming sadness in her mother's eyes. She had turned to her husband and cried into his chest for quite a while. Megan and Patrick had gone in to see her next, and Megan had a similar look to her when she emerged. They had offered to let Porter go in, but he'd declined. He wanted desperately to see her, but felt that he should allow her family as much time with her as possible before he had his turn. So her parents went in to visit again before they would go home to get some sleep. Leaving the hospital was not on Porter's short list of things to do, so he would give them have as much time as they wanted without intruding.

"Thanks." He stood up and took a deep breath. "Megan?"

"Yeah?" She turned back around towards him.

"What am I walking into in there? How bad is it?"

Megan took in a deep breath and then let it out in one big gust. "Mostly, she just looks like she's sleeping. But she has some pretty decent bruising on her face and there's a bandage around her head. Her arm's in a sling. It's the machines that are the scariest. The ventilator is the worst part." She walked over to him and rubbed her hand up and down his arm. "She's going to be ok, Porter. She's the strongest person I know and there's no way she'd let a little bump on the head keep her down long. But she needs you in there."

"I know. I just wanted to be prepared." She gently squeezed his arm and then she and Patrick left the waiting room.

He walked towards her room, willing himself to take slow and even breaths, trying to keep calm and not lose his composure. He got to her door and could already hear the faint beeping noises coming from within. He placed his palm on the door and tried to gather the strength to push it open. He closed his eyes and all he saw was Ella, laughing on the beach, hair bowing in the wind, smiling at him. No matter how nervous he was to see her right now, he knew he had to be there for her, and seeing her smile in his mind was the last bit of strength he needed to walk through her door. The door opened silently and Ella slowly came into view.

Porter drew in a shaky and uneven breath, unprepared to deal with the emotions seeing her lying helpless in a hospital bed would evoke in him. He stepped into the room letting the door close behind him. He was completely lost and didn't know how he was supposed to handle any of this.

The ventilator was definitely the worst part. Every few seconds he heard the muffled sound of air being pushed through the tube. Her chest was rising and falling in time to the machine. Each breath the machine took for her, took a little bit of his breath away. He knew it was necessary for her to be in this state for her to heal, but she looked so fragile like this. He had to look closely to see the strong willed woman who had told him off that first night he met her.

She looked much like Megan had described: arm in a sling, bruising on her face, and bandage around her head. A flash of anger came over him when the thought about the bruising which, from what the officer had described, probably was a product of Kyle rather than the robbery. He took a tentative step towards her bed and tried to focus on the things about her that were unmarred.

Her blonde hair laid beneath her, fanned out in its usual golden halo, peeking out from the bandages around her head. Her hands were still small and delicate. He looked at the hand that lay by her side and he stepped up the side of the bed to hold it. He sat next to her, gently took her hand in his, and brought it to his mouth laying a small kiss upon her knuckles. The instant his lips touched her skin, a dam inside of him broke, and there was nothing in the world that could tear her hand from him. Tears streamed down his face as he held her hand to his mouth, to his cheek, to his forehead. It was the only piece of her he could grasp on to, and he felt like he needed to keep it close to him. He held back sobs, trying to keep himself as together as possible, but he was slowly losing ground. Seeing her in the hospital bed, broken and unconscious, only brought terrible thoughts of loss to his mind. Suddenly he was very afraid.

"Ella, baby," he said between shuttering breaths, holding her hand to his cheek. "Please, I need you to be ok." He placed another kiss on her hand and gave in to all the emotions rushing at him. He cried into her hand, sitting at her bedside, listening to a rhythm of beeps. "You need to wake up soon, Ella. I need to see your eyes and know that you are going to be all right."

He cried like he'd never cried before. Gasping sobs led to aching moans. Whispered pleas led to silent prayers. He cried until he felt like he had no more air in his lungs and no more energy to even stand upright. Eventually, exhaustion took over and he fell asleep hunched over with his head lying on the edge of the bed, Ella's hand clasped in his.

He woke to the sound of the door closing. When he

looked up he saw Ella's mother standing just inside the door. She was wearing different clothes than before and she looked at him with a small smile on her lips. Porter looked at the clock above Ella's bed and noticed he'd been asleep for at least a few hours, and he felt it. He was still tired and his body ached from the strange position he'd been sleeping in, but he felt less panicked. Sleep had eased his nerves slightly.

"I'm sorry. I didn't mean to bother you," Ella's mother whispered. Porter placed a chaste kiss on Ella's hand.

"That's ok. I've taken up way more time than I should have anyway," Porter went to stand up and she waved him back down.

"Nonsense. You stay as long as you want to."

"Thank you, Mrs. Sinclair," Porter said as he sat back down and resumed holding Ella's hand.

"Please, call me Susan."

"Thank you, Susan."

Susan came to Ella's bedside and brushed her hand over Ella's hair, then down her cheek. She leaned over Ella and kissed her on the forehead, eyes closed. She took the chair on the other side of Ella's bed and sat down looking right at Porter.

"Megan told me about how you and Ella met, but I wouldn't mind hearing the story from you," Susan said with a smile.

"Well," he started, rubbing one hand over the days' worth of growth on his face, "she showed up at my mom's bar last Friday and needed some help getting to her rental house after her car battery had died. My mom volunteered my services and I took her to her house and got her settled." Porter grinned at the memory of the two of them bickering in his truck; she had been feisty from the beginning.

"And she had told you about Kyle at that point?" Susan asked.

"Yes and no. She had told my mom a detailed version while she was having a drink, but then told me a more abbreviated version on the way to her house, more out of frustration than anything else." Susan shook her head to herself.

"I cannot believe Kyle would do that to her."

"He doesn't seem to be making very wise decisions lately," Porter said through gritted teeth.

"No, he doesn't," she said quietly. "Megan says that Ella has fallen in love with you. Is that true?"

Porter looked down at his hand holding hers, unsure of where this line of questioning was going. "I hope so," he answered. "I mean, I believe so." Susan tilted her head to the side and looked at Porter with critical eyes.

"And how do you feel about her?"

"I love her more than I ever thought it would be possible to love anyone," he said without a second of hesitation. A slow smile spread across Susan's face.

"Of course you do; she's very easy to love."

"The easiest thing I've ever done was fall in love with Ella. She wasn't convinced as easily as I was though. She was dealing with a lot of guilt over how quickly her feelings were growing. I think it was hard for her to justify the idea of loving someone so quickly; for whatever reason she felt like she was doing something wrong."

Susan nodded her head as if she understood what he was talking about. "Ella has always had an incredibly strong moral compass and I can see how she would fight her feelings for you not wanting other people to judge her. It seems, however, that you did a pretty good job of convincing her to move past those feelings."

Porter laughed a little to himself. "Actually, it was my mom that made the most effective argument to Ella. I think she was on the fence, but then my mother took it upon herself to talk to Ella about everything and that night she came back to me," Porter said with a sad smile on his face.

"She sounds like a woman I'd like to meet."

"Well, as soon as I tell my mom what happened I'm sure she'll be here to worry over Ella in person." Susan smiled at that.

The door opened and a nurse walked in holding an I.V. bag of fluids.

"Oh, look who's awake this time," she said looking right at Porter. The nurse was a short and round woman in her late fifties with short, spiky, brown hair. "All night, every time I came in to check her vitals you were sound asleep holding her hand. It was the cutest thing." The nurse spoke as she switched out I.V. bags.

"I'm sorry, I didn't mean to fall asleep here. I hope I didn't cause any problems."

"Oh no, Dear, but I did have to take her hand from you to get her blood pressure." The nurse moved around Ella, checking her vitals, adjusting her IV lines, taking her temperature.

"Is everything ok with Ella?" Porter asked.

"She is doing just fine. Her vitals have been stable all night and soon they will take her to do another CT scan to see if the swelling is coming down like it should be."

"And what about her gunshot wound?" Susan asked.

"Oh, that is doing just fine as well. I know it sounds scary, being a gunshot wound and all, but she got really lucky and the bullet missed everything important. It's still going to be a little painful healing, but she really could have had a lot more damage. As far as gunshots go, this is the best one she could have. The CT scan is scheduled for a few hours from now. I will be back in a little while to check her again." The nurse left the room and the door closed behind. Porter turned to Susan, suddenly enraged thinking about someone pointing a gun and Ella. He was equally bothered by the fact that he wasn't there to protect her.

"Have you spoken to the police about the robbery? Have

the found the person who did this?"

"They really don't have much to go on yet. Without being able to talk to Ella, all they really have is the video footage from Poppy's surveillance cameras. I will forever thank the heavens above that Ella had that security system installed. If she hadn't, who knows how long it would have been before someone had found her."

"I totally agree with you. Although, I would have found her about ten minutes later when I showed up." Porter shook his head. "I am very glad that I wasn't the one who found her though. I am not sure I would have handled that very well."

"What do you mean? Why would you have been the one to find her?" Susan looked confused.

"Ella had called me before she went into the store. She and Kyle had a fight and she indicated that it had gotten physical. She was really upset. I got in my car and left right away to meet her at her store." Porter looked back at Ella and paused for a moment. "I tried to get her to call Megan and go over to her house, but she said she didn't want to bother her. If she had only called her, none of this would have ever happened." He rubbed his hands over his face in frustration. "If I had just come back with her, none of this would have ever happened."

"What makes you think that Kyle had gotten violent?" Susan asked, almost in a whisper.

"She was crying. She said she had tried to leave the apartment, but he wouldn't let her. She also said that he hurt her jaw." Susan's eyes darted over to Ella's face where the dark bruises were wrapped around her jaw. Her hand came over her mouth and new tears welled in her eyes. She jumped out of the chair and left the room. Porter looked back at Ella, feeling a little guilty that he had upset Susan. A few minutes later Megan came in. She was looking just as upset as her mother had.

"Porter, the police are on their way and they are going to

want to speak to you," she said.

"Ok, that's fine. I expected as much."

"I think there's been a misunderstanding. I assumed that either you or Ella had reported Kyle. When he was here last night I guess I thought he'd already been questioned." Porter's eyes became wide and crazed.

"The police don't know what he did to her?"

"Not unless you're the one who told them."

"The only cops I've seen since I got here were at the scene, and at that point I was so focused on getting to Ella it didn't even occur to me to tell them about Kyle."

"I know. Everything was crazy."

"I didn't even see a police officer here last night. I was waiting to see her, and then I fell asleep."

"Ok. Everything is ok. Will you talk to the police? Make sure you tell them everything."

"Of course I'll tell them everything. I didn't do this on purpose. Everything has just been so out of control. It just slipped my mind. I mean, I pretty much kicked the shit out of him."

Megan smiled. "Yes. Yes, you did." Porter stood up from his chair, leaned down to give Ella a kiss on her forehead and then headed for the door.

"I'm going to go talk to your mother. I feel terrible for upsetting her." Megan nodded.

"She is in the waiting room with my dad." Porter found them sitting in the uncomfortable chairs along the wall of windows looking out over the river.

"Mr. Sinclair," Porter greeted Ella's dad with a nod as he entered the room.

"Please, call me Robert." He stood up to shake Porter's hand.

"Robert, Susan, I am so sorry I didn't tell you or the police about Kyle. With everything that happened yesterday, it didn't occur to me that Kyle hadn't been questioned by the police. I really didn't give much thought to Kyle after I saw him in the waiting room."

"Yes," Robert said slowly, "Megan told us that you took matters into your own hands." Porter stood up a little straighter and squared his shoulders.

"Yes, Sir. And I would do it again in a heartbeat. There's no excuse for putting your hands on a woman. And if someone puts their hands on the woman I love, they better be prepared for me to put my hands on them. And my feet for that matter."

Robert smiled and patted Porter on the shoulder.

"I agree. And thank you." Porter nodded his head.

"Again, I am very sorry I didn't mention Kyle earlier. I should have."

"Don't worry, Porter. The police are on their way to question you and Megan about Kyle. There was a lot going on last night and you were so upset. We'll get it figured out." Susan's face went from went from compassionate to frightened and she brought her hand to her mouth. "You don't think Kyle could have shot her, do you?" She said, turning to her husband.

Robert wrapped an arm around her shoulders and rubbed her arm up and down, trying to soothe her. "Honey, I don't think Kyle could shoot anyone, but at this point, I couldn't really put it past him. Let's give the police the information and let them do their job. They'll find whoever did this to her."

Porter was chastising himself for even letting Kyle leave the hospital. At the time he was sure he would have killed him if he didn't leave, but now he just wished he had kept calm so that the police could question him. If Kyle was the one who shot her, and he just let him walk away, he'd never forgive himself. Suddenly there was a pit in his stomach, and his heart was thumping so hard that he could feel the pressure in his brain. He turned and went back to Ella's room.

Once inside he looked to Megan. "Do you mind if I have

a minute alone with her?" His eyes were pleading with her to give him some time.

"Of course not, I'll just be outside." She stood and gave her sister's hand a squeeze, and then left after giving him a supportive pat on the shoulder. He walked back to the chair he had vacated just minutes ago, but he felt like he'd been gone for hours. He was drained, emotionally and physically. He rested his elbows on the bed and his chin on his hands, wanting to just look at her. She did look just like she was sleeping. She even looked somewhat peaceful. She was deep in a restful sleep and his only wish was that when she woke, she would be well again. He sighed and took her hand in both of his, kissing the top of her hand, inhaling her scent which still had the lingering essence of vanilla. His lips smiled against her skin.

"Even in the most sterile environment, you still smell of vanilla, my love." He placed her palm on his cheek and tucked her hand in the crook of his neck. He stretched his hands up along her arm, hugging the one part of her body that was free to him. He wanted to crawl in the bed with her, but knew that wasn't the wisest idea. He looked up at her closed eyes, breathed her in, and willed her to come back to him.

"Baby, we need you now more than ever. You're the only one who knows what happened, and who's to blame. I'm not going to rest until the person who did this to you is being held responsible." He sighed and dropped his gaze back down to the bed. "I promise if you make it through this, I will spend the rest of my life protecting you, Ella." He felt the tears threatening again, but this time the tears were for him, not for Ella. He didn't know if he would ever extinguish the feeling of guilt; he didn't know if he even deserved to be rid of it and he was sure that as long as Ella lay in a hospital bed it would be impossible to escape it.

About a half hour later, Megan and her mother came in and Porter decided to give them some space.

"I'm going to head down to the cafeteria for a little bit, get some coffee or something. Can I bring you back anything?"

"No, thank you," Susan replied and Megan just gave him a warm smile. Porter made his way through the maze of the hospital, only having to ask an orderly once if he was on the right track to the cafeteria. Once he was there the sight of food made him feel even emptier. He knew he should probably eat something, but he couldn't convince his body to take anything in besides coffee. He sat a small table with his coffee. The table was near a window and he spent some time sipping and looking out over the busy city, watching cars roam around on the streets like ants. Boats were gently gliding along the river, some big and some small. The small ones were inconsequential, while the bigger ones caused a ruckus and stopped traffic while bridges were lifted. He couldn't help but think about how, at this moment, his life was stuck at a bridge that was lifted. Some big boat has come along and halted all the progress he'd made with Ella in the last ten days. He was on one side of the bridge and she was on the other. They were both stranded on either side and he was fighting like hell to get back to her, and he was hoping she was on the other side doing the same.

He rubbed his hands over his face, trying to break apart his depressing thoughts. He pulled his cell phone out of his pocket and dialed his mother, dreading the conversation they were about to have.

"Hey, Honey, how are you doing?" His mother asked. Porter exhaled loudly, not sure how to begin to tell his mother what had happened to Ella.

"Mom, I'm in Portland. Something's happened to Ella."

"Oh my goodness, Porter, is she ok? Are you ok?"

"I am ok, yes. Ella is not." Porter paused and took a deep breath. "Mom, Ella's store was robbed last night and she was there. She took a gunshot to the shoulder, but also hit her head."

"Oh my word, Porter, I'm so sorry." He could hear his mother start to get upset and knew tears were forming in her eyes.

"Her brain was bleeding and swelling, and they took her in for surgery to try and relieve the pressure on her brain. They got the bleeding and swelling to stop, but now they have to get the swelling to go back down." He could hear his mother crying quietly into the phone and he loved her even more for loving Ella so much. "They have put her into a medically induced coma." An audible cry came from his mother this time, and he winced knowing his mother was losing it and he couldn't be near her to comfort her.

"Oh, Porter. I am so sorry. You must be going crazy."

"I am losing my mind here, Mom. She is just lying there and I just want to hold her, but I can't. She looks so fragile. I'm trying to be strong for her, but I can't help feeling like she's slipping away from me."

"Oh, Honey, she's there. She can hear you and feel you there. She wants to come back to you but she has to heal first. Do you want me to come there and be with you?"

"Mom, besides Ella waking up and being ok, you being here is all I really want right now."

"Done. I will just tell the staff what's happening and I will leave. Do you need me to bring you anything?" Like a switch had been flipped in his head, he was suddenly filled with anxious need.

"Yes, in fact I do. Can you go to my house and on my bed there should be something from Ella. Can you bring it with you?" He had gone directly to his shop after Ella had left and hadn't even seen the present she had left for him on his bed. He needed to see the last piece of herself she'd given him, needed it to feel close to her again, if only for a moment before the reality of their situation came crashing back down around him. He would give anything for a temporary distraction from this world of unclear futures and questionable endings.

"Of course. Do you want me to bring you an overnight bag too?"

"Thanks, Mom. That would be great." Porter told his mother which hospital they were at and gave her directions.

"See you soon, Sweetie," she said as they hung up the phone.

"Drive carefully, Mom. Love you."

"Love you too, Son."

He hung up the phone and saw the picture on the screen of his phone that he had taken of them on the beach during their picnic. He was looking at the camera, smiling like an idiot, but she had her head turned and was looking up towards him. All he saw in her eyes was love. She was looking at him like he was the most important person on the planet. The picture made his chest ache. She was so beautiful and in that picture she was all his. It was the only picture of them together and he wished he would have had the presence of mind to look down to her as well. To look into her eyes and convey what he was feeling for her. He quickly emailed to picture to himself just to make sure he had a copy of it somewhere for safe keeping.

Porter sat in the cafeteria for a while longer, trying to gather up enough energy to find Ella's room again. He was so tired. His eyes burned and his muscles ached. He had never felt this level of exhaustion before. He was going to need to find a way to recharge soon or else he would be no good to anyone. He stood up, refilled his coffee cup, and started his quest to find Ella's room again.

Chapter Twenty-One

Porter

When Porter returned a detective was waiting to talk to him. Porter walked the detective through the entire situation and the detective took noted feverishly on a tiny notepad, stopping him at intervals to ask him questions.

"And Miss Sinclair specifically mentioned that he had hurt her jaw?" He asked.

"Yes, she told me that he had hurt her jaw, and she tried to tell me something else but she was too upset, I never got the rest of it."

"Did she mention if he had a gun?" The question made Porter's blood run cold.

"She never said anything about a gun."

"Based on what you've said, I can charge him with assault, but unless she can id him as the shooter, or the surveillance video can give us an id I can't get him on attempted murder. I will process this and get a warrant out for him."

"Do you think he's the one who shot her?" The detective looked down at his notepad for a moment and then met Porter's eyes again.

"I can't say. But if she was assaulted by her ex, and then just happened to run into another asshole that shot her, I'd say she has the worst luck I've ever seen." Porter shook his head, understanding what he was alluding to.

"Let me know if there is anything else I can do, or any more questions I can answer."

"Thanks for your time, and good luck to you."

"Thanks." Porter shook the detective's hand and went to check on Ella.

Ella had been taken for a CT scan, brought back to her room, and no nurses or doctors could give anyone any answers. The nurse had told them that the doctor would talk to them when the results were back. Until then they were playing musical chairs in Ella's room: trading spots, letting everyone have their own moments with her, making sure she was taken care of, talking to her and keeping her company.

Porter was sitting in the waiting room, leafing through a magazine when he heard his mother's voice.

"Porter, there you are! This hospital is built like a labyrinth."

"Yes, it's a little confusing," he said as he kissed his mother's cheek. She gripped him in the biggest hug that her small frame could muster. He felt the hug was as much for his benefit as hers. When she pulled away he saw her wipe a single tear away from her eye. He rubbed his hand down her back, trying to comfort her.

"Mom, these are Ella's parents. Susan and Robert Sinclair, this is my mother, Tilly Masters." They rose from their chairs to shake Tilly's hand.

"It's very nice to meet you, Tilly. We've had a day or two to get to know Porter and you must be so proud of the man you've raised," Susan said, giving Porter a warm and sincere smile.

"Yes. He is the light of my life. We've both grown so fond of Ella, too. I never got the chance to have a daughter, but she is exactly the daughter I would want. She is so smart, and sweet, and thoughtful," her words trailed off and she looked troubled. "How is she doing?"

"She had a CT scan a few hours ago. Now we're just waiting for the results," Porter replied.

"Has she improved at all?" Tilly asked.

"Not really. She's been pretty stable, but they are keeping her sedated until the swelling in her brain goes down. That's what the CT scan will tell us."

"Would it be ok if I saw her?" Tilly asked Ella's parents.

"Of course, I will just go tell Megan and Patrick," Robert

said with a smile.

Once Tilly and Porter were in the room with her, Tilly immediately started crying again. Much like everyone else who had visited her, Tilly sat on the side of the bed where Ella's free hand rested. Tilly wrapped her hands around Ella's and just looked at her for a few minutes.

"She is going to be just fine, Porter," his mother said after a while.

"She has to be," he nearly whispered.

"How are you holding up through all of this?" She asked him, looking straight into his eyes. Porter sat quietly for a moment, collecting his thoughts.

"I can't get over the fact that if I had just gone home with her yesterday, none of this would have ever happened. If she doesn't pull through this, if I lose her, I will never be able to get past it."

"None of this is your fault, Porter. There's only one person responsible for this and the police will find them. I know you're protective of Ella, but you can't blame yourself for any of this. Ella wouldn't want that."

"What if she never wakes up, Mom? What if I only get to have her for a week and then she's taken from me forever? What was the point in all of this?"

"You have to believe that she will be ok. She will be ok, Porter. She just needs some time to rest. You need to be here for her and be strong for her. Talk to her. She can hear you. She needs to hear your voice." With that, Tilly stood up and walked past him towards the door. She rested her hand on his shoulder as she passed. "I know it's scary to think of living without her, but she's still here, and she's right in front of you. Don't give up on her now." As his mother left, he turned his attention back to Ella and moved over into the chair his mother had just vacated.

"I'm petrified here, Ella. I never thought I would love someone the way I love you. I really didn't think I was capable of feeling anything that even came remotely close to love." He wrapped his hands around hers, kissed her knuckles gently, and rubbed his thumbs back and forth over the back of her hand. "When you wake up, we're going to figure this out. We're going to be together one way or another, Ella. You're going to marry me and I am going to put beautiful babies in that gorgeous belly of yours." He brought her hand up to his face and leaned his cheek against the smoothness of her skin. "I will build you your dream house and we will spend our lives together in that house, loving each other, being happy, until forever. I will make all of that happen for us, Ella. I promise. All you have to do is come back to me."

At his words, although small and miniscule, he felt Ella's fingers squeeze his hand. His head shot up to her face at the movement. Even though he knew she couldn't wake up under all the medication, he knew right then she could hear him and that she was fighting her way back to him. He started crying fast, happy tears. For the first time in thirty-six hours he had a ray of hope, a sliver of optimism that everything was, in fact, going to be all right.

He spent the next few hours watching Ella sleep, never letting go of her hand, talking to her about anything and everything. His mother and Ella's family came and went, taking turns visiting her, but never asked him to leave. They seemed to respect his need to be near to her and he thought that, possibly, they also believed that she needed him to be near her just as much.

When the doctor finally came to talk about the CT scan results, he requested that everyone leave Ella's room and they all met in the waiting room.

"Please tell us some good news, Doctor," Robert said once everyone was seated.

"I do have good news," he said as a collective sigh breezed through the room from everyone. "The swelling in Ella's brain has dissipated overnight and her brain looks healthy and normal."

Susan's hand came up to cover her mouth as happy sobs escaped, and Robert rubbed circles on her back. Megan hugged Patrick, both smiling, and Tilly laid a reassuring hand on Porter's shoulder. His relief coursed through him like wildfire. They would get their forever.

"The bleed in her brain is gone completely, as well. I am very pleased with the progress she's made and I feel if another CT scan in the morning shows similar results we can start to wean her off the medication keeping her sedated."

"So she'll wake up then?" Megan asked, hopeful.

"Well, Ella has still had some significant brain trauma. There is no way we can anticipate if she will suffer any adverse side effects from the injury. There is just no way to be sure or give you any indication what state she will be in once she comes out of sedation. Once the medicine is out of her system she could wake up in a few hours or she could wake up in a few days. The CT scan results are very good news, but I need everyone to be aware of the issues Ella could still encounter."

The light happiness that had taken over the room quickly retreated and darkness came again with the warning from the doctor. Porter had been so focused on Ella waking up, it hadn't occurred to him that here could be problems past just getting her to open her eyes.

"What are the possibilities, Doctor?" Robert asked.

"The brain is a fickle and unpredictable thing. It is possible that when Ella wakes up she won't be able to talk, or walk, or remember how to feed herself. It is also possible that she will wake up and be completely fine. There is no way to predict what state she will wake up in," the doctor paused, "if she wakes up at all." Gasps were heard from everyone. The doctor held up his hands, "We have every reason to believe she will wake up and make a full recovery. I just need to prep you for all possible outcomes."

"Thank you, Doctor," Robert said gravely.

"We will give Ella another CT scan first thing in the morning. If everything comes back OK we will take her off the medication, and we will go from there. Until then, however, it would be a good time for everyone to get some rest. Ella is completely stable and she will need everyone to be at their best once the real test begins tomorrow."

The doctor stood, shook Susan and Robert's hands and nodded at everyone else.

"I think we will take the doctor's advice and go home to rest up for tomorrow," Susan said.

"I'm just going to go and say goodbye to her before we head home too," Megan said. Patrick followed her into the hallway.

"Porter, Tilly, you are both more than welcome to come with us and stay at our house tonight," Robert said as he placed his arm around Susan's shoulders. Tilly looked up at Porter, waiting for him to take the lead.

"Mom, you should go with them and get some rest. I am going to stay here," he said knowing he was going to get a fight from his mother and possibly Ella's mother as well.

"Porter, you heard the doctor, we all need to get some rest to be here for Ella when she wakes up." Tilly said, pleading with him. Porter placed his hand on her arm, trying to mollify her.

"I did hear the doctor and I understand what he said. The fact of the matter is I am not going to sleep any better being away from Ella than I will being here with her. You go ahead, get a good night's sleep and I will see you in the morning." Susan stepped forward towards him and he fully expected her to try and talk him into leaving. She surprised him when she placed a hand on his arm and leaned up to kiss his cheek.

"Try to get some sleep and take care of my girl for me," was all she said as she walked passed him.

Porter walked his mother to her car and got the overnight

bag she'd packed for him. It had been a rough day and he was looking forward to getting cleaned up and then keeping Ella company. When he got back to her room, he set the back down on a chair and opened it up looking for his tooth brush. He came across an envelope with his name on it. He looked at it quizzically and flipped it over, hoping there would be some clue as to who it was from. He didn't recognize the hand writing. It then dawned on him that the envelope must be the gift Ella had left for him on his bed. He continued to stare at it, trying to figure out what in the world he should do with it. You have to wait until you miss me so much you can't take it anymore. When you feel like I might slip away from you and all you want to do is hold me in your arms. Then, and only then, can you open it.

Porter desperately wanted to read the letter and it almost hurt physically to leave the envelope sealed, but he wasn't ready to give up on her yet. She was farther away from him than his head or heart felt comfortable with, but she wasn't slipping away. She was going to come back to him. He tucked the envelope back in his bag, urging himself to remember now wasn't the time to lose hope.

After he had cleaned up a little and was feeling a little more like himself, he settled into the uncomfortable chair he'd spent so much time in the last day or two. He leaned forward, studying Ella's face, rubbing his hands up and down her arm. He talked to her, telling her all about what they would do together once she was healed.

"We can go on a tropical vacation anywhere you like. As long as you wear a bikini, I will follow you anywhere. We can lounge around on the sand, with fruity drinks in pineapples. We can swim in the blue waters and make out in the ocean. We will rent a cabana and make love as the waves come crashing on to the shore. We already know we both love the sound of the sea."

Porter sighed and rubbed his hands over his face. His

eyes burned with fatigue and he had a hard time keeping them open. He looked over at the flat and hard surface of the bench-seat intended as a bed for family with dread; it looked uncomfortable and far away from Ella. He wanted nothing more than to hold on to a piece of her while he slept, to make sure she knew that he was there with her, and also just to feel her next to him. He vowed to himself that once this was all over, and she was healed and in his arms, they wouldn't be spending any nights apart. He settled for leaning as far over onto her bed as possible without disturbing her, pulling her hand into his body tangled with his hands under his head, using their entwined hands as a pillow.

"I love you, Babe. I cannot wait to see your beautiful eyes open. Come back to me sooner than later, ok? I'm going to be waiting for you, right here." Porter drifted off to sleep with the rhythmic beeping of heart monitor keeping time with the ventilator. He woke a few times during the night when nurses would come in to check her vitals. None of them asked him to move or indicated that him half-lying on her bed was an issue, so he tried to ignore them to the best of his abilities, drifting in and out of consciousness. He didn't dream, but he did see images of a smiling Ella float around in his mind, memories of smiles she'd gifted him with over the last week and a half. He saw her eating cheesecake on his couch, running towards him wearing only a white comforter, kissing him goodbye the last time they'd been together.

When he eventually woke up completely, the nurse gently shook his shoulder.

"We're going to take her for her CT scan now." Porter inhaled deeply and rubbed his face, trying to focus on what the nurse was saying.

"She's getting her CT scan now?" He asked, still trying to get his brain to comprehend her words.

"Yes, the doctor wanted to get her in as soon as possible.

She should be back in about an hour."

"All right." Porter stood up and placed a feather-light kiss on Ella's forehead, and then stepped back giving the nurse enough room to wheel the hospital bed out of the room. He pulled out his cell phone to check the time, noticing it was still pretty early. He decided to text his mom and Megan to tell them what was happening, a little upset he didn't have Susan or Robert's phone numbers to link them in.

Ella was just taken for her CT scan. The nurse said she should be back in about an hour. Just an FYI. Could one of you please tell Susan and Robert? Thanks, see you both soon.

Porter took the time he had by himself to shower in the bathroom attached to Ella's room, and grab a cup of coffee and bagel from the cafeteria. When he made it back to Ella's room, he was pleased to see she had returned. The nurse informed him that the CT scan went well and that the doctor would be back soon with results.

"Dr. Andrews is anxious to get Ella off the ventilator and the medication, so he should be by soon to give his orders. If the CT scan looks good, we should be proceeding soon," she said happily. Her smile was contagious and her optimism was greatly appreciated by him. He felt himself lighten at her words and squeezed Ella's hand. He wanted nothing more in the world to see her bright blue eyes open up and he felt like today could be the day his Ella came back to him.

Ella's family quickly started arriving, everyone asking Porter for updates. He told them all what he knew, but everyone was waiting for the doctor to come with the official news. Dr. Andrews came into Ella's room late morning, and asked Porter and Susan to join the rest of the family in the waiting room.

"Ella's CT scan looks great," he stated as soon as everyone was huddled together. "There is no evidence of swelling or the bleed. I am going to have her taken off the ventilator and the medication within the hour." Ella's mother's hands covered her mouth, as she laughed and cried at the same time. Everyone seemed to be smiling and laughing at the good news. "I am going to need to ask you all to stay out of her room until the nurses can get her situated without the ventilator. Once she is settled, we are going to request that only one person be in the room with her at a time. Coming out of this type of sedation can be confusing and scary for patients. So once she starts to come around, we will be asking that only Ella's mother be in the room." Everyone nodded, taking in every word the doctor was saying. Porter was a little upset that he wouldn't be able to be there for Ella when she woke up, but he could understand why having Susan there was important. He would get his time with her.

"We have every reason to believe that Ella will wake up and make a full recovery, but I still would like you all to remember that there are still risks. She's not completely out of the woods yet. However, I am very pleased with her progress and we should be optimistic that there will be no repercussions from the head trauma. She is a strong woman, a fighter for sure."

Porter's heart swelled with pride at the doctors words. He had never met a stronger woman then Ella and he was so lucky to have her. Even though he hadn't slept well in days, and had been on an emotional roller coaster, the energy and strength the doctor's words had brought him made him feel like he could run a marathon.

The six of them sat in the waiting room, energy buzzing around them, grasping on to the hope of good news when Ella woke up. All of the Sinclairs were busy texting and calling extended family, giving updates and taking well wishes. Porter sat next to Tilly, glad that his mother was here for him, and appreciated the fact that she had now closed the bar for two days to be here and support him and Ella. He took his mother's hand, brought it to his mouth, and kissed it. She gave his and a squeeze.

"I love you, Baby Boy."

"I love you too, Mom."

"She is going to be so glad to see you, Porter. I will make sure she knows how you never left her side, and that you've been with her throughout this whole ordeal. She is lucky to have you, Son." Porter smiled down at his mother.

"Thanks, Mom."

After a while, a nurse finally came into the waiting room.

"Ella is off the ventilator. Again, until we can evaluate her progress and medical condition once she wakes up, you are welcome to visit her one at a time."

Porter had been with her all morning and didn't want to monopolize all of the time the Sinclairs had with Ella. He had all this pent up energy, waiting for something that might not even happen soon, and he needed to occupy himself.

"Mom, I'm going to go for a walk."

"Do you want me to go with you?"

"No, it's ok. I think I'm just going to get something to eat and stop by the gift shop. Do you want me to get you anything from the cafeteria?"

"No, thank you. I am fine."

"Ok, call me if anything happens while I'm gone."

About an hour later Porter returned with flowers from the gift shop, hoping they would make Ella feel better once she woke up. Robert looked up from his chair in the waiting room and smiled.

"Susan is in there now, but she wanted you to get some time with her before she woke up. You can go in there now if you'd like," Robert said.

"Thanks, I think I will." Porter walked to the door and gave a gentle knock before opening it and stepping in. He placed the flowers on the rolling tray next to Ella's bed and he smiled at how they instantly made the room happier.

"Hello, Porter," Susan said. "I was just telling Ella how I think she's finally found the right man to spend her life with." She looked over at him and smiled. "Over the last two days I have watched you with her, seen how you've taken on all of the burden of her incident, and tried to just make everything as easy for her as possible. I don't think I've ever seen anyone look at Ella the way you do. I almost believe that you need her just as much as you need air to breathe." Porter was taken aback by her words, not expecting them, but he felt a little bit of weight come off his shoulders as a wave of tension he didn't realize he was holding rolled off of him.

"That really means a lot to me, Susan. I know it was a bit of a shock to find out that Ella and I were together and I wish it could have been under better circumstances. But I love your daughter more than anything and being here with her right now is exactly where I am supposed to be. I am where Ella is. It's as simple as that." Susan stood up and hugged him. As they embraced, she took a deep breath in and slowly let it out.

"I'll let you have some time with her," she said as she backed away from him. He saw her try to wipe a tear away without him seeing and it made him smile knowing that her mother approved of what was happening between them; it was just one more hurdle they wouldn't have to face once this whole ordeal was over.

He looked over at Ella and took in a sharp breath. Without the ventilator, he could once again see her perfect mouth.

"There you are, Babe. I've missed that mouth," he said as he leaned down and pressed a small kiss to the very corner of her lips. His hands cradled her face and he felt another knot of tension release, not realizing how good it would feel to see her face free from machines. "You are so beautiful." She still lay peacefully asleep, but now she very much reminded him of the carefree woman in his bed just days ago instead of the robbery victim he'd been so worried about. He brushed a piece of hair off her forehead and took a peaceful moment to simply appreciate how gorgeous she was. As he used his eyes to strategically commit every one of her features to his memory, he noticed her eyelids started to move and it looked as if she was squinting with her eyes closed.

"Ella? Baby?" his heart rate spiked rapidly and his fingers became useless as he tried to punch to call button for the nurse. Adrenaline pumped through him as he watched Ella start to move her head to the side and her eyelids fluttered open. A buzzing noise came through the speakers on her bed.

"Is there something we can do for you?" A disembodied voice asked.

"Please come quickly. She's waking up," He said with urgency. He turned back to Ella. She faded in and out; her eyes opened for fractions of a second at a time. "Ella," he said as he gently rubbed the back of his hand over her cheek. The nurse came in the room right as Ella opened her eyes fully and looked around the room in confusion, still processing what she was seeing.

"Sir, I am going to have to ask you to leave now." Porter looked back and forth between Ella and the nurse. He knew this was protocol, but being so close to her as her eyes were opening, he didn't know if he could leave her now. "Please, Sir, it's time to go."

"I'm right here, Ella. I'm not going anywhere," he said as the nurse all but pushed him towards the door. With one last look he retreated from the room. As he left he saw two more nurses and Dr. Andrews walking towards Ella's room, moving swiftly with urgent purpose. He watched them go into her room and tried to ignore the gnawing pain in his chest from wanting to be with her. He turned towards the waiting room and when he went in all eyes came to his face. He must have had his shock showing because Susan shot up from her chair. "She's waking up," was all he could say. Susan ran out of the waiting room, no doubt headed for Ella's room. He sat down next to his mom and felt her trying to comfort him by rubbing circles on his back.

He sat there for what felt like days. Time crept by slowly and quietly. Porter felt like he could have counted individual grains of sand as they fell through an hourglass. He was being tortured; he was sure of it. Finally a nurse came into the waiting room and everyone looked at her expectantly. Their eyes pleading with her to give them hope, news, anything.

"Megan?"

"Yes?" Megan answered with confusion in her voice.

"Come with me, please," the nurse said curtly. Megan stood up and followed the nurse back to Ella's room. Porter let out a frustrated groan and stood up to start pacing the room.

"What the hell is going on in there? Why hasn't anyone come out to update us?"

"Porter, honey, I am sure they are just checking her out, giving her a chance to get acclimated. Everything is going to be fine, just be patient."

"Patience is something I'm familiar with mother. I've waited thirty-two years for Ella to even come into my life. I'm just having a hard time with the last hour or so. I just need to see her eyes, talk to her, tell her I love her."

"You'll get your chance. Just let the doctors do their job." Porter let out a loud breath, and continued to pace around the room. Just as he talked himself out of barging into Ella's room demanding to see her, Megan came into the waiting room. She looked at the floor and nervously fiddling with her fingers.

"Dad, you can go in and see Ella. She's asking for you,"

she said gesturing towards the doorway.

"She's awake? And she can talk? What's going on Megan?" Porter demanded as Robert left the room to go see his daughter.

"She is awake and she can talk, but she still seems pretty confused," Megan said finally looking up at Porter.

"Can I go see her?"

"Not yet, let's give her some time."

"Fuck! Megan, please, I need to see her!" At his harsh words Patrick stood from his chair and moved in between him and Megan.

"Calm down, Porter," Patrick said sternly, holding his arm out towards him.

"Porter, you watch your mouth!" Tilly chastised from her chair.

"I promise you, Porter, as soon as the doctors think it's a good idea for you to see her you will be allowed in. Right now we need to do what's best for Ella. I know you love her, but you need to calm down and stop making demands." He looked at her, trying to calm down his breathing.

"I'm sorry Megan. I am really not trying to be an ass. I just miss her," he said sadly. "Knowing she is in there awake and not seeing her is killing me."

"I know. Don't worry about it. Everything will be ok." Megan and Patrick sat down again, and the four of them began another agonizing wait for any news about Ella.

Finally, Dr. Andrews came into the waiting room. Porter stood, along with everyone else.

"Doctor, how is Ella doing?" Porter asked.

"Ella is doing well. She is coming in and out of consciousness, which is typical after being on this medication. This last time she woke up, she was conscious for about twenty minutes and was answering questions and following commands. It would seem that she has retained all of her speech abilities and as far as we can tell, she is able to move normally. There doesn't seem to have been any detrimental or irreversible damage in that way."

Porter exhaled a breath that he felt like he'd been holding for days. He shook, endorphins pumping through his system from the news he'd been waiting to hear since she was brought to this hospital. He needed to sit down, and his body moved backwards until he found a chair to collapse into. With his elbows resting on his knees he held his head in his hands and focused on taking deep and even breaths.

"She's ok?" He finally managed to choke out.

"She seems to have dodged most of the complications these types of brain injuries can cause." Porter's head rose slowly to meet the doctor's eyes.

"Most?"

"Yes, unfortunately, there does seem to be some retrograde amnesia."

"Retro-what?"

"Retrograde amnesia."

"What does that mean?"

"Sometimes when these types of brain injuries occur the brain shuts certain connections down. As doctors, there's only so much we understand about the brain and most of the time the way it works is still a mystery. Where memory loss in concerned, there are two types. Someone either loses the ability to make new memories, more commonly known as Short Term Memory Loss, or they lose old memories, also called Retrograde Amnesia. In Ella's case, she has lost some of the memories in the past."

"Is it permanent?"

"Not always, although there is no proven way to 'cure' this type of amnesia. Usually when a patient gets their memory back it is random and not linked to any kind of specific treatment."

"But there are ways to treat it?"

"There are methods to encourage recall, yes. Hypnotherapy, counseling, simply looking through old photos or visiting memorable locations."

"No medication? No operation?"

"No. Unfortunately, there are no known medical treatments used to bring back lost memory."

"I want to see her." Porter stood up from his chair and began to march towards her room. Dr. Andrews took a step in front of him and put a hand up to meet his chest.

"Right now, Mr. Masters, that is not a good medical choice to make for Ella. She is in a fragile state at the moment and any disruption to her emotionally is not advisable." Porter stared so deeply into Dr. Andrews eyes, he was surprised the doctor didn't shrivel up onto the floor or burst into flames.

"I am going to see her. I haven't been sitting here for days just for you to tell me what's best for her emotionally. There is nothing better for her than me." Porter could feel his heartbeat pounding in his neck and he knew he looked like he was about to lose control. He wasn't so sure himself that he wasn't teetering over the edge.

"Mr. Masters, again, with her memory loss, seeing you wouldn't be in her best interest. If you cannot accept this and still intend to enter her hospital room, I will have to call security and have you forcibly removed from the building."

"What the hell does her memory loss have to do with keeping her away from me?!"

"It's you, Porter," Megan interjected, looking at the ground, avoiding all eye contact. "You're the memory Ella lost. She doesn't remember you."

Epilogue

Dear Porter,

If you're reading this letter, it's because something has happened between us. I told you specifically not to open this letter unless you felt me slipping away, so I assume we've had a fight or some nonsense. I was hoping to write you this letter to preemptively bypass any stubbornness on my side (I've been accused of being stubborn by a certain handsome man I know). But seriously, if you've opened this envelope, I've made a mistake.

I want you to know that there should never be any doubt in your mind that I want to be with you, that I want us to be together. What we have, our relationship, is bigger and more important than any problems we may be going through at the moment. So, even though circumstances are pushing us apart or perhaps even I am pushing you away, I want you to fight Porter. Fight for us. Fight for me. Don't let me slip away. Don't let me give up and please don't give up on us. I don't know if I will always have the determination to keep marching on when obstacles get in our way. I will always want you, but I won't always be strong enough to tell you that or remember how much we are supposed to be together. You will need to remind me.

I am positive I am the one running and that you are hurting. I can't tell you why I'm losing faith in us, but please just don't give up. Just remember that I will always love you, no matter what.

There has never been another man in my life that I have loved with the depth of feeling or sense of need as I have with you. You are my heart. You are my soul. And you are sexy as hell.

Don't lose me, Porter. Don't let me slip away.

I love you, almost as much as you love me.
Come and get me,
Ella.

The paper that Ella used to write her letter on was soft and supple. That tends to happen when too much handling occurs. The natural oil from hands seeped into the paper causing it to feel almost like leather, making it appear to be deceivingly strong even though constant handling made the paper fragile.

Porter read the letter from Ella hundreds of time since he left her at the hospital eight weeks ago. Ever since the day that Ella woke up and had no memory of him, or the beach, or breaking up with Kyle, or even finding Kyle with another woman; Porter was at the mercy of Ella's family. Her parents were adamant that even though they knew that Porter loved her, they thought it was best not to pressure Ella into talking to him or even telling her he existed. Unless she remembered him on her own, they were not going to let him see or speak to her. They promised that if Ella regained her memory they would contact him. They made it clear he was not to contact them or Ella.

Megan was a little more understanding of Porter's position. In the beginning, she would send him updates on her progress, let him know how she was doing. But as the weeks waned on, she had less and less to say to him. Ella still remembered nothing of him or the time they spent together. Porter was optimistic that, given time, her memory would return. Surely, the memories of what they shared together, those eight days at the beach, were so permanently engrained in her mind they would eventually surface and one day he would get a phone call from her and all would be repaired. But each and every day that passed wore him down and eventually he found himself struggling.

When he got to the bottom of the pit of darkness that he usually resided in, he pulled out her letter and read it over and over again. Sometimes he cried because he missed her and felt her absence so deeply that his chest and arms ached for her. Sometimes he yelled and threw things against the walls of his house that betrayed him with memories of her.

She was everywhere in his house; she was shrieking up the stairs running from him playfully, she was in his bed haunting him with memories of loving her, she was waiting for him on his couch every day when he walked in the door. How could he go and get her if she had no idea who he was?

Today, however, he read her letter on the beach. He had tried to stay off the beach since her accident, not wanting to be reminded of the times they had spent there together. But today he felt a pull to the ocean and, inevitably, Ella. He read the letter while listening to the waves, trying desperately to hear Ella's voice speak to him. Today, a new piece of the letter stood out to him. You will need to remind me. How could he remind her if they won't let him speak to her? Remind me. He could hear her, calling to him, asking him to help her remember. To remind her.

Available Now

Never Far Away
Book 2 in The Never Series

Acknowledgments

Here is where I feel like I will start to sound like every other author on the planet.

To my dear husband, Demian, without your support and encouragement, our house would be cleaner, our children wouldn't miss me, and we would have more money in our bank account because I wouldn't be drinking so much coffee. However, when you gave me free reign to do this, and follow my heart, you gave me the greatest gift. I hereby bestow upon you one "Follow Your Dream" coupon, which you can cash in whenever you have something completely out of left field you want to pursue. I promise to support you 100%, and show you all the love and devotion you've given to me since this whole process started.

Brook, what you have done for me and this book is nothing short of incredible. The book might not have even gotten finished had you not been so wrapped up in it. I was fueled by your enthusiasm and driven by your feedback. You've been my best friend since forever, and I can't wait to share more of my crazy stories with you, until you tire of reading them! I am so excited that we both are doing something we love, and that we can support each other.

Matt, thanks for pouring the wine and hating Kyle with such raging passion. Can I get a Grande mocha for 'Not a Pervert'?

Krysta, your talents and gifts made Never Close Enough so much better. I cannot express how much I appreciate all the time and effort you contributed to this endeavor, and I am forever grateful that you agreed to be a part of this book.

Finally, Mom, thanks for all the support you show me in anything I venture in to. I could have been writing an owner's manual to a car and I am sure you would have been just as excited and proud. Thanks for watching my kids so I could write in peace and quiet and for listening to all the updates I excitedly told you about (and will continue to bombard you with). I am so lucky to have you.